THE SLICING EDGE OF DEATH

THE
SLICING EDGE
OF DEATH

Judith Cook

St. Martin's Press
New York

Library of Congress Cataloging-in-Publication Data

Cook, Judith.
The slicing edge of death : who killed Christopher Marlowe? /
Judith Cook.
p.   cm.
ISBN 0-312-10011-6
1. Marlowe, Christopher, 1564–1593—Fiction.   2. Great Britain—
History—Elizabeth, 1558–1603—Fiction.   3. Dramatists, English—
Fiction.   4. Murder—England—Fiction.   I. Title.
PR6053.O5196S57   1993
823'.914—dc20   93-24281   CIP

First published in Great Britain by Simon & Schuster Ltd.

First U.S. Edition: October 1993
10 9 8 7 6 5 4 3 2 1

This book is for my grandchildren:
Joshua, Daniel, Sam and Kate.

1

No, 'tis not so deep as a well, nor so wide
as a church door; but 'tis enough, 'twill
serve . . .

Romeo and Juliet   Shakespeare

THERE WAS NO REASON why anyone, least of all
William Bradley, should have known that 18
September 1589 was to be the last day of his life. To the
regular customers of the Bishop Tavern, on the corner of
Gray's Inn Road and High Holborn, the sight of the
landlord's son, drunk, belligerent and spoiling for a fight
was commonplace: drink merely aggravated a basically
unpleasant personality. Bradley spoke first, fought second
and thought, if he ever got around to it, a good deal later.

The object of his wrath on this occasion was the writer
and poet Thomas Watson, a genial and easy going man not
known for causing trouble. Nor was the Bishop one of his
regular drinking spots. In fact, the clientele of that tavern
had dwindled markedly since William had returned to
London some two years previously. His father, a small,
rat-like man, was unable to restrain his son who, in
appearance and temperament, took after his dead mother.

There was only a handful of customers drinking in the
taproom when William lumbered in half-way through the
morning, smelling of stale drink and sweat, as he had fallen
asleep in his clothes. He was already muttering that he
would get satisfaction from Master Watson that very day,
though when a bored drinker asked what the man had
done to offend him, Bradley responded only with
incoherent raving since, to be honest, he could not
remember much about the previous night – except that the

1

man Watson had upset his dignity. He had also been accompanied by an unpleasant, smooth-tongued young fellow to whom he, Bradley, had taken an instant dislike.

Finally, having drained a tankard of ale, belched loudly, wiped his hand across his face then down the front of his greasy doublet, he took down his rapier from the hook on which it was hanging by its belt and strapped it on. He now had only an hour or so left to live.

He stumbled blinking out of the Bishop (the taproom was short of light), and made his way towards Hog Lane where he knew his quarry had lodgings, striking north up the Gray's Inn Road. The street was busy as usual and his progress slow as he barged his way through the pedestrians, treading on toes and elbowing his way through the crowds, leaving a trail of enraged citizens in his wake. Then, in an effort to move faster, he stepped into the middle of the road, nearly getting himself run down by a carriage coming in the opposite direction.

At last, puffing and panting, he arrived at the end of Hog Lane at its junction with Bishopsgate. He now had a problem, since he did not know where Watson lived and the Lane was full of lodging houses. The first two people he accosted had never heard of Thomas Watson, while every third person seemed to be a visitor who had never set foot in London until that morning. He stood, breathing heavily, looking wildly up and down the length of the Lane.

Suddenly his eye lighted on a slender, dark-haired neatly dressed young man who was walking briskly towards him. Surely that was the fellow he had seen with Watson on several occasions, including last night? The young man in question was going in search of breakfast, leaving behind him, in a tumbled bed, a snoring, fair-haired lout who, he thought ruefully, had appeared much more attractive in candlelight. He was, therefore, somewhat surprised to find himself grasped suddenly by the arm. He looked up, then swiftly away again after receiving the full force of Bradley's stale breath in his face.

'Here, you,' said the latter, 'you know Thomas Watson, don't you?'

The young man struggled unsuccessfully to release himself. 'So?'

'Where is he?'

'I haven't the faintest idea. We don't lodge together. Why do you want to know?'

'Because I want to teach him a lesson, that's why.'

The young man weighed Bradley up through narrowed eyes; fleshy and overweight, stupid certainly, but, from what he had heard, more skilful with the sword than might appear. Watson, on the other hand, was a man of words rather than action.

'Well?' bellowed Bradley.

His victim wrenched his arm free and stepped back. 'I can't help you. Why not go to Whitehall? He is often at Court these days.' At which he made to go. Baulked of finding Watson, Bradley suddenly remembered something he had heard about this particular young man.

'Sodomite!' he shouted.

There was a pause.

'What did you say?'

'I said "sodomite". You're a dirty little sodomite.'

Chistopher Marlowe turned back with a pleasant smile then, whipping out his sword slit Bradley's shirt neatly down to the waist. 'Well now,' he said, gently, 'will you stand there until I cut through your points as well and your breeches fall down so we can all see your disgusting arse?' This was not at all what Bradley had intended. It was obvious that there was nothing for it now but to fight.

Within minutes the two were going at it hammer and tongs up and down Hog Lane. The bystanders reacted in the usual way. The more sensible left the scene as quickly and quietly as possible. Others, less timid, flattened themselves against the house walls, loathe to leave while such a show was being provided. This smaller and more vociferous group followed the action at close hand, laying bets with each other as to the outcome.

In spite of his bulk, Bradley was no mean swordsman but Marlowe was better. He was also fitter and, within a comparatively short time, Bradley was bleeding from a flesh wound to his arm and he was also running short of breath. He might still have lived if matters had not taken an ironic turn. For it was then that his real quarry, hearing the clash of swords from the backyard of his lodgings, strolled out to see what the trouble was, just at the point when Bradley stepped back to wipe the sweat from his face. His eye lighted on Watson.

'Oh,' he grunted, 'so you've come at last. Well, now I'll have a bout with you.' He turned on him and Watson, suddenly aware of the hazard, fumbled for his own sword.

'For God's sake leave him to me,' shouted Marlowe, but it was too late. Watson drew his own weapon, to the delight of the bloodthirsty watchers, and turned to meet Bradley.

At this stage another man, emerging from a house nearby, took in the scene and decided something should be done. Taking aside a young lad from the candlemaker's, who was watching the action, eyes aglow, he told him to cut along at once and fetch the constables. When the lad seemed set to argue he told him that if he did not do as he was told, and that at once, he, Master Robert Poley, would have a word with his master; at which the lad fled into the Bishopsgate.

Taking on a new and less-skilled opponent seemed to give Bradley a fresh lease of life and he began forcing Watson relentlessly towards the ditch at the Finsbury Fields' end of the Lane, Marlowe, unable to intervene, following close behind. Eventually Watson found himself with his back against a wall, only yards away from open ground, where Bradley could finish him at his leisure. He had already suffered two nasty flesh wounds to his thigh, which were bleeding profusely. Aware that the moment of victory was at hand, Bradley could afford to take his time. He grinned from ear to ear.

'Take a good look at me, Master Watson. It's the last

4

sight you'll ever see.' At which point he spread his arms wide.

'Now!' shouted Marlowe from behind.

Watson automatically lunged at Bradley's exposed chest with his sword, running him through. A look of intense astonishment crossed Bradley's face as he fell, first to his knees, then to the ground. He died still looking amazed.

'Oh my God,' panted Watson. 'Have I killed him?'

'I sincerely hope so,' replied Marlowe. He bent down and listened to Bradley's chest. 'Jesus, what a stink! Yes, he's definitely gone.' He went over to his friend who was shivering. 'We must get those wounds of yours seen to.'

'I didn't mean to kill him,' said Watson. 'But if I hadn't struck then, I'd have been dead.'

'You wouldn't. I'd have stabbed him in the back before he had chance. I told you to leave him to me.'

It was at this point that the constables arrived on the scene and took them both off to Newgate.

* * * *

At the inquest held some days later, Master Thomas Watson explained how he had been the recipient of an unprovoked attack from William Bradley and how he had killed him, by running him through with his sword, only to save his own life. The sword, he affirmed, had originally cost some three shillings and four pence. Precise details were very important. Master Christopher Marlowe then explained how he had been waylaid by Bradley when going about his business and how a fight had also been forced on him. The jury, having viewed the body, cleared both men on the grounds that they had acted only in self-defence.

Unfortunately, they had no powers to release them from prison and Sir Owen Hopton, in whose jurisdiction the affray took place, decided they should remain in Newgate for a while as an example. There were too many easy street fights.

However, on 1 October Christopher Marlowe walked

free from gaol, after appearing before William Fleetwood, the London Recorder, on a bail of forty pounds offered by two securities.

'Why do you always have the devil's own luck, Kit?' asked the unfortunate Watson, left behind in the squalid room they had been sharing. The wounds in his thigh had festered and he was running a fever.

'Because I always give the devil his due!' Marlowe reached in his pocket and gave all the money he had to their gaoler. 'See my friend has a doctor, man. And enough to eat. There's sufficient to pay for both and if you pocket it yourself I'll see the Governor knows of it.' Then, turning to Watson, he added: 'Cheer up, Thomas. You'll soon be out of here. And I promise I'll organise a splendid party to celebrate it.'

So, making a bundle of his few belongings, he threw it over his shoulder and walked out, a free man. He now had no money at all so his first port of call would have to be the Rose Theatre.

2

Sweet speeches, comedies and pleasing
shows . . .

Edward II Marlowe

IT WAS A COLD, but bright, February day when
Thomas Watson emerged at last into the outside world.
Still limping from the injuries to his thigh, he made first for
his lodgings, greeted his landlady, who cried when she saw
the state of him, washed the stink of the gaol from his
person and rolled up his filthy clothes to be thrown away.
There was, as promised, to be a party for him that night in
the Anchor Tavern on the Bankside, but first he would go
to Court and see what employment he might obtain from
those who used his services when they needed an
appropriate verse.

He had difficulty finding any of his patrons for the
Court was in dissaray. Early that morning Sir Francis
Walsingham, Secretary to the Privy Council, had dragged
himself to his office from his sickbed in defiance of the
warnings of his doctors and in spite of the pleas of his
family. He knew, without their dismal warnings and grim
faces, that time was rapidly running out for him. He was
dying, worn out in the service of the Queen to whom he
had given everything. She called him her 'Moon'.

Of all that he had done, he was most proud of the setting
up of a professional secret service, one that no longer had
to rely only on a riff-raff of hired informers, disgruntled
menials and dissatisfied foreigners. He had brought in new
blood, well-trained *agents provocateurs*, brilliant young
spies handpicked from the Cambridge colleges. What
would happen to them now? The man who wanted to be

7

his successor was already hovering in the background, desperate to get his hands on his confidential files. There were one or two names he thought it better should be removed while there was still time: certainly that of his own nephew's closest friend. He reached into a drawer in his desk, but found that first his fingers, then his arm, refused to respond properly. He tried to get to his feet to call for help but his legs crumpled under him. Half an hour later his secretary found him lying there, raised the alarm and had him carried to his bed. He tried, desperately, to communicate, to tell his secretary there was at least one name which should be erased; but the stroke had left him bereft of speech.

Even as Walsingham was carried to his chamber and put to bed, there were those who hurried to seek out the Lord of Burleigh, William Cecil, Lord Treasurer of England and Chief Secretary of State, to inform him of what had happened.

Burleigh received the news with the correct expressions of concern, asking if all that was needful was being done. He was assured that it was.

'Is he aware of the gravity of his condition?' he enquired.

'I do not know, my lord,' replied the clerk who had brought the news.

'Surely he has been advised to make his final dispositions and seek God's forgiveness?'

'Unhappily that isn't possible, sir. He can no longer speak.'

Burleigh was scarcely able to conceal his satisfaction. So the spymaster was finally silenced, as good as dead already. He turned again to his informant.

'Fetch my son,' he said.

'That won't be necessary, father.' The speaker had come quietly along the corridor, as was his habit, to stand unnoticed, like a dark shadow. The eyes of father and son met in mutual and complete understanding. The Lord of Burleigh allowed himself a small, satisfied smile.

'It would seem, Robert, that you are about to achieve

what you have long been waiting for.'

* * * *

For the fair-haired young man knocking loudly on the door of the Rose Theatre, it would also be a day to remember, the day when, he hoped, he would be taken on as an actor by a real London company, the day he would achieve his dream.

The door was finally opened by the irritated Gatherer. 'All right, all right, I came as fast as I could. Can't hear a thing with all this going on.' He gestured behind him where carpenters sawed and hammered on the stage. 'Anyway, what do you want? You can surely see there's no flag flying. No flag, no performance.'

'I have to see Master Henslowe.'

'Does he know? He's a very busy man.'

'Not exactly. But I have a letter for him.'

The Gatherer scratched his groin. 'You'd best come in then.' He held the door open and Richard passed through into the auditorium and stared around spellbound at the sheer size and magnificence of the Rose. He turned to ask the Gatherer where he might find Henslowe, but the man had disappeared.

So, he was here at last! For a moment his mind returned guiltily to his family in Warwickshire; for all they knew, he might be dead. The son of a respected wheelwright in the village of Luddington, he had had the good fortune (as his mother continually reminded him) of having been sent to the local grammar school in Stratford, even though, as the only son in a family of girls, he would be following his father into the family business. People will always need wheels (as his father ceaselessly reiterated).

So he had completed his education, and embarked on a lifetime of making wheels, when the Earl of Leicester's Players came to Stratford *en route* for Kenilworth Castle. It was love at first sight. This, he decided there and then, was where his future lay. He was consumed with a desire

9

to become an actor. Prudence dictated he gave himself time for reflection, and this might well have been the case, had not the Earl of Oxford's Men followed hard on the heels of the Leicester company, bringing with them *The Spanish Tragedy* by Thomas Kyd. Richard went home and told his father there would be no more wheels. He was determined to become a player. His family were outraged.

Had he lost his wits, been put under a spell? Was he setting out to bring his father to destitution, his mother to her grave, his sisters to beg at the roadside? When this failed, the terrible fate of John Shakespeare's lad, some years ahead of him at school, was pointed out to him who, after a disgraceful marriage, had run off to London to go with the players *and had never been heard of since*! By this time the Oxford Men had moved on to Gloucester. It was now or never.

In the small hours of the morning, Richard crept out of the house and set off along the Evesham Road. He arrived in Gloucester, tired and dusty, to present himself to the Players and plead for work. He was lucky. Sickness had reduced the company while on the road and, they told him, if he was prepared to help out with the copying of parts and play any small roles which came his way, then they would accept him. At the end of the week he helped them pack their carts with the baskets of clothing and props, climbed in beside his fellow actors, and set off on the road to Bristol.

Now, two years later, he had amicably parted company with the Oxford Men and set off to seek his fortune in London, armed with a recommendation from the company's Bookkeeper to Master Phillip Henslowe, owner of the Rose Theatre on the Bankside. Yet now he had actually arrived he felt his courage evaporate.

Such was the activity that it was some time before he was able to attract any attention, but finally he was noticed by one of a group of actors who were sitting with a man who was obviously the company's Bookkeeper, for he was reading a script which they were following from rolls of paper in their hands. The actor excused himself and came to the front of the stage.

'You look lost.'

'Can you direct me to where I can find Master Henslowe?'

'Certainly. Is he expecting you?'

Once again Richard replied that he was not, but that he had a letter for him. The actor nodded then called to an apprentice who was passing by. 'Show him up to Master Phillip's office, will you?' The lad shrugged, clambered down the ladder at the side of the stage and said 'follow me'. 'Thank you,' said Richard to the actor, but he had already returned to his rehearsal.

The lad took him out of a side door of the theatre, across a yard, and into the neighbouring warehouse from which Phillip Henslowe, entrepreneur, timber merchant, Bear Pit keeper and theatre owner, ran his business. The apprentice banged on the door at the top of a flight of stairs. When a voice from within barked 'what now?' he called out that there was someone to see him, then fled.

Cautiously Richard opened the door. It was a large room with windows overlooking the Thames and it was very chilly, being heated only by a small fire, for Henslowe did not like to waste money unnecessarily on fuel. Richard saw in front of him a large, fleshy man, wrapped in a fur-lined robe. He waited for a reaction to his arrival, but nothing happened. Henslowe was deep in his accounts and continued writing for several minutes while Richard shifted from foot to foot, the only sounds in the room being the entrepreneur's stertorous breathing and the scratch of his pen.

He looked up suddenly. 'Well? What do you want?'

Richard handed over the letter without speaking; Henslowe read it carefully then, without saying anything, got up from his chair and left the office. Richard heard his heavy tread descending the stairs and wondered what he should do next. Was he meant to stay? Was it the end of the interview? For some minutes he employed himself

looking out on to the river and across to St Paul's. It was
no longer sunny, but clouded over and the river ran oily
grey past the wharves and watersteps. I must have been
mad to have come here, he thought. He imagined having to
return to the Oxford Men admitting to dismal failure; even
worse, crawling home and pleading to become a
wheelwright. He was still plunged in gloom when he heard
the sound of feet again, this time ascending the stairs. The
door was thrust open and Henslowe reappeared, this time
bringing with him the actor who had spoken to him from
the Rose stage.

'So you want to join my company, young man?'

'Yes, sir. I've played a good many parts now, and have
had some praise and . . .'

'No doubt, no doubt,' Henslowe cut in, 'but I am
already in the process of enlarging this company for in due
time we are to join with Lord Pembroke's Men, which will
make us the biggest company in London. We will not be
short of players. What do you say, Simon?'

Simon Pope knew his cue for Henslowe, when he had
fetched him from the theatre, had shown him the letter,
pointing out that the Earl of Oxford's Bookkeeper was one
of his oldest acquaintances and a man to be trusted.
Perhaps they could give the boy a chance, as he was good
looking and still had his teeth; that is if he did not cost too
much.

'I think we might find room for one more. What roles
have you played?'

Relief flooded through Richard. 'A good many probably
not known to you, since they are only country pieces, but
of recent months Hieronimo's son in *The Spanish Tragedy*,
Michael in *Arden of Faversham*. Oh, and the Dauphin in
the play of *The Famous Victories of Henry the Fifth*. I've
also helped the Bookkeeper with the writing out of parts.'

Henslowe appeared to give the matter due thought then
said, 'Very well, we will take you on trial. Ten shillings a
week when you play in London, five shillings if you go out
on the road.' By Richard's standards the sum was

outstanding. 'Most of your costumes will be from our own wardrobe but you will be expected to provide shoes, boots and other such and keep yourself, without getting into debt, please! I am not happy when I have to bail out indebted actors from the Counter Prison.' He then settled himself back again at his desk, took up his quill and continued writing as if he were alone in the room. The interview was at an end.

Simon Pope touched his arm and together they went back down the stairs. 'What do I do now?' Richard asked.

'Have you friends or family in London?'

'No. This is my first visit. Someone I knew at school left to become a player, but no one has heard anything of him for several years and I've no idea where to look for him or even if he ever reached London.'

'You can stay with my wife and me for a few days then,' said Simon, briskly. 'We usually have bed for an actor if necessary, as well as giving a home to two of the apprentices. We live nearby and in a little while I'll tell Jenny to expect you. Once you've found your feet there'll be time enough for you to find suitable lodgings.' He picked up the bundle Richard had left at the bottom of the stairs on his arrival. 'Is this yours? We'll take it over to the theatre with us while I introduce you to everyone. Later we'll go on to the Anchor Tavern. There's to be a celebration tonight for Tom Watson.'

'Who is he?'

'Is he not known in the country? He's a poet and a good one.'

'What is the celebration for?'

Simon smiled. 'He's just been released from Newgate.'

'From Newgate!' Richard stopped in his tracks. 'What did he do that he was sent to prison?'

'Why, he killed a man – he and Kit Marlowe between them.' On saying which, he slung Richard's bundle over his shoulder and led the way back into the theatre.

3

I must have wanton poets, pleasant
wits . . .

Edward II Marlowe

FOR RICHARD, RUSHED BY Simon Pope from
pillar to post, the next few hours passed like a mad
dream of names he was unlikely to remember, details of
plays in repertoire and plays to come, followed by a visit to
the Tiring House where the Wardrobe Master, a crabby
fellow, measured him for costumes. Then came a brief tour
of the theatre, to a running commentary from Simon.

'Whatever you do,' he puffed (for they had climbed up
to the top tier of the building), '*never* fall sick.'

'Why not?'

'Because Phillip Henslowe fancies himself as a doctor
and will dose you with horried cures. I was once stupid
enough to tell him a headcold had left me deaf and unable
to hear what the other actors said. He treated me with a
mixture of boiled worms and goosegrease. And when Will
Hunt, that's our clown, complained of a thick head after a
night's drinking, Phillip threatened him with a mixture of
vervain, fennel and peppercorns steeped in the urine of a
boy, at which he left the couch where he was lying in a
single bound, saying he was completely restored to health!'

Lastly, Simon took Richard down to the stage itself
where he was introduced first to Peter Hobday, the
all-important Bookkeeper, and then to the great Edward
Alleyn, leading actor of the Lord Admiral's Men, and
Phillip Henslowe's prospective son-in-law.

Ned Alleyn was at his most dignified, a long, dark
velvet gown over his stuff doublet and breeches, a fine,

white lace ruff around his neck. He regarded Richard thoughtfully. 'Master Henslowe has told me what you have done . . . you have played Lorenzo, I hear? Well, we will try you in that next week when *The Spanish Tragedy* is performed again. I would also like you to learn these.' He thrust a handful of rolls, many dog-eared and worn, at Richard. 'No doubt our Bookkeeper has told you to learn them as soon as possible. See to it that you do.' He turned to go and then was struck by a thought. 'Ensure when you are on stage, if you will, that whatever happens you *never* block the audience's view of me – from anywhere in the theatre. Keep that always in your mind.' With that he swept out.

Richard stared at the bundle of play rolls in his hand, feeling cold at the pit of his stomach. 'Don't be too daunted,' Simon told him, 'it's most important you learn first the parts in those pieces we perform most often. I'll tell you which they are, then you can add in the others as each play comes along; but it's as well to keep up with the learning. There's such a demand for new plays these days that it's all too easy to fall behind.'

'I can't imagine how I'm ever going to remember them all. And there's so little time. I can see I'll be up half the night just reading these – the Bookkeeper said I ought to learn the part of Michael in *Arden of Faversham* by tomorrow. I didn't say I already knew it for I thought it would look well if it seemed I'd done as he asked!'

Simon smiled. 'You seem to have learned something from your travels on the road, but now we'll go to the Anchor. Don't worry, I've told Jenny we'll be late to bed tonight.'

They left the theatre and made their way along the Bankside, Richard still wondering if he would wake up and find it all a dream.

'What's he like?' he asked, suddenly.

'What's who like?'

'Sorry. Kit – Christopher Marlowe. I've heard of his great plays of *Tamburlaine*, of course, but what kind of a playwright would *kill* a man?'

'It's easy to see you've spent most of your time in the

15

country! London's a dangerous place and fights are not uncommon. It was Watson, though, who struck the fatal blow, not Kit; not that he wouldn't have been more than capable of it. What kind of a man is Kit? Brilliant, difficult, adder tongued, dominates any company he's in . . . anyway you'll see for yourself tonight. He's bound to come.'

Most of the Rose actors had arrived before them and the room in which the celebration was to be held was very full. There were others too, as well as actors, including several women, none of a respectable sort. It was barely possible to make out individuals through the smoke of the guttering candles and the many tobacco pipes; even so there was one man it was impossible to ignore.

'Who on earth is that?' asked Richard, in a low voice pointing to an outrageous person in an extravagantly slashed green doublet which had seen better days. His red hair was greased to stand in a point, a foot or so behind his head, while at the end of his pointed beard there hung a pendant jewel. He was lounging at a table in the middle of the room, one foot resting on it. Beside him, her hand on his thigh, sat a handsome-looking woman with large eyes, so dark they were almost black, and a quantity of coarse, dark hair falling down from its pins, dressed in a shabby, orange velvet gown. The lady had obviously been crying. They made a striking couple. 'Is it Christopher Marlowe?'

Simon roared with laughter. 'No, that's Robin Greene. He'll be mortally offended he's been taken for Kit.' He motioned to a drawer who was passing by. 'Two quarts of ale, boy.'

The red-haired man looked round at the sound of his voice. 'Ah, Simon, you're well? And who's this?'

'A new player, just joined our company. Richard Crawley, meet Robert Greene, known to us all as Robin: poet, playwright, writer of scurrilous pamphlets, expert on the ways of the wicked . . . and the lovely Emma . . .'

'. . . his mistress.' Greene picked up a feathered hat from the pool of ale in which it was lying and swept it across his

16

chest as a sign of courtesy. 'I will not get up, I fear if I do I will fall over.' He nodded at Emma who was still staunching her tears. 'It has been a trying day.'

'What's the matter?' enquired Simon.

The lady turned a furious face on him. 'I'm with child.'

Greene yawned. 'So are half the women in Southwark but they aren't crying about it. Anyway I'd have thought an old hand like you wouldn't have been such a fool.'

Emma hit him hard on the knuckles with a battered fan. 'I'm twenty-seven years old and started whoring when I was thirteen. It's only the second time I've been caught. What are you going to do about it?'

'I've told you. Go to one of the old women and get yourself a potion.'

Emma hit him again. 'The last girl I know who did that died of it. It's your child.'

'Richard mistook you for Kit Marlowe,' Simon broke in, wickedly.

'Kit . . .!' Greene, who had just taken a mouthful of wine, choked on it.

At this point the drawer returned with the two pots of ale, giving Simon a chance to take the embarrassed Richard away from the scene. 'Don't take any notice. Robin always seeks to be the centre of attention and Emma can look after herself. For years she was the mistress of Dick Tarleton.'

'The great clown?'

'A great clown and a great man, a man of infinite jests. Even after he married he ensured Emma was never in want and gave her a house. He died Armada Year, the seizure taking him while on a visit to her, much to his family's chagrin.' Richard looked across at the couple. Greene was buried in his tankard, while Emma was looking at the ravages weeping had made to her face in a small piece of broken mirror. 'She comes from a tough family,' added Simon, 'her brother's a notorious highwayman known as "Cutting Ball Jack"!'

'Is this man Thomas Watson here?'

Simon looked round the room. 'Not that I can see. No, I

think not yet.'

'What happened, why did he kill a man?'

'It was this way. September last he had some kind of a quarrel with an innkeeper's son, William Bradley. Why the two fell out I don't know, but Bradley was always a roaring man. Well, it seems he went looking for Watson but couldn't find him.' A door opened behind as he spoke. 'He couldn't find Watson, but ran into Kit Marlowe instead and called out some insult or other . . .'

'Sodomite!' said the man who had just come through the door, loudly. The whole room fell silent and all turned to look at the speaker. 'He called me a sodomite. True, possibly, but I didn't care for the way he phrased it.' Thus it was that Richard saw Christopher Marlowe for the first time.

'Poseur!' called out Greene, waving his glass at him. Marlowe bowed. 'Thank you.' Richard had never before been in a room with two such extraordinary men, though Marlowe was very different in style from Greene. He had penetrating dark eyes in a pale, finely boned, intelligent face with a small beard. His hair was silky and well cut and he wore a velvet doublet in the fashionable colour known as 'tobacco', slashed with copper silk. His shirt collar, for he wore no ruff, was of the finest white lawn and spotlessly clean. He looked like a court gallant and he immediately dominated the gathering without any of Greene's affectation. Someone handed him a glass of wine and he thanked them, as his eyes raked the room. 'No sign of poor Tom yet, then? Ah well . . .' He turned to the two actors.

'I seem to have spoiled your story, Simon. I must make amends.' He called over to the drawer and ordered more wine.

'I hear Watson was fortunate not to have died at Bradley's hands,' commented Simon.

'No. I would have made sure that didn't happen. I was behind Bradley and would have knifed him first.'

He passed on into the room, stopping to talk to friends and acquaintances, until he reached the table at which

18

Greene sat. The meeting was watched with interest for the intense rivalry between the two was notorious. Emma was, once more, sniffing into her handkerchief. 'Greetings again, Robin, and you Emma. Why the tears? Do get her to stop, there's a good fellow, I can't stand weeping women.'

Greene yawned again elaborately. 'It seems I've fathered a brat. Oh, for God's sake stop bawling, Emma, I need looking after myself. Never feel well these days.'

'Pox worrying you?' enquired Marlowe, silkily.

'Could be, don't know.'

'*You* need looking after?' Emma spat then, picked up the red shawl which had fallen to the floor, draped it around her shoulders and stood up. 'Need me? The only need you have for me is to whore for you, to keep you in drink. That's going to have to stop soon with the child coming.'

Marlowe smiled. 'But, as we all know, you're so good at it, Emma.' Greene laughed while Emma, now totally enraged, picked up his glass and threw the wine in his face. 'Bravo!' said Marlowe, clapping his hands as Greene wiped it away.

'Why won't you be kind to me, Robin? Why won't you marry me?'

Greene looked at her blearily. 'You must be drunk. Give me one good reason why I should.'

'Because of the child, because I want a name for it.'

'You're a fool. Anyway, you know very well I'm married already.'

Marlowe was enjoying every moment. 'So you are, of course, Robin, so you are. And where is the good lady?'

'Last time I heard she was back home in Norwich. With the child. Haven't seen her since I spent the last of her dowry. Pretty bitch, though, hair of a true flaxen.'

'No one here who matters would know you already have a wife,' Emma broke in angrily, 'living as she does in the country.'

'Don't fancy gaol for bigamy. Anyway she might be useful one day. She's still got money. God, I need another drink.'

It was obviously useless. 'Go to hell,' shouted Emma, finally. 'Robert Greene, *gentleman*, Master of Arts of Cambridge . . .'

'. . . and Oxford,' broke in Marlowe. 'Never forget Oxford. He claims to have been there too.'

She turned on him in fury. 'Who asked you, you . . . you . . . you're not even a proper man!'

Marlowe threw back his head and laughed and the scene ended. Someone produced a lute and began to sing in a pleasant tenor voice. Emma pushed her way to the door then, noticing Richard and liking what she saw, stopped to ask who he was.

'I've a spare room in the attic if you're looking for lodgings,' she offered. 'You can have that if you'll pay me rent for it. Don't look so long-faced, you won't be asked to share it with the customers. Anyway, Robin doesn't like me bringing them home, he says it degrades him.'

'It's very . . . er . . . civil of you,' Richard replied.

'Well, think on it. I've had better than you content to lodge with me,' and so saying she left.

It was now very hot and very late and the singer could hardly be heard above the noise. Richard was just on the point of saying to Simon that, in spite of Watson not having appeared, he would retire for the night and try and learn some lines, when the reason for the celebration finally walked through the door, full of apologies. He was greeted with a rousing cheer.

Marlowe stood and raised his glass. 'Welcome back, Thomas.' There was a slight uneasy pause, then Watson smiled and went over and embraced Marlowe. 'You always come off best, Kit.'

Marlowe smiled. 'I do. I do.'

Plates of food appeared, along with bottles of canary wine. Richard gave up all thought of leaving and, having finally drunk enough to give himself confidence, set about making the acquaintance of some of his fellow players, during the course of which he noticed that the dreaded Bookkeeper was well on in drink and therefore unlikely to be smartly off the mark the following day, except that it now *was* the following day . . .

In a room packed with performers, it was no wonder that there were soon other singers, including an elderly man who nobody knew and who had slept by the fire throughout the preceding racket. Waking suddenly and determined to take part, he lifted up a quavering voice and began a ditty, the first line of which was 'I wish that I had silver balls, I'd clank around the town . . .' but could not remember any more and slumped back again into his comatose state. There was also poetry, good and bad. Thomas Watson refused to be persuaded into performing; Robin Greene wanted to oblige, but was too far gone to make himself understood. 'Come on then, Kit,' called out Simon. 'Why not give us one of your naughty translations of Ovid!'

Marlowe, his pale face now flushed with wine, laughed and without further prompting climbed up on to his bench. There was much shushing and calling out until the room fell silent and he began:

> And eagerly she kissed me with her tongue,
> And under mine her wanton thigh she flung,
> Yea, and she soothed me up and called me 'Sir'
> And used all speech that might provoke and stir
> Yet like as if cold hemlock I had drunk
> It mocked me, hung down the head and sunk . . .
> Nay more, the wench did not disdain a whit,
> To take it in her hand and play with it.
> But when she saw it would by no means stand,
> But still drooped down, regarding not her hand,
> 'Why mock'st thou me,' she cried, 'of being ill,
> Who bade thee lie down here against thy will?
> Either thou'rt witched with blood of frogs new
>   dead
> Or jaded come'st thou from some other's bed.

There was a roar of applause. 'When did you write that?'

one of the actors called to him.

'When I was at Cambridge studying for Holy Orders.'

There was another shout of laughter. 'Is that how you spent your time?' Simon called out.

'Poetry, learning, fornication. What else is Cambridge for?'

The excitement and noise were dying down. People began to drift away home, while those remaining talked together quietly, which is how Richard came to overhear the odd exchange between Marlowe and Watson.

The two men had been deep in talk, then Marlowe had leaned back on his chair, stretched, yawned and said, 'So, you've been to Whitehall. What gossip have you from that sink of lies?'

Watson clapped his hand to his brow. 'God have mercy! All this has put the news clean out of my head.'

'What news?'

'That Sir Francis Walsingham is sick and close to death.'

Marlowe stared at him. 'You are sure of this?'

'Certain sure. It is the talk of the Court. God knows how I came to forget, but being so tardy and then seeing everyone again . . . It seems he can't last long and there's much gossip about who will be his successor. They say Robert Cecil can't wait to step into his shoes.'

Marlowe rose to his feet, instantly sobered. 'I must leave for Scadbury at once.'

Watson eyed him. 'You'll go to Scadbury, even at this late hour? Surely there's no such urgency?' But Marlowe was not listening. He stood up and reached for his cloak.

'What is it to you if Sir Francis dies? It's his nephew you have for patron and you can only benefit from the old man's death. It is known Tom Walsingham will inherit everything.'

'We'll meet tomorrow, Thomas,' said Marlowe abruptly and left without another word.

Richard intended to ask Simon if he knew what it was all about, but somehow the words did not come out in the right order and when he staggered to his feet he found the room would not keep still, but kept spinning around him in a most disturbing way. Simon caught him under the arm and guided him towards the door. 'Come along, lad, you're for your bed. I doubt you'll be learning many lines tonight.'

The cold air finished Richard completely and he vomited in the gutter. Later, as he lay in bed listening to the apprentices snoring on the other side of the room, two of the night's events continued to circle in his head – Kit Marlowe's reaction when Watson had told him Sir Francis Walsingham was dying, and the roar of laughter that had greeted his own response to Robin Greene when the latter had asked where he came from and he had said 'Warwickshire'. It brought the house down. 'Don't mention that word,' Marlowe had advised. Why not, he had asked, what's wrong with Warwickshire? 'Nothing,' Marlowe had replied, 'so long as I'm aware, apart from its being the origin of Master Shakeshit which is what upsets dear Robin. He just doesn't care to hear the place mentioned.'

He was still musing on the mystery when he passed into oblivion.

4

Matters of import aimed at many
Yet understood by none.

Massacre at Paris   Marlowe

'A S I WORK THROUGH the mountains of papers
left by my predecessor, I begin to wonder if there is
anyone left in England who he did not employ in his secret
service at one time or another. It has taken me months to
get this far.' Robert Cecil looked up at his secretary from
behind the paper in question. A fanatically tidy man, he
intensely disliked clutter. 'You may sit.'

John Dowling did so. It looked as if it were going to be a
long evening and he would need to warn the clerks, eager
to go to their suppers, that they were likely to be working
for a good while yet. He looked across the desk and saw a
small man with cold eyes, his large ruff hiding, so far as
was possible, his crooked shoulder. Robert Cecil, son to
the great statesman the Lord of Burleigh, right-hand man
to the Queen, of whom it was widely rumoured – by those
who mocked and whispered in the corridors of Whitehall
Palace – that such was his nature that when he pissed his
urine turned to ice. 'Well?' Cecil looked at him again.

'Sir Francis did become somewhat obsessed, sir, but then
he did originate the system and so was extremely proud of
it.'

'Humph . . . the expense alone is enormous. It must be
possible to dispense with many of these people, some of
whom appear to be of very low ability.' He riffled through
the pile of papers nearest to him. 'For instance, here's a
Nicholas Skeres receiving regular payments although he
doesn't seem to have had anything to do for years.'

24

Dowling considered for a moment. 'Skeres . . . yes, he's worked closely with Poley. Assisted him in the vital work he undertook in connection with the Babbington Plot.'

'It says here he drinks too much.' He continued pulling out names. 'William Baddy, James Taylor, Richard Baines . . . I see he hasn't exerted himself for a long time either. What kind of role does he play?'

'He's primarily an informer, sir. Mingles in public places, listens to what people say.'

'Is he a gentleman?'

Dowling thought again. 'He so describes himself. His origins are quite unique. He was a recusant, attended the Catholic Seminary in Rheims for several years, was ordained by Bishop Chalon, actually priested! Then he seems to have lost his enthusiasm for the priesthood and Catholic plots.'

Cecil gave him a keen look. 'You seem remarkably well informed.'

'It was my special task for Sir Francis.'

'Why did Baines leave the Roman Church?'

'He's always refused to say. He must have done something to incur the displeasure of those for whom he was working, as he was imprisoned within the seminary, and was then sent to the common gaol. When released, he sent word to Sir Francis offering to sell him information on all the plots being hatched over there and Sir Francis agreed. Oh, and he also had the idea of poisoning all the wells in Rheims, but it never came to anything.'

'Poisoning . . . is he deranged?'

Dowling allowed himself a smile. 'I think he wanted to show his zeal once he'd changed sides.'

'Well, well, we'll keep him for now. Robert Lang . . . he can be paid off, Thomas Morgan . . . there's a note here to the effect he's received money both from us and the French. He seems to have disappeared though. Do you know where he is?'

'He was imprisoned in the Bastille in Paris. It seems he upset the French too.'

Cecil slapped his hand down with impatience. 'There are too many amateurs.'

Wondering to himself just how long all this was going to take, Dowling agreed then added, 'Sir Francis did try and improve the quality of agents. It was entirely his own notion to start recruiting among the undergraduates at Cambridge University. It was considered to be a most innovative idea at the time.'

Cecil stood up and walked over to the fireplace. It was late spring but the room was always cold and a fire burned in the grate. In reality, he relished his task. Expected to die any time, Walsingham had lingered on for weeks, his prolonged demise watched by Cecil with mounting impatience. There was little he would not have done to step into Walsingham's shoes and he was acutely aware that he was only *Acting* Secretary to the Council, for the Queen had still not formally agreed to the appointment. He turned again to Dowling.

'I think we must go through all the names again, retaining only those who are obviously likely to be of use in the future and ridding ourselves of the rest – one way or the other'. He gave a thin smile. 'Especially any whose loyalties might be in any way in doubt. If one side can buy a man, why not another? Now, what of Robert Poley?'

'He has a good knowledge of who is of value and who is not. Sir Francis thought him the most brilliant man he had ever engaged, whether as courier, double agent or *agent provocateur*. Anthony Babington had total trust in him, so securely had he wormed his way into his affections, to the point that when they came to arrest him he wrote to Poley telling him to flee for his life and thanking him for 'being so true' . . .

Cecil returned to his desk and resumed his seat. 'It is said that when Babington was hanged, drawn and quartered, Poley stood among the crowd and smiled at a job well done. I would like to see him.'

With some relief Dowling realised he was about to be released and so stood up. 'That can easily be arranged. He's

26

recently returned from the Low Countries with despatches and can be sent for.'

'See he's brought here tomorrow morning then. You may go – oh, and tell the clerks that I want the lists of accounts they are copying tonight.'

As Dowling reached the door there was a discreet tap. He opened it on one of his young clerks who said something to him in a low voice. Cecil looked up again from his papers and sighed. 'Well, what is it?'

'It seems Thomas Walsingham is here to see you, sir.'

Cecil's mouth set in a line of annoyance. 'You'd best send him in.' Dowling opened the door wider and ushered in the man who had been standing behind it, before leaving himself.

Thomas Walsingham was handsome, tall and straight limbed, everything that Cecil was not and the two had disliked each other intensely since they were both up at Cambridge. All they had in common was their nearness in age and the fact that they were both the sons of great families; but whereas Lord Burleigh was still very much alive and in command of his, Thomas's father had died, swiftly followed by his elder brother, Edmund, leaving him heir to great estates and one of the finest houses in England, Scadbury Manor. Now it seemed he would inherit yet more wealth. Thomas could thus do much as he pleased and had so far refused the pressure being put on him to marry. Some said it was because of his friendship, his very close friendship, with the poet Christopher Marlowe, to whom he was patron, that made him turn away in irritation whenever the matter was brought up.

Cecil rose from his seat and greeted Walsingham. 'You would like some wine?' Walsingham nodded his assent and Cecil went to a cupboard in the corner and produced a wine bottle and a single, beautifully cut wine glass. Noting Walsingham's look he said, 'I do not drink myself when I am working and I have much to do even at this hour of the night. It is a great burden.'

Walsingham uncorked the bottle and poured himself a

glass of wine, then went and sat in the chair facing Cecil. 'And one you could not wait to assume, for my Uncle was scarce coffined before you rushed to sit in his place.'

Cecil, refusing to rise to this, asked blandly, 'To what do I owe this honour, Thomas?'

Walsingham did not answer directly. 'It is said that your appointment has yet to be approved officially.'

Cecil regarded him coldly. 'That is so. But in the meantime the work must be done and I am doing it.'

'A formality, I'm sure. It is also said that so eager were you for the post that you have agreed with Her Majesty that you will work without remuneration until such time as it is approved. I fear, knowing her miserly inclinations, that if that is the case you are likely to work unpaid and so unacknowledged for many years.'

'I am a busy man, Thomas. I do not imagine you have ridden to Whitehall from Scadbury merely to pass on to me palace gossip.'

'I will come to the point then. As you know, my uncle confided in me some of his affairs and also that I was used by him to recruit suitable men for his service.'

'You were particularly busy, it seems, at Cambridge. I never knew. In those days I concerned my mind with other matters and, anyway, we were several years apart. I still do not see where this is getting us.'

'Merely that I take it my services will no longer be required and have, therefore, come to you seeking confirmation.'

'You are not looking for employment then?' asked Cecil, smoothly.

'You know very well I'm not. I merely wish to know where I stand.'

'Then you can set your mind at rest. I do not think you will be needed again in such matters. If I have cause to change my mind then I will, of course, inform you.'

They looked at each other across the desk. Walsingham saw a crook-backed, humourless machine of a man, driven by ambition, Cecil a handsome dilettante to whom

espionage was an amusement, ranking equally with hunting, writing verse or visiting the play house; which prompted a thought.

'You are patron, are you not, to the poet Christopher Marlowe who was at Cambridge with us?'

'I am. It has been one of the great pleasures of coming into my inheritance that I have been able to assist him. He can come to Scadbury whenever he pleases, my door is always open to him.'

'Your bedchamber door, too, I hear.'

Walsingham raised his glass in salute. He waited for what he was sure would come next, but it did not. Instead Cecil added, 'I hear he is having great success in the playhouses.'

'He is indeed. Have you not seen any of his work?'

'I do not greatly care for drama. I have seen a number of pieces played at Court, some of which had a certain amount of style, but nothing, I think, by Marlowe.'

'His plays of *Tamburlaine the Great* are magnificent, especially as they are acted by Edward Alleyn of the Lord Admiral's Company. His latest piece, though, is a comedy of sorts, *The Jew of Malta*.' Walsingham drained his glass and stood up. 'I will away then, Robert. You should go to the playhouse sometime, it would interest you.'

'Possibly. Perhaps you're right, perhaps I should know what dangerous ideas are being purveyed there to the gullible.'

At the door Walsingham turned. 'Do you always see only the dark side of matters?'

'Always,' replied Cecil and once more returned to his papers.

5

... a devilish exercise

Dr Faustus Marlowe

ROBERT POLEY WAS STILL in bed when the messenger from Robert Cecil banged on the door of his
lodgings in Hog Lane. His landlady screeched up the stairs
that he was wanted at once on urgent business and, blinking
in the light of day, he tumbled out, dragging on his breeches
on the way to the door; he found the young man with the
letter tapping his foot, impatiently awaiting his reply. Poley
broke the seal and read. He was to present himself before
Acting Secretary Robert Cecil at noon that day. 'Tell your
master I'll be with him anon,' he barked. 'You don't need to
stand there and wait. I'll make my own way.'

Upstairs, he plunged his head into a basin of cold water,
shaved as best he could, then rummaged in the wooden
chest beside his bed for a clean shirt. As he had only been
back in England a day he had given most of his town
clothes to his landlady to be washed. His breeches and
doublet were still travel-stained but they would have to do.
Finally, after dragging a broken comb through his hair, he
picked up his hat and went out. It must, he thought, be
well after ten. The quickest way would be to walk down
Hog Lane to Bishopsgate Street, then turn right and
continue until he reached the watersteps at London Bridge,
where he could take a boat for Whitehall. It was a warm
sunny morning and Hog Lane was so crowded that he
continually had to give way to the women, usually in pairs,
carrying baskets of washing on their way to spread it out to
dry in the nearby fields. One of his close neighbours, a
young man whose dark hair was already receding from his

high forehead, gave him a greeting as they passed each other and Poley returned it, only remembering afterwards who he was – a young actor from the Lord Chamberlain's Company, no doubt on his way to Burbage's Theatre. Someone, he could not remember who, had told him his neighbour now fancied himself as something of a poet and playwright as well as an actor.

Although Bishopsgate Street was noisy and full of traffic, there was more room to move and as he walked towards the river at a steady pace he had plenty of time to think about the coming meeting. It had been bound to happen, in fact he had expected it sooner. New brooms always sweep clean and Cecil would be going through Sir Francis's files with a toothcomb checking every detail of every agent employed in what some called a devilish exercise.

He reviewed the last years. The highpoint had, obviously, been the part he had played in the plot hatched by the inept Anthony Babington, yet another Catholic attempt to put the ageing Mary Stuart on the throne of England. Sir Francis had been quite specific as to what he wanted: Mary Stuart's head, literally. Poley's role was not only to inveigle his way into the ranks of the plotters but to encourage them by every means possible to go ahead with their rash plans and this he had accomplished to perfection.

Well, Babington and his friends had gone to their terrible deaths at Tyburn and Mary Stuart to the block (though it was said that to the last Elizabeth had hesitated putting her name to the death warrant) and the realm was the better for it.

He reached St Paul's church and made his way to the steps. Half a dozen boats were jockeying for custom, the air blue with the language of the notoriously foul-mouthed boatmen. He motioned to one fellow, asked his fee, then, ignoring the oaths of the rest, tossed him a coin, climbed in and told him to take him upriver as quickly as possible.

The Babington Plot might well have been the highpoint, but there had been some, well, difficulties since.

31

How much was known to his employers? Probably most of it, since they were all encouraged to spy and report on each other. After all, he had been put in gaol. And for such a ludicrous thing too. He cursed the day that, for once, he had allowed his feelings to get the better of him.

A vision rose in his mind, a picture of a blonde, white-skinned, buxom charmer with hot blue eyes: Joan Yeomans, wife to an elderly cutler. He had noticed her as soon as he moved into his lodgings. Indeed, he could scarcely miss her, for she often lounged at her door in a distracting manner, or leant, enticingly, out of her window watching the busy street. They exchanged lingering looks. He smuggled a note expressing his admiration. The cutler was old, tired and away all day in the City, the lady bored, frustrated, much alone in the house.

She granted him increasing favours until the day came when she promised him the last. She was down to her shift and he untying the points of his breeches with shaking hands when she suddenly burst into tears.

'We can't, we mustn't!'

Oh no, thought Poley to himself, not an attack of conscience *now*! 'What is it, my bird?' he enquired.

'Adultery is a mortal sin. What will I say to God on Judgement Day?'

Poley considered this the least of their problems. He was also tired of taking his pleasure with paid whores and he had become sexually obsessed with Mistress Joan. He *must* have her. He was suddenly struck by a brilliant idea.

'You know,' he said deviously, 'that there are those of the old religion, the Catholic faith, who would say you are not married at all.' He fastened his eyes on the hem of her short smock.

'Of course I'm properly married. It was a grand occasion. Everyone was there.'

'No, you don't understand. You see in the eyes of older people, your marriage is invalid since it was not performed according to the Roman rites. No,' he said as she began getting up from the bed, 'listen to me. Now suppose I find

32

a Catholic priest and marry you myself? Then, in the eyes of God, if not in those of the world, it might be said that it is you and I who are truly man and wife, not you and Master Yeomans.'

It was a blatant piece of casuistry, but then the lady was equally enthusiastic to consummate the relationship. 'Do you think that would do?' she asked, doubtfully.

'Of course. I will arrange it myself. But in the meantime, surely . . .?'

Reassured, she swiftly removed her smock and flung herself back on the bed in what could only be described as an abandoned pose. But she had insisted on the carrying out of the bizarre arrangement and the two were duly 'married' by a lapsed Catholic priest who owed Poley a favour.

There had followed several weeks of exciting afternoons on the lady's bed, until the day when the cutler, arriving home unexpectedly, caught them *in flagrante delicto*. He had locked the door on the outside, called a constable, and while the lady burrowed under the bedclothes and sobbed, Poley found himself hustled off, half-dressed, to the Marshalsea Prison on a charge of 'alienation of affection', from which he had only escaped by . . . but there was no further time for recollections, for they had arrived.

He knew his way to the Secretary's Office; he had been there often enough. He was greeted by Dowling who, after tapping discreetly on the door, opened it and ushered him into Cecil. Cecil was busy scanning a document, his brow puckered. After a few minutes, Poley sat down opposite him whereupon Cecil immediately put down the paper and regarded him coldly. 'I did not ask you to sit.'

'I did not think it necessary,' Poley responded. Cecil looked him over, carefully concealing his interest in the agent Francis Walsingham had described as the best he had ever employed. He saw a neatly dressed man of medium height, his hair a mousey brown, his face not one that would stand out in any way from those around him, which was, in part, why he was so successful; but it was necessary to put him in his place so that there would be no future misunderstandings. 'Remember in future that you will remain standing until I say you might sit.'

'Sir Francis was not wont to stand on such ceremony.'

Cecil's fingers rapped the desk. 'I am not Sir Francis!' Then he turned again to the paper he had been reading. 'I trust your mission to the Low Countries was successful?'

'The papers are already with Her Majesty.'

'You've been much employed in such work, I see, and a good deal else over the years. Sir Francis commended you highly, especially with regard to the Babington business.'

'I played my part to the best of my ability. The death of the Queen of Scots has saved the country a deal of trouble.'

Cecil gave him a keen look. 'You've not entirely kept clear of trouble yourself, have you? I note you were imprisoned, albeit briefly, owing to some kind of liaison with a married woman. How did that come about?'

So it *was* in his record; best brazen it out then. He gave Cecil a man-of-the-world smile. 'She was a comely woman of a coming-on disposition and I was, I readily admit, foolish.'

'And went through a form of marriage with her,' continued Cecil, disbelievingly, 'though she was another man's wife; a form of marriage celebrated by an illicit seminary priest at the house of one Moss the Tailor, in Wood Lane.'

It seemed all was known. 'The lady had scruples, and I used the priest, who has long since lapsed and become an informer for us, to persuade her she was still a spinster in the eyes of God, according to the Catholic Church. If you know this, you will also know that the case never came to court for it soon turned out that her husband was more concerned that it might be his money to which I was attracted, rather than the charms of his wife, until I informed him I'd given the slut some one hundred guineas during the course of our relationship. On hearing this, he withdrew the case.'

'So I note . . . and was reconciled through the gift from

you to him of a large silver bowl.'

Poley bowed his head. 'The wages of sin!' Surely Robert Cecil had not brought him all the way to Whitehall to discuss a romp with a cutler's wife that had been past history these last two years?

Cecil stood up and walked round the desk until he stood over him. 'Of more concern to me is that you were once brought here on business, which was never satisfactorily explained, to do with a book written about the Earl of Leicester, a matter on which you were questioned by no lesser person than Sir Francis himself.'

This was much more serious, but Poley was schooled in the art of not showing his feelings and, without hesitation, he replied, 'Then if you know that, you will also know that after two hours of his hard questioning I confessed nothing.'

'The note says you put him to "great heat", that you "grinned like a dog" throughout, and that when he pressed you about the whereabouts of the information he required, saying that he knew very well that you knew of it, you told him . . .'

'I told him that I will swear and foreswear myself a hundred times rather than ever accuse myself in such a manner as might do me harm. It is, you might say, my credo and I have ever found it to be a sound principle.'

Cecil returned to his desk. 'Well, we will put it behind us now. I've sent for you because it is not clear from Sir Francis's records the true worth of some of those employed on the Queen's most secret business and my secretary tells me that your opinion is to be trusted. I would, therefore, know more of them.'

The worst was over; inwardly Poley sighed with relief. 'I'll try my best to help you.'

Cecil produced a list. 'Richard Baines? Is he worth retaining?'

'Yes, for certain classes of work. He is something of a bragger, but you'll go farther and fare worse in the collecting of useful information – bearing in mind that, at the last, he'd sell his own mother to save his skin, so it's best he's never put to such a test. Should you wish to be rid of him, then it must needs be the knife in the back alley.'

'Good!' Cecil ran his finger down the names. 'Nicholas Skeres?'

'Nick's reliable so long as he's strictly watched. He's been useful to us in the past and might well be again. I think I can safely offer to vouch for Nick.' He mentioned a dozen or more names, on each of which Poley gave a brief opinion, then he put the list down. 'And Christopher Marlowe?'

'Our gentleman playwright? Now, there's a very different proposition.'

'We were both up at Cambridge together,' said Cecil, thin-lipped, 'though he was some time behind me. He is no born gentleman, his father's a cobbler. The "gentleman" came with his Master of Arts degree, which he obtained, I now learn, at the express request of my predecessor on behalf of the Privy Council, for the University were refusing to grant it, as he had been absent from his college for two periods, absences he refused to explain. Of course I did not know until the death of Sir Francis that Tom Walsingham had recruited Marlowe while still an undergraduate and that during his absences from his studies, he had spent time in Rheims, passing himself off as a disaffected Catholic wishing to study for the priesthood. I now know also that he was one of a number similarly brought into his uncle's service by Thomas Walsingham. You look sour.'

'I've never understood this passion of Sir Francis for recruiting Cambridge gentlemen.'

Cecil considered this. 'My secretary tells me it was because Sir Francis thought to make his secret service more "professional".'

In spite of himself Poley rose to his feet, unable to control his anger. 'Professional? The true professionals are those who spend their whole lives in the business, who are willing to dirty their hands, not Cambridge academics who turn to it as to a game of chess. What do they know of those who earn their bread by it? The "Cambridge Spies", the cossetted gentry invited into the business as if it were some diversion to set beside hare-coursing or playing the lute! Anyway so far as I'm aware, Marlowe's done little of late, his time being almost entirely taken up with his theatrical ventures.' He could not conceal his contempt. 'A suitable employment for a Cambridge man.'

Cecil coughed. 'As I pointed out, I am a "Cambridge man" myself.'

Poley became suddenly aware of how far he had pushed matters.

'However,' he continued, thinly, 'I have much sympathy with your point of view. I do not consider espionage to be a matter for amateurs and all too many of the "Cambridge spies" cannot be considered as anything else. But you must also agree that it was necessary to find persons of a higher calibre than hitherto. Now, if you will, read this.'

It was an account of the fatal night in Hog Lane. 'I knew of this when it happened,' Poley responded. 'Indeed, I not only saw the fight myself but sent for the Constables to stop it. Unfortunately they didn't arrive until after Bradley was dead – not that he was any great loss.' A further paragraph noted that Marlowe was a member of the School of the Night, an esoteric circle hosted by Sir Walter Raleigh, given over to the discussion of science, mathematics and theology. The School was currently under surveillance.

There was a silence then Cecil asked, 'How . . . safe . . . is Marlowe?'

Poley did not reply straight away. 'He drinks, heavily,' he said, finally. 'He has a predilection for young boys, and it is also said that he and Tom Walsingham have been lovers since Cambridge days.'

'That is not an answer. Men can drink and fornicate yet still be loyal.'

'He has continued to undertake tasks from time to time, usually when he has run short of money, and I agree with what is written here that there has been no complaint about his work. But, as you know, I have been much out of the country of late. Frankly, I do not know.'

Cecil picked up a small bell on his desk and rang it. 'Your information has been most helpful.' Dowling appeared immediately from an outside chamber. 'Add to your notes that I shall be increasing the payments made to Master Poley.'

Poley felt gratified. He had survived the interview with flying colours. 'You are very generous, Master Cecil.'

'I am generous only to those who render me good service. You may leave us again, Dowling.' The secretary, aware that there was more to come, had stood by wanting to hear what Cecil had in mind, and so left with some reluctance. 'The Queen, Poley, is ageing fast. The threat from Scotland now is of a different kind. The Stuart faction will not seek to do by plotting what they know will be achieved by natural means when she dies. Whatever the Queen might say publicly, James will be her heir and no doubt there are already those making overtures to ensure his favour when he succeeds to the throne. There is work for you there . . .'

'And Marlowe? Since he no longer has Sir Francis to whom to turn directly, he might well come to me again particularly if his funds run low. Should I offer him work? What do you want me to do?'

Cecil considered this. 'If you wish. In fact, that might be a good notion, for in future I would have him watched. It is as well to anticipate trouble. At best he is hot tempered and quick to fight and I'm told he has become overweeningly arrogant: a dangerous combination. As you see, he dabbles in esoteric studies with Sir Walter Raleigh and his mentor, Harriot. He has a powerful friend and patron in Thomas Walsingham although, since the death of Sir Francis, he no longer has the same influence at Court. Yes, I would like you to make Marlowe your especial charge alongside those who look to Edinburgh. You are free to go, but report anything untoward you might discover about Marlowe direct to me. Remember. Direct to me!'

6

'What is your profession?' said Roberto.
'Truly sir,' said he, 'I am a player.'

Groats-worth of Witte   Greene

THE DECAYING HEADS ON pikes which adorned
both sides of London Bridge held a horrible
fascination for Richard. He had seen them first when
Simon Pope took him out to show him some of the sights
soon after his arrival. Their first port of call had, naturally,
been St Paul's great church and he had drawn Richard's
attention to the heads as they crossed the Bridge. He tried
to forget them, however, after walking through the
crowded aisles of the church and paying his sixpence to
climb to the top of the tower. 'Be careful,' Pope had
warned, as he clutched the rail at the summmit, 'that
wood's as rotten as your dead grandfather. Kit Woodroofe
vaulted over the rail some months ago and broke his neck.'
   'Why was that?' Richard had enquired.
   'Oh no reason except that he was blind drunk!'
   Now Richard saw the Bridge, and consequently the
heads, every day for, after tactfully refusing Emma Ball's
offer of accommodation, he had found lodgings near St
Paul's. He had been happy staying with the Popes in their
small house, chosen by them since it backed on to the Paris
Gardens where Jenny Pope could take her two small sons
to romp and play. But he had not wanted to outstay his
welcome with them and he was aware that he was
becoming very fond of Jenny Pope, so much so, that when
she saw where his easy affection was wandering, she told
him gently of her love for her husband and how they had
met.

'Simon came to Oxford with the players and father took me to see one of the plays. He gave me a good education at home – I could read by the time I was five – and we both enjoyed the theatre. Afterwards we talked with Simon and, well, it was love then and is still love now. Father was upset at first, he thought the daughter of a Chancery Clerk deserved better than a player, but we won through in the end.' She put her arm round him and gave him a sisterly kiss. 'I hope you'll make as good a match one day.'

She had waved him off to his new lodgings with a bundle of necessities she had put together, telling him he was always welcome to visit or dine with them at any time. So he had arranged his room to his satisfaction and, after several months in London, felt he had truly arrived. Later, he would look back on those early days as a golden age; for that was before the shadows fell.

On this particular morning he was feeling somewhat apprehensive. Less than an hour before, one of the company's apprentices had arrived at his lodgings with a note. It was from Peter, the Bookkeeper, informing him that due to an unfortunate accident which had befallen a member of the company, Richard was wanted to rehearse the role of Theridamus in *Tamburlaine*. He sent the boy on his way, dowsed his head under the pump in the backyard to clear it (for he had spent too long in the tavern the previous evening), crammed down a dry crust of bread and searched among the tattered rolls beside his bed to find the part.

Having scanned it, he stuck it in his belt and set off for the Rose. Once again, at the entrance to the Bridge, he found his eyes drawn to the heads.

Treason doth never prosper: what's the reason?
For if it prosper, none dare call it treason.

The soft voice from behind startled him. He turned to find the author of *Tamburlaine*.

'No, they aren't my lines, they're Sir John Harington's, but neat, don't you think?'

40

Marlowe still made Richard deeply uneasy. 'I'm not sure what they mean.'

'What they say. Take those baubles up there. Suppose any one of them, and those of like mind, had succeeded in a plot to kill the Queen and had ensured the coronation of either Mary Stuart or her son. Do you not think they would have been richly rewarded? And who would have stood against them, said openly then that they were traitors, richly deserving of death? Very few.'

'You're very cynical.'

'I am indeed.'

'Who are they?'

'It's hard to tell now. I think the one picked clean by the crows is Antony Babbington, an innocent fool gulled by dreams of knight errantry into a Plot, every detail of which was known to Francis Walsingham from the first: nay, more than that. You might say it was hatched in Whitehall.'

It was all to much for Richard. They began to walk through the jostling crowds on the Bridge.

'So,' continued Marlowe, 'our gallant Earl of Essex is to go to Normandy to fight beside Protestant Henry. And the sweaty fellows in the taverns rake their memories for the words of our own Henry's Agincourt Song and dream of death and glory.'

'Surely there can be no greater honour than to die in battle?' Richard had conventional views on such matters and had clear and recent memories of his father, and others, drilling on the river bank in Armada Year in case they had need to fight the Spaniards.

'The accolade of "honour" strikes me less forcibly than does the word "die". I have little wish to be the most honoured man in the graveyard.'

'Would you not fight then for Queen and country?'

Marlowe considered the question. 'There are more ways of doing that than merely hacking away at some fellow with a pike.'

They reached the Bankside and turned towards the

Rose. Richard's feeling of trepidation at taking on his new role doubled at the prospect of Marlowe actually being present while he rehearsed. However, when they reached the theatre, he disappeared in the direction of Henslowe's office.

The stage was still being cleared from the previous day's performance of *The Jew of Malta*. Henslowe was a great man for special effects and there were a dozen trap doors from which smoke, fire – and actors – could issue and these were being reset for a different play. The stagehands were struggling with the mighty cauldron, Henslowe's favourite *coup de théâtre*, which rose from a trap as if by magic, belching smoke and surrounded by flames, and in which the wicked Jew was boiled in the grand finale. It was proving difficult to remove.

Henslowe was not in his office, but in the auditorium, in deep conversation with Robert Greene. It seemed some bargain was being struck.

'Twenty nobles!' Henslowe's voice rose in incredulity. 'You ask *twenty nobles* for this new piece?'

Greene was unrepentant. '*Orlando Furioso* is the best play London will see this year.'

'It's certainly the most expensive play London will see this year or any other. Have you any idea what it will cost to put on?'

Greene shrugged. 'Ah, but think how many people it will bring in! You've not put on anything new for months, have you?' He yawned, elaborately. Henslowe considered the matter. It was true, he had no new work to offer for some time, whereas over the river, in Burbage's Theatre, the new playwright, Will Shakespeare, was proving a definite draw. It was actually Henslowe who had given Will his first chance as a writer and the lad had produced a rather routine blood-and-thunder epic, *Titus Andronicus* but it had not gone down particularly well and he had not encouraged him to write any more.

'Very well,' he said, grumpily. 'Come to the office and you can have your money.'

Richard had learned a great deal very quickly. The experience of playing before small crowds of country yokels, marvelling at any kind of performance, had not prepared him for appearing on a huge stage watched by upwards of two thousand people, the better-off packing the galleries, the groundlings filling the raked floor of the pit. London audiences were noisy, aggressive, talkative, their attention all too easily distracted. They brought with them pies and bottled ale, bought oranges from the fruitsellers (which they would throw at the actors if they did not like the play) and haggled with the dozens of whores frequenting the pit seeking trade. Pickpockets and cutpurses were rife and often there would be uproar when it was realised a purse had been stolen. On the other hand it was also necessary to gain the approval of the sophisticated and wealthy who patronised the playhouses in increasing numbers.

The actors had proved good friends to him. Simon Pope, who had taken to the new lad, had been a fount of wisdom. From Will Hunt, the company's clown, he had learned a great deal about the art of timing, that of making up the face from the epicene Dick Hoope. Above all, from Ned Alleyn, he had learned to speak great words.

But while he assimilated theatrical knowledge quickly enough, he remained curiously naïve compared with most of the other actors, who had either grown up in London or had joined the company as apprentices and soon learned to be streetwise. Little shocked them. It was a divide he found hard to bridge.

Overawed by the acid-tongued Greene and the terrifying Marlowe, he was charmed by the gentle soft-voiced author of the most popular play in the repertoire, *The Spanish Tragedy*. Thomas Kyd was a complete contrast to the other two playwrights, kind, helpful and extremely modest as to his own undoubted talent, and he had proved helpful in making suggestions to Richard as to how he might interpret a variety of parts. When Richard had thanked him, adding that he was the only playwright he had met so far who did not frighten him to death, Kyd had sighed and shaken his head.

'Kit and Robin call me a hack, a mere scrivener, which is, indeed, my trade, for you can't pay your way without money and there's not enough to be made from writing plays unless you've a rich patron. Robin and Kit and Tom Watson and Nash call themselves the 'University Wits' and mock me for not being one of them. Which reminds me,' he added, 'Kit owes me half the rent of the room we share in Norton Folgate.'

'You share lodgings with Marlowe?' asked Richard, in some surprise.

'Heaven forbid! No, it's merely a room in which we both work, but I'm thinking of trying to find one on my own. He works in such an untidy manner, leaving his papers all over the place then coming in and rummaging among mine for them, so leaving all in confusion. And he's *very* distracting.'

Richard laughed. 'So I can imagine.'

Kyd paused for a moment. 'He talks, especially in drink, of things about which I'd prefer not to know. He belongs to some society of gentlemen who call themselves the School of the Night, men who seek to find falsehoods in the Bible, debate the very existence of God and study mathematics. Some say they even practise necromancy. I find it frightening – and dangerous.' He then abruptly changed the subject.

The young actor was jolted out of his reverie by the Bookkeeper asking if he intended staring into space all day. 'Right then, there's no time to lose,' he said. 'As you know, this is usually Ralph's part. The idiot got involved in a tavern brawl last night and isn't fit to be seen. I'll warn you now, Ned Alleyn was far from pleased at rehearsing today as it was. He doesn't yet know it will be with a new actor.'

At that moment Alleyn appeared and it was obvious he was in a tetchy mood. He and Henslowe had had words over the purchase of Greene's new play, and it had taken the intervention of Henslowe's stepdaughter, Joan, to make the peace. A plain, but practical, girl, she was now officially affianced to Alleyn and had considerable influence with him. Peter cleared the stage of stagehands and called for quiet while, at the same time, listening to Alleyn's morning grievances.

Theridamus is a bold warrior but Richard had never felt less confident than when he strode on and said his first line: 'Where is the Scythian, Tamburlaine?' Nothing happened. Alleyn was still haranguing Peter. He tried again, then again, finally bawling his line at the top of his lungs, prompting Alleyn to respond, testily, 'Yes, yes, I can hear you, you've no need to shout. Can't you see I'm busy?' Then, apparently continuing his sentence, added: 'What seek'st thou, Persian? I am Tamburlaine.'

Only belatedly realising he had begun, Richard rushed into the next few lines until he reached 'or meant to pierce Avernus' darksome vaults and pull the . . . pull the . . .'

'Triple-hounded Dog of Hell,' prompted Peter.

'If this actor is not ready, why is he here?' roared Alleyn. 'Where's Ralph whose role this is?'

Peter saw there was no hope of concealing what had happened. 'There was a brawl.'

'A brawl?' You know Master Henslowe's views on actors who brawl. I still fail to see why he hasn't appeared.'

'All right, Ned, you'd better hear the worst. He's got two black eyes and has lost his front teeth. I fear that'll make him hard to hear, even if we could paint around his eyes.'

Alleyn gave a petulant sigh and returned to the dialogue, Richard gradually gained more confidence. Just before noon Marlowe lounged into the theatre. His eye had been taken some days before by a new apprentice, Jamie, a lad with long fair hair and girlish features and he had come in search of him. Alleyn had just reached:

And we will triumph over all the world,
I hold the fates bound fast in iron chains,
And with my hand turn Fortune's wheel about,

45

And sooner shall the sun fall from his sphere,
Then Tamburlaine be slain and overcome.

'Bravo, Ned!' shouted Marlowe. 'Magnificent! But you could hardly fail with such language. So, Richard, you're playing Theridamus. Where's Ralph?' They told him. Marlowe regarded Richard critically. 'You'll need a more suitable costume. And for God's sake pad him out.' Then he added, 'You look more like a country tailor drilling for the Warwickshire militia than a great Persian warlord!'

The rehearsal had, to all intents and purposes, ended. 'I must go,' said Alleyn. 'There are problems at the Bear Pit. Walk him through it, Peter, and for Jesus' sake, boy, remember your lines.'

As he left the theatre he almost collided with Emma coming in. She was deathly pale, her body now swelling with the growing child. 'Have you seen Robin?' she asked, in obvious distress.

'He left Phillip Henslowe some time ago,' replied Marlowe, 'jingling a large number of coins in a purse. Try the Anchor or the Falcon or any other tavern, brothel or gaming house. He looked like a man set on spending money.'

Emma looked so white that Richard wondered if she'd been seeking Greene to send him for the midwife. 'Are you sick?' he asked.

'No, it's not that. It's my brother. He's been arrested and taken to Newgate.'

When Richard had first heard that Emma's brother was the notorious highwayman Cutting Ball Jack he had dismissed it as theatrical exaggeration but he had learned later that it was true.

'Well Emma,' said Marlowe, dispassionately, 'he must have known the odds and so must you. Highway robbery's always a hanging matter.'

'But he was the best, the very best. Chief Foist before he was twenty. The best Upright Man on the road.' – 'That's thieves' cant, my innocent', Marlowe told Richard. – 'He looked after me right from when we were barefoot children in the street, stealing what we could. What am I to do? I must find Robin.'

Richard felt desperately sorry for her. 'Come on, I'll help you look for him.'

'Thank you.' She put her hand on his arm. 'You're a kind soul.'

* * * *

Within a month the comparative peace enjoyed by the Rose company was shattered by two enormous rows, rows which left Henslowe without either of his most famous playwrights.

Rehearsals had begun for Greene's *Orlando Furioso*, a play which stretched the capacity of the Lord Admiral's company to the full, both artistically and technically. They were hard at it one morning when a man Richard had not seen before strolled into the theatre. Simon hailed him cheerfully.

'Ralph, my old friend! Here, all of you, meet Ralph Wilkins, late of Lord Pembroke's company.'

Wilkins bowed, elaborately. 'Now with Richard Burbage and the Lord Chamberlain's Men.'

It was at that point that Henslowe arrived to see how his money was being spent. The rehearsal continued, watched, shrewdly, by Wilkins, until there was a pause.

'Of course,' he called to Simon, 'what you really need is a new play.'

'What do you think we're doing?'

'Well – certainly not a new play.'

They stared at him. 'Of course it's new,' said Will Hunt, the clown. 'Haven't you seen the playbills posted all over the town? It's Robin Greene's latest and it's cost Master Henslowe and the sharers a fortune.'

Ralph laughed. 'Then you've been gulled!'

Henslowe bustled over. 'What are you implying Wilkins . . . it is Wilkins, isn't it? As an actor, you hardly need telling that the company is busy and I would prefer there were no strangers in the house while we work on this new play.'

'But that's what I'm trying to tell you. It *isn't* a new play.'

'I can assure you it is. I paid Robert Greene twenty nobles for it. More than for any other piece performed here.'

'Twenty nobles! That's what Greene was paid by Lord Pembroke's Men when we took it on tour last summer. Twenty nobles for a *new* play. Oh, I can assure you it's true,' he continued, as Henslowe looked fit to explode. 'I was in it. I'll quote you some lines if you like.'

So it was not a rehearsal of *Orlando Furioso* Greene saw when he strolled into the theatre that afternoon but the real life Henslowe Furioso in his office, an interview from which he emerged having been told it would be a long time – if ever – before he would be welcome anywhere within spitting distance of the Rose again. Even Greene privately admitted to himself that he had probably gone too far.

It was the unfortunate Ralph Wilkins who, inadvertently, provoked the second quarrel too, this time between Henslowe and Marlowe. A few days later many of the actors, in common with half the population of London, had gone to see the Earl of Essex ride out on his way to France. As Marlow had predicted, the taverns emptied to cheer the Queen's own favourite, as memories of England's past victories in France, the battles of Agincourt, Poitiers and Crecy flooded back, along with tales of the great heroes, Henry V, and that emblem of English chivalry, the mighty Talbot.

They had all returned to the Rose, accompanied by Wilkins, for he was not needed by Burbage until later that day. He was loudly singing the praises of their actor-playwright, whose trilogy on the life of Henry VI was receiving a rapturous response. Indeed, during the next two months they would be adding two other Shakespeare pieces to the repertoire, the history of Richard

Crookback and a comedy based on a farce by Plautus about two sets of identical twins. Will, boasted Wilkins to Henslowe, who had accompanied the party, was unstoppable. Henslowe listened, said little, but the wheels whirred in his head.

They had obviously whirred to some effect as Marlowe was to discover when he arrived at the Rose that afternoon with his friend, Thomas Nashe. There was discussion of the campaign in France (Marlowe had not joined the joyous crowds) and broad support for helping Henry of Navarre, at which Marlowe made one of his gnomic remarks. 'I'm sure the government has its reasons for doing so, not least the debt Secretary – or more accurately, Acting Secretary – Cecil owes to Henry regarding his cousin, Antony Bacon. And Her Majesty, too, of course.' But as he did not amplify this, talk turned again to Shakespeare.

'What do you think of him, Kit?' asked Nashe.

'Phillip put on *Titus Andronicus* a couple of years when we were still at the Curtain Theatre. I can't say I rated it very highly. Also, if you recollect, Phillip, you had to bring me in to cobble together his first attempt at a play of Henry VI. I understand he has "revised" it and added two more, God help us. I can't think what they must be like and lack enthusiasm to find out.'

'Then possibly you should,' broke in Henslowe, 'for these plays of Henry and his she-wolf wife are, I'm told, filling Burbage's Theatre.

At which Nashe added, enthusiastically, 'Surely you remember my telling you only last week, Kit, that I'd seen them? Shakespeare still has much to learn, but to see brave Talbot walk once more! Oh, think of the joy it would give him, that Peril of the French, to know that after lying two hundred years in his grave, he triumphs once again, his exploits washed in the tears of ten thousand spectators; who imagine, in Dick Burbage, that they actually see him come bleeding from the battlefield.'

'How poetic,' said Marlowe, unpleasantly.

'Wilkins tells me,' continued Henslowe, relentlessly, 'that soon Burbage will be putting on his play of Richard III. There seems to be a fashion, nay a demand, for plays about kings. I wonder you haven't recognised it.'

Marlowe who had, as usual, been lolling back on a bench, leapt to his feet, white with rage. 'Are you classing me with this . . . this *peasant* from Warwickshire? This ill-educated yokel? The only reason for his so-called success is because the playhouses now will take anything.'

Henslowe was unimpressed. 'It seems the people don't share your view. I've been watching Shakespeare of late with interest. It's a pity you've not done likewise. Rather than this petty show of spite, you might be better employed turning your own undoubted talents to the history of a king.'

'So!' Marlowe, very softly. 'You want a play about a king. You think I can't write such a piece as well as some pretentious actor? I, who gave you, *Tamburlaine*! Very well, I'll give you a history of a king, a history beside which Shakespeare's will be soon forgotten.' He snatched up his cloak. 'Phillip, you've the mind and soul of a shopkeeper.' Then he added, 'I'm tired to death of the lot of you. I'm for Scadbury.' And without even waiting for Nashe, he swept out.

On his way home that night Richard once again looked at the heads. They seemed to be mocking him.

7

Beware the rope's end . . .

The Comedy of Errors   Shakespeare

IT WAS TIME HE was back in town, thought Marlowe. The months at Scadbury, following his quarrel with Henslowe, had been both pleasant and creative and he had, indeed, completed a play about a king, a play which had already had its first production, not at the Rose, but on tour with Lord Pembroke's Men. Now he would offer it to Phillip. He wanted a play about a king? Then he would give him one with a vengeance, a play dealing with the life and times of Edward II, who had had not one, but two, homosexual lovers (both depicted in the piece in some detail) and who had ended his life held down on a table in a squalid dungeon while his executioners plunged a red-hot poker into his bowels . . . a nice touch.

So his summer had been spent enjoying the pastoral hospitality of Tom Walsingham, friend, patron and, nowadays, only occasional lover. He had a fine room in which to write, a world away from the squalid attic he shared with Kyd – which reminded him; he must go back there sometime and collect the various books and papers he had left behind. Busy days had been followed by pleasant evenings listening to Tom's musicians, entertainment which had prompted him to write verses for them to set to music. Scadbury offered an idyllic, apparently unchanging world, though even that could no longer be counted as certain, for Tom was under increasing pressure to marry.

Now he was restless, drawn once again to the life of the Bankside. With the onset of hot weather most of the playhouses had shut, their companies touring the

51

provinces. But now they would be back in town, with rehearsals due to start at the Rose for *Edward II* and he wanted to be there. Also, since he and Tom were now affectionate friends, rather than lovers, he felt the need for more direct stimulation; his mind wandered to the pretty, golden-haired Jamie in the Lord Admiral's Company.

He also needed money. Tom, generous to a fault, would always give him anything he asked but he disliked being so totally beholden. It was time, therefore, to seek again other kinds of work.

He did not give any of these as reasons for his decision to return to London when, one fine September morning, he went to seek Tom out. He found him in close conference with one of his retainers, a tenant on his estate and a man Marlowe disliked and distrusted. He was well aware that it was not unusual for a wealthy and important man to have such as Ingram Frizer around him, one who lived on his wits and on the edge of what was legal or even strayed beyond it to the other side. A man who would see to his master's best interests and who was not too fussy about the methods he used, whether to bring in unpaid rent or useful gossip or to undertake a less than honest land deal, a useful whipping boy on whom all the blame could be shifted if anything untoward occurred.

It was not this side of Frizer that offended Marlowe but the way his whole personality changed, depending on the company he kept. In his own world he liked to play the role of the accomplished confidence trickster, or, as Robin Greene would call it, a 'coney-catcher' or 'cosener', making money on the side by duping the 'gulls' or innocents, conning them out of their money using a whole host of doubtful methods. If you came across him in one of the inns in Kent or the taverns of the Bankside he would most likely be the centre of an admiring circle as he boasted of his latest trick, a real Jack-the-Lad, up to anything. Yet, as soon as he set foot in Scadbury he changed completely. His attitude to Tom Walsingham was sickeningly sycophantic, horribly obsequious. It was said too that at home his wife, a real dragon, wore the breeches and ruled him with a rod of iron. When Marlowe had spoken to Tom of his feelings about Frizer, he had laughed. 'He's a rogue and a scoundrel, I know, but he has his uses and he amuses me.'

Recently Marlowe had begun to wonder if Frizer might not have other irons in the fire, unknown to his employer, for he had been surprised to find him one day in the company of Nick Skeres. Skeres was a man he had come across before in other circumstances, plying a different trade; but then Nick too had also been part of that world of low-life cosenage.

When Marlowe entered the room Frizer, aware of his dislike, had cringed and bowed, sweeping the orange hat he held in his hand (for he was a showy dresser) down to the floor before offering, silkily, to go away at once and leave his master and his friend alone.

'That won't be necessary,' said Marlowe. 'I'm here just to say that I've decided to ride into town for a few days.'

Tom immediately put aside the rent rolls he had been discussing with Frizer. 'Why the sudden haste?'

'There are matters I need to see to. I've lain here in your lotus land long enough, Tom, but the immediate reason is to go to Tyburn to see Cutting Ball Jack turned off.'

'Is this some friend of yours?'

'I hardly know him, other than as one of the best of the highwaymen. But he's the brother of Robin Greene's mistress and I thought it might be amusing. His wit and his purse have kept him from the gallows for months, but now, I hear, he's to hang in the morning.'

'Well, each to his own taste, Kit. As you know, mine doesn't run to standing in a packed and sweaty mob watching petty criminals dangle from the rope's end. Will you be returning soon?'

'Probably. I'll send you word, I promise.'

He rode across the great courtyard and over the drawbridge, for Scadbury still retained its moat, through parkland bathed in an early autumn haze, down the marvellous tree-lined avenue planted by Tom's grandfather and out into the Kent countryside. Although only twelve miles from London, Scadbury was indeed a world away from the narrow, noisy, close-packed streets he loved. He took one last breath of scented country air and turned his horse towards the city.

By the following morning he had found himself new lodgings, for he had left owing rent to his landlady in Hog Lane, enjoyed a night of debauch and was up betimes to follow those making for one of the capital's most popular entertainments: a public hanging.

Although he reached Tyburn in good time there was already a good crowd, attracted by the execution of such a well-known criminal and there was a brisk trade in bottle ale, fruit and ballads of the sinner's repentance variety. He stationed himself as near as he could to the gallows, as today the hangings were all of the straightforward variety, no disembowellings and quarterings. There followed some delay, for it was the custom for the carts carrying the condemned to stop outside the George and Blue Boar in High Holborn so that they could enjoy a last drink.

At last they rattled into sight, to a roar of approval from the crowd. Cutting Ball Jack was riding in the first on his own, a privilege accorded to his status. In the second cart sat a sad little group, one of which was a strikingly beautiful young girl with the vacant gaze of the simpleton. 'Her's the witch from Epping,' Marlowe's neighbour informed him, gratuitously. As the procession arrived at the scaffold, Marlowe caught sight of Emma. She was pushing as close as she could to it, tears streaming down her face.

The arrival of Cutting Ball Jack provoked an enormous cheer. He had dressed himself for death in his best, a scarlet velvet doublet, thrown open to reveal a spotless white shirt. In his hand he carried several posies from the dozens that had been thrown to him by women. Ballad makers were already filling their purses with 'The Last Words of Cutting Ball Jack, Lately Hanged at Tyburn'.

The hangman motioned to him that he was to go first. As he began to mount the steps, he saw Emma and leaned down to her, almost touching her outstretched hands, before she was pulled away by a constable. A pretty black-haired girl called, 'Remember me, darling?' and he turned and smiled at her, then threw her his posies.

'Speech, speech!' bayed the crowd, and one man succeeded in passing up a flagon of ale. Jack downed it.

'Friends,' he called out. There was a sudden hush. 'Friends, there is little enough I can say. I thank you all for coming to see me make my farewells to this life.' The parson kept for these occasions stepped towards him. 'I thank you, not that. I have no wish to repent of my sins on the gallows. There are many who have done worse than I that the law cannot touch. Save your prayers for others who need it more, like that poor, idiot girl there.' The crowd, baulked of a deathbed repentence, began to grow restive. The executioner came forward and Jack put his hands behind him to be tied, but waved aside the blindfold. The executioner then asked for the ritual pardon.

Jack smiled. 'Why not? We all have our job to do and this is yours.' The signal was given, the rope was jerked, at which point a young man, who had been standing close by, suddenly leapt up and grasped the highwayman's feet, pulling down with all his strength. Emma let out a howl of anguish. It was all over in seconds, much to the disgust of the mob who turned, in fury, on the young man, but he had disappeared. Marlowe had no interest in the fate of the other poor wretches, nor did he feel able to comfort Emma. He noted that there was no sign of Greene who had left her to face this, like most things, on her own. As he was pushing through the crowd he came suddenly face to face with Nick Skeres.

Although they had known each other for years, theirs was not a close acquaintance; work had drawn them together and, on occasion, when Marlowe could find no better companion, he drank with Skeres. He was a thin fellow of about thirty with receding fair hair; not a particularly noticeable man. It was strange he should come across him, having only thought about him the previous day. They greeted each other, then Skeres said, "Ere, Master Poley's been lookin' for you.'

'He must know if I'm not in town I'm likely to be at Scadbury.'

'I told him that but he said he'd no truck with Walsingham. He said, though, that if I was to see you then to tell you he'd got work if yer wanted it and that he was in his old lodgings 'til the end of the month. Aren't you stayin' to see the rest of the show?'

'No. I must go to the Rose. Thank you, Nick, I'll seek Poley out. If you see him today you can tell him I'm back in London.' He began the long walk to the Bankside in a thoughtful frame of mind.

* * * *

The tour of the Lord Admiral's Men had proved little short of disastrous. The weather being hot and dry, there was an abundant harvest to take up the time and energy of the countryfolk. Nor was it much better in the towns; audiences were small and unresponsive and eventually the actors had run out of money. In fact, so dire had the situation become, that to avoid being arrested as vagrants or sturdy beggars they had had to sell props, costumes, even some of their own clothes to meet the bills for their lodgings.

Only Ned Alleyn, canny as ever and seeing what was likely to happen, had despatched his best coat, white-and-silver waistcoat and two pairs of velvet breeches to Joan, his betrothed, by the first carrier he could find who was making for London. Although their marriage had been agreed as a sensible business arrangement, the couple had become genuinely fond of each other and the autocratic Alleyn was coming to rely more and more on his 'mouse', as he called Joan; she now adored him.

So it was a tired and somewhat depressed group of actors

56

that had reassembled back at the Rose to face the wrath of the wardrobe master.

'Is this all there is?' he demanded, furiously, as he raked about in the bottoms of the costume baskets.

'You know very well we had to sell nearly everything,' replied Simon Pope, wearily, 'we had no money left.' He hated leaving Jenny and the children at the best of times; to leave them only to return tired out and in debt was deeply mortifying.

'We didn't only have to sell the costumes,' added Richard, 'many of us had to sell our own clothes as well. Except for Ned Alleyn, of course, he managed to send his back home before it came to that.' Richard had lost his fresh-faced boyish good looks on tour, along with the innocence of his early days with the company.

Never a merry soul at the best of times, the Wardrobe Master grunted, 'you'd best have stayed here.'

'With no work?' broke in young Jamie. 'We aren't sharers like you. How would we have lived with the theatres closed? It was too hot, there was the harvest, and people just stayed away.'

'Nor did it help,' added Simon, 'that Lord Pembroke's Men were touring the same places immediately before us with Kit Marlowe's play about Edward II. Audiences hated it and it rubbed off on us, even in towns where we're usually welcomed, like Coventry. They didn't even seem to want pieces like *The Spanish Tragedy* and *Crack Me This Nut* which usually go down so well in the provinces.

The wardrobe master shrugged. 'So they were disappointed in this piece of Kit Marlowe's?'

'No,' said Richard in support of Simon, 'they were horrified by it, so much so that when we set up they accused us, before they had ever seen our playbills, of bringing in more such filthy and depraved stuff. Parsons preached against us from the pulpits! The groundlings threw bottled ale at us in Leicester and in Warwick I was hit by a pie. I was so hungry I'd have eaten it too, except that it was rotten. Wherever we went we were blamed for *Edward II.*'

'It seems that word had got round of Will Shakespeare's royal plays with the heroic Talbot in one and the Crookback villain in the other,' snarled Will Hunt, whose clowning usually ensured his popularity everywhere, 'and they were looking for more of the same, instead of which they were treated to . . .' He broke off.

'An exhibition of unbridled lust between a King of England and not one, but two minions! Oh, I know all about it for I have had to read it,' grumbled the Wardrobe Master. 'If Master Henslowe is determined to put the piece on here, as he seems to be, then he needs his wits seeing to. Anyway, I haven't got all day, I'd best go and see what is left in the wardrobe for *Tamburlaine*, I suppose I should be grateful you left some costumes here. Now there is, if I recall, a tawny satin doublet with gold lace, a pair of carnation satin breeches, a woman's gown of gold cloth . . .' He disappeared muttering to himself.

'Do you still have your lodgings safe?' Simon asked Richard.

'It seems so, but I'll have to ask Master Henslowe for an advance of money in order to pay for them. Do you know, when we got to Warwick, so close to my home, I was near to going back to my father and asking him to make me a wheelwright after all. At least Will Shakespeare is successful!' He had still not managed to catch up with his old schoolmate. On every occasion he had tried, Will had either been working in his lodgings on a new play and so unwilling to be disturbed, or visiting his family in Stratford.

Gradually the whole company assembled, to be harangued by Henslowe on their lamentable performance on tour, knowing he would have to advance most of them money to enable them to survive; although it was noted that he did not include Alleyn in his diatribe. Next came Peter the Bookkeeper, who listed the plays that would be presented during the next two or three weeks, a programme which included the new (to London) *Edward II* for which he then handed round the rolls. Henslowe had, in truth, had severe doubts about it, fully aware of its provincial reception, but after much thought and some discussion with Alleyn had decided to take a risk. He needed a play about a king, and a new play from Kit Marlowe, and London audiences were far more sophisticated than their country cousins. It would have been better for everyone if Marlowe had allowed him to put the play on first at the Rose, but Marlowe had been determined to punish him for comparing him with Shakespeare.

So it was that Marlowe walked in to the Rose to the words of his own contentious play. Richard had rather hoped he might be cast either as Gaveston, Edward's first favourite, or his enemy, Mortimer, but the first had gone to an actor of more experience and Mortimer to Simon and he had to make do with the Earl of Lancaster. Alleyn, of course, was to play Edward.

The scene being rehearsed was that between Edward, his wife Isabella (played by young Jamie), and Gaveston, when the Queen is trying to regain the King's affection. Whatever the exigencies of the tour, Jamie had returned from it with increased confidence while retaining his prettiness. There was no sign of his voice breaking and, if he was lucky, he might still have two years or eighteen months to play. He even managed to look convincingly regal as he turned to Gaveston with contempt on the line, "'tis thou who robb'st me of my lord'. Marlowe watched with keen interest, sharpened by attraction and speculation; not all the boys successful in women's roles were attracted to their own sex.

He knew he looked well, thanks to Tom's generosity, and his clothes contrasted sharply with the shabby garments of the actors. Tom had been generous over the summer and he now sported a deep-blue velvet doublet and breeches, his usual fine white shirt and soft leather riding boots. He sat and watched without saying a word until the rehearsal was at an end then, seeing Henslowe hovering in the background called out, 'Stop lurking there, Phillip. How do you like your play about a king?'

Henslowe shook his head. 'I have grave doubts over the

59

piece, Christopher, grave doubts. Perhaps you've not heard, hidden away in Kent, what happened in the provinces?'

'Word did reach me from Pembroke's Men. But what can you expect of provincials? I am aware it could hardly be called a success.'

'Nothing was,' said Richard, 'but your play didn't help any of us. We had to sell everything to get back to London.'

'I knew of that too, even "hidden away in Kent". You came out of it all right, though, didn't you Ned? I was told you sneaked all your possessions back to town before your creditors could lay hands on them. Well done!'

Ned Alleyn gave him a speaking look and then disappeared with Henslowe to discuss the business of the Bear Pit, his expertise on the matter having been sadly missed in his absence.

'You've just ridden from Scadbury?' enquired Simon.

'No. Tyburn.'

Several actors, about to depart, turned back at this and Will Hunt enquired what had taken him there.

'Why Cutting Ball Jack, of course, Emma's brother. Did you not know he was to be turned off this morning?' There was a general murmur of dissent. Simon's thought turned at once to Emma and considered it might be well to tell Jenny what had happened, for the girl must be in dire need of comfort. Greene would be of little use, and now Emma had another responsibility. It was not yet a year since she had given birth to a boy, a weak and sickly child, to whom his father had given the singularly inappropriate name 'Fortunatus'. 'Was Em there?' he asked.

'Yes, though without her puny infant. A creature not long for this world, I imagine.'

'Nor his father either if all I hear is true,' responded Simon.

'Indeed, they say he gallops apace to his grave, a bottle in one hand, a lady's placket in the other. You know he called the boy Fortunatus? Fortunatus!'

'How did – er – how did Jack . . .' began Will Hunt.

'How did he die? Oh, with great aplomb, as you might

imagine. Usual type of thing . . .' He was suddenly aware that they had all fallen silent and only then did he realise that Emma was standing in the doorway. The child was in her arms and she was accompanied by another woman.

'Why, Emma,' began Richard, 'we thought you'd still . . .'

'There's no point, now it's over, as no doubt Kit has told you.'

'Where's Robert?' asked Simon.

'Drunk, of course. Even though the sickness eats him.' The child set up a thin wailing sound. 'Here, Nell, he seems to be hungry again already.' Nell took the baby from her, sat down and, unlacing her gown, began to feed him. 'I've lost all my milk,' continued Emma, 'and he still takes little else. Nell's child was stillborn so she's food enough for him.'

'Aye and to spare,' said Nell, settling the child more comfortably. 'Mine looked a bonny boy, too, as big again as this one was. Yet God saw fit to decide he would never draw breath. He sucks so weakly still, come on little one.'

Richard came over and put his arm around Emma. 'We are sorry, Emma, all of us.'

'Sorry? Are you? Have you any notion what it was like? I pushed up as near as I could to the cart when it reached the gallows. He saw me and we tried to touch one last time, but they stopped us. I was so close I could smell his sweat through his shirt. Then they pulled me away.

'He was gallant to the last. He refused to say he was sorry for what he'd done; he said there were others, worse than him, the law couldn't touch.'

'I thought that rather well said,' commented Marlowe, 'I hope I'd say as much myself in similar circumstances.'

'Don't go on,' begged Richard, 'you'll only upset yourself more.'

'They shit themselves when their necks break, did you know that? They're degraded even in death, but he was luckier than some. One of our friends had already given the executioner a guinea to allow him to pull on his legs so he'd die quickly. But they won't cut him down until tonight, he must hang as an example.' Very quietly she began to cry. 'I must see to his burial. There's a priest who'll turn a blind eye to who he was and what he did for a handful of coins.'

Hard-pressed as they were, all her listeners put their hands to their purses and gave her what money they could. She thanked them. 'We were left orphaned as children, you know. What else could we do to survive? He stole and I sold myself in alleyways for fourpence.'

'Very affecting,' said Marlowe, strolling over to Jamie and putting his arm round him. 'Quite a tract for our times. Come, Jamie, let us go to the Ordinary and I'll buy us both some dinner.'

The two women stood up and made ready to leave. 'The child sleeps,' said Nell, 'I'll take him back with me while you do what you must.'

'Did Emma's brother leave any wife or mistress behind to mourn him and share her grief?' asked Jamie.

'Not that I know of,' said Marlowe, 'many doxies but no wife, so no doubt there'll be a gaggle of women around the grave tomorrow.'

'I'll send Jenny to her,' said Simon and left.

'Emma always said that the women would never leave him alone,' remarked Richard.

'Oh, he was a pretty fellow.' Marlowe began toying with one of Jamie's long curls. 'Golden-haired and skin as smooth as a girl's . . . not unlike this boy here. Very different from poor Em, I fear they must have had different sires. Well, we'll away, I'm starving.' At the door he said, 'There was a certain irony this morning. I happen to know that the friend who did him the greatest service, pulling his legs so he died fast, loved him beyond the love of any woman.' He pulled Jamie close to him. 'Not that Jack appreciated it!'

* * * *

Much later, after he had arranged for Jamie to come to his lodgings that night, he went in search of Robert Poley. He needed both the money and the amusement the work provided.

8

Then pour the stars down Plagues . . .

Much Ado About Nothing   Shakespeare

THEN CAME THE PLAGUE.
For two years it was to ravage London, bringing terror to the streets, filling the graveyards and sending those who were fortunate enough to have the choice into the countryside; although its tentacles spread even there. For months at a time it closed the playhouses, forcing the players' companies out on to the road for sheer self-preservation. By February 1592 the Rose, the Theatre and the Curtain were all dark.

While it was naturally accepted that life was uncertain and death rarely far away, the wholesale slaughter wrought by the disease was altogether different. A man might leave his home in the morning, only to be brought back lifeless on a bier that afternoon, dead from a knife wound or the cut of a sword in the street. A woman might scarcely have time to rejoice at the safe delivery of a son or daughter before she was stricken with child-bed fever. But Plague stalked the city relentlessly and impartially, visiting young and old, the palaces of the rich as often as the warrens of the poor, removing whole families in a single night.

Many turned to God and those who had attended church irregularly, and only then for fear of being fined, now exhorted the Almighty on their knees to bring them through it. Some, like Master Henslowe, turned to medicine, dosing his reluctant family with a specific composed of rue, southernwood and elderflower, mixed with bats' blood and steeped in wine. Others eagerly bought Master Simon Kellawaye's pamphlet, *Defensative*

Against the Plague, noting that the most sensible piece of advice was probably *fuge locu* – flee the place!

Many of those that could did indeed leave London, even though it meant fretting over those left behind. Simon Pope sent a reluctant Jenny and the boys to her father in Oxford, writing to her whenever it was possible pleading that she stay there until there was, at the very least, a lull in the spread of the sickness. Phillip Henslowe, who stoutly refused to join the exodus out of London, wrote to Ned Alleyn in Worcester, where the Lord Admiral's Company was spending a few days, assuring him that all was well with the family and the 'mouse' he had left behind on the Bankside. He was putting his faith, he told Alleyn, in hearty prayers to the Lord Jesus, 'that we shall have again a merry meeting', and that while they naturally stood in fear of the Plague, they thanked God in his mercy for their good health.

'Yet,' he wrote, 'all round about it has been in almost every house and whole households have died, yet my friend the bailiff escapes though he smells monstrously of fear, for there have died this last week in general 1603 souls, which has been the greatest number yet, and as for other news of this and that I can tell you none but that Robert Browne's wife in Shoreditch and all her children and her household are dead and her doors shut.' Robert Browne, an actor with Worcester's Men, was on tour in Germany and so would not know of his tragedy until his return. 'Mouse' added a note to the letter of a more cheerful kind. The joiner had been to measure up for a new bedstead and she had dyed his orange stockings as requested but had not been able to buy the cloth for his new doublet as all the markets were closed. She had also tried to sell his horse but as no one would give her more than £4 for it, she had sent it to the country until his return.

* * * *

There were those who could have left London but did not

choose to do so; men burdened with the affairs of state, like Acting Secretary Robert Cecil.

He was now at the centre of a complex web of which his interest in Marlowe formed only one strand. Central to his strategy was the downfall of Essex, the power of whose family and faction almost rivalled his own. Rich, spoiled, the object of the Queen's besotted affection, Cecil knew that it was only a matter of time before, with judicious assistance, Essex could be destroyed. To this end, following Walsingham's precedent in the Babbington Plot, he had a double agent within the Essex household, a man called Richard Chomley. Then there was the question of Walter Raleigh and his School of the Night.

Here, too, he had to walk carefully, for Raleigh was also held in high esteem by the Queen. Cecil disliked him personally, disliked his extravagance – Raleigh had recently been taken to court for his elaborate dressing, having presented himself before Her Majesty literally covered in pearls – and was deeply suspicious of his intellectual questings. However he now had his own contact in the School of the Night, Matthew Cobham, and it was Cobham who had given him the piece of news he now revealed to Robert Poley, with the nearest he ever came to showing amusement.

'Raleigh – contemplating marriage?' Poley responded, with incredulity. The Queen's attitude to favourites who married was notorious.

'It would seem he is involved in a lengthy and serious affair with Elizabeth Throckmorton, one of the Queen's own ladies. I cannot imagine the Throckmortons settling for anything less.'

'And this more than mere Court gossip?'

Cecil coughed in the way he did when he found a subject somewhat unsavoury. 'My informant saw him with the lady, under a tree. It seems little doubt that – er – congress was taking place. The lady's skirts were up around her waist and Raleigh's breeches down around his ankles. I am told that the lady's faint protestations of "oh Sir Walter", turned to what sounded like "switter, swatter" repeated many times . . . I think, therefore, we are in a position to deal with the School of the Night at any time we choose. I shall watch carefully to see if there is a marriage.

'Now, to more urgent matters. Essex is making overtures to Scotland. I must know more. I do not entirely trust Chomley. Make it your task to encourage him to confide in you.' He paused. 'I have heard nothing from you of late about Marlowe.'

'Marlowe undertook courier work for me last year. We are in touch. I will contact you, as promised, the moment I decide we must take action.'

Cecil rose to his feet to end the interview. 'I do not like these writers of plays. Dangerous ideas can be promulgated in the name of entertainment.'

* * * *

There were those who could not leave London even had they wished. Greene had moved out of Emma's house, sick, he told her, of the child's wailing and her nagging and lack of looks, and had taken lodgings with a shoemaker and his wife. He spent his days either hunched in his bed, writing feverishly or, when he felt strong enough, in his old haunts, the taverns and brothels of Shoreditch or Bankside, now thin of trade. He took little heed of the Plague, for death now stood always at his shoulder, as the pox continued to eat into him. The end would be the same whether he was hustled out in the night to the death cart and thrown into a Plague Pit or carried, more decently and with less haste, to a nearby churchyard.

Emma remained in her little house and prayed for the survival of the frail Fortunatus, now an unsteady toddler (for he had been slow to walk), clutching at her skirts and demanding her attention. Clients were few but she took what she could where she could for the alternative to risking the Plague was starvation.

By July most of the touring companies had disbanded,

waiting hopefully for the reopening of the playhouses and Simon left thankfully for Oxford and Jenny, while Richard, unsure what to do, finally decided to risk returning to London, for Henslowe had written that he was hopeful the worst had passed. He presented himself once more in Henslowe's office. Henslowe, without receipts either from the Rose or the Bear Pit had concentrated on the other string he had to his bow, his timber business, and his desk, usually strewn with his inventories and accounts for the Rose, was heaped with papers to do with elmboards and bundles of laths. After the usual greetings, Richard asked him if he could advance him a little money until the Rose opened once again.

'*If* it opens again . . .' grumbled Henslowe. 'They say that by August it might well be possible but I don't know, I don't know at all.' Richard's heart sank. 'But you could be useful. Peter has been taking the opportunity to renew many play rolls and I will pay you to assist him. That way you make yourself useful and I do not have to advance you money without knowing if I will ever get it back.' So it was that walking back to his lodgings, his arms full of rolls for parts in such diverse pieces as *Titus and Vespasia*, *The Comedy of Donnaracio* and *The Pinder of Wakefield*, Richard ran into Tom Kyd.

'How often have I had to undertake such a task,' he told Richard, 'and much else of far less interest, like legal documents and church sermons but, thankfully, it's now behind me for I've found a patron.' Richard congratulated him. Kyd was struck by a thought. 'Why don't you come and share my workroom with me? There's ample room for two and I imagine it might be difficult for you to find the space in your lodgings.'

'What about Kit Marlowe?'

'Oh, he told me he no longer wanted to share it months ago, yet he's *still* not collected all his papers. I warned him the last time I saw him that the next time it's cold I'll use them to light the fire!'

'Is he in town?'

'If he is, I haven't seen him. I imagine he's at Scadbury, away from the Plague. He told me he was working on another play, one that would surpass anything he had ever written before.'

So Kyd took him over the river to the workroom he had, close by St Paul's, a spacious attic with a large window which let in plenty of light.

'How much would you like me to pay you towards your rent?' asked Richard.

Kyd waved it aside. 'Happily, thanks to my patron, I've now sufficient funds and know very well what it's like for a young man to be dependent upon the vagaries of the playhouses.' He remained mysterious as to the identity of his patron, and Richard did not press the point. So a comfortable routine was established. Every day Richard walked over the bridge (averting his eyes) to spend his time laboriously copying out the seemingly never-ending rolls, while across the room Kyd crossed and recrossed sheet after sheet as he worked on his play.

Kyd had a fund of knowledge of old plays and plots and was only too happy to share his enthusiasm. He showed Richard a play he had written for Henslowe some years previously, a story set in the court of King Claudius of Denmark and his stepson, Prince Hamlet. Although he began it, as he had *The Spanish Tragedy*, with a ghost calling for revenge, it had not proved anything like as popular with the audiences, who had joked later in the taverns about yet another bad actor in a white sheet clanking chains and moaning 'revenge'. He was finding it difficult to get right and had decided to make one last attempt to see if he could make it work. 'It's a good story,' he told Richard, 'it should be possible, but perhaps I'm not the right person to do it.'

One morning, needing to clear a bigger space for a particularly large bundle of rolls, Richard knocked over a pile of papers which had been gathering dust in a corner. As he picked them up and tried to re-arrange them in the order in which they had been put, he glanced idly over a

JUDITH COOK

yellowed, dog-eared pamphlet. It was obviously old and the print had faded but it seemed to be some kind of treatise denying the existence of the Holy Trinity. It was an odd thing to find in Kyd's room.

He was still musing on it, when the playwright arrived.

'What've you got there?'

Richard jumped guiltily. 'I'm sorry. I knocked over the papers in the corner. I've tried to put them back as I found them. I was just reading this.'

Kyd laughed. 'Oh, don't worry. Those are Kit's papers, the ones I told you he'd never collected.'

Richard felt a great sense of relief. 'So this awful thing isn't yours?' He handed the pamphlet to Kyd.

'No, indeed it is not.' He sighed. 'You can see why I find Kit's views so alarming. Put it back where it was and pay it no mind. It's got nothing to do with us, thank God.'

A gentle soul, Kyd had never been a great frequenter of taverns, not least because he had become weary of being the butt of the savage humour of both Marlowe and Greene. Now the Plague made most people think twice before mingling with others, but it was still necessary to eat and drink and the two would sometimes dine together. The liking Richard had immediately felt for Kyd became a real affection. He felt he alone understood his own feelings about London and the actors' world in which he now lived.

After such a supper Richard would walk back again over London Bridge, to fall into an exhausted sleep whereupon a mad procession of kings, ghosts, soldiers, clowns, wanton women and proud queens, Robin Hood and the Queen of the Fairies, Persian kings and boiling Jews, would march round and round inside his head.

Once or twice they came across Robert Greene, a macabre, emaciated figure, the red hair of which he had been so proud now thin, greasy and straggling down his back, his eyes burning in a white face, tinged with a greenish hue from the stained doublet dyed in his favourite colour, goose-turd green. Once, too, Richard had found

70

Emma, looking tired and ten years older than her age, wearing a dirty, spangled red gown, standing with the other whores outside St Paul's. He had pressed some coins in her hand and, when she offered to take him home, had told her it was for the child.

* * * *

During the first part of that Plague summer, Marlowe had indeed retreated to Scadbury, nor had he any wish to leave it, he was so carried away with his new play. Raleigh had given him a copy of the *Faust Book*, recently published in Germany, which, he told him, should appeal to him, dealing as it did with a man who could raise demons and who sold his soul to the devil. Marlowe had laughed and taken it with him to Scadbury as a diversion to read beside the lake. He read on and on until the dusk had fallen around him and Tom came seeking him for supper. Here, in Faustus, he had found the ultimate protagonist, a being with whom he could utterly identify, a man arrogant and reckless enough to challenge God himself, selling his soul not only for power, but for unlimited, infinite, knowledge. Who would not willingly sell his soul for such a bargain!

He had been totally caught up and swept along by Faustus; through him he could explore all those forbidden subjects which were of such consuming interest to the School of the Night: the new sciences and mathematics, the sheer scope of man's intellect, the movement of the stars and the planets, the truth, or otherwise, of man's belief in God. He wrote eagerly to Thomas Harriot, most brilliant of mathematicians, seeking more information.

No other play had come so easily; he wrote on and on, hardly stopping to eat, refusing even to join in the entertainments on the summer evenings, impelled by some unknown force to complete the work. Only to realise, of course, that because of the Plague it could not be performed, at least not in London.

So he had agreed with Henslowe that it should be tried

out by one of the touring companies, then presented at the Rose as soon as that theatre re-opened.

Afterwards he suffered, as he always did after an intensely creative period, from boredom, lack of direction and an irritable restlessness which the peace of Scadbury only exacerbated. In normal circumstances he would have thrown himself into several weeks of debauchery until the mood left him, but these were not normal times. He could eat and drink his fill with Tom, drink to intoxication without let or hindrance but it lacked the edge and danger of the seamy, crowded taverns, packed with thieves and coseners and he found he missed, too, the theatrical gossip and the wit of the actors and his fellow poets.

Nor, at Scadbury, could he drown himself in venery. He needed the stimulation of new blood and the chase. His passionate affair with young Jamie had been abruptly brought to a halt when the Lord Admiral's Company left London. He cared for the boy, though in no way could reciprocate his devotion, but it might well be months before the Rose re-opened and the company returned.

So it was that he took his chance with the Plague and returned to London, a London half empty, from which most of his friends and acquaintances were absent, and it was in this frame of mind that he turned, yet again, to Robert Poley. He had never either liked or trusted him and knew the feeling was mutual, but he had had his uses and at one level he could appreciate Poley's expertise, the brilliant amateur recognising the true professional. So, having nothing better to do, when Poley had suggested he might again undertake some simple tasks for payment, he agreed.

Twice he acted as a courier, taking despatches to the Low Countries (and enjoying for a few days the delights of Amsterdam) and he had also read through and made out summary from a sheaf of reports from agents on the situation at the Catholic seminary in Rheims. The latter brought back, for the first time in years, memories of those heady days spent in France, disguised as a recusant Catholic student, when he should have been attending to his own studies in Cambridge.

Nothing since had quite matched the excitement of taking such risks, of acting so persuasively that he had totally convinced the seminary that he was, indeed, a recusant student bound for the priesthood, able and willing to plot against his Queen. It had been as if he were pitted against masters in a marvellous game of chess. Sir Francis had been delighted with the reports he had sent back from Rheims, even more so with the information he had brought to him on his return to England. He had learned of other interesting matters too, while in France, but these he had chosen not to divulge to his employer. It was always as well to keep back some information for possible future use – if it became necessary.

It still amused him to think of the fuss his absences from college had caused, the long faces of his tutors and that of Dr Norgate, the Master, when they told him he would not be granted his MA as he had not fulfilled the College's residency requirements – or how all these solemn men had had to eat their words at the express command of the Privy Council, as shown in its letter to the appropriate University authorities.

'Whereas,' Walsingham had written, 'it was reported that Christopher Marlowe was determined to have gone beyond the sea to Rheims and there to remain, their Lordships thought it good to certify that in all his actions he has behaved himself orderly and discreetly, whereby he has done her Majesty good service, and deserves to be rewarded for his faithful dealings: Their Lordships request that the rumour therefore should be allayed by all possible means, and that he should be furthered in the degree he is to take this next commencement. Because it is not her Majesty's pleasure that anyone employed as he has been, in matters touching the benefit of his country, should be defamed by those that are ignorant of the affairs he went about.' It was signed by no less personages than the Archbishop of Canterbury, the Lord Chancellor, the Lord Treasurer, the Lord Chamberlain, the Controller of the

Queen's Council and, of course, Secretary Francis Walsingham himself.

'Orderly and discreetly.' Well those days were gone. Since the fight in Hog Lane he had kept himself out of overt trouble for some time but when visiting London briefly, at the beginning of May, to give his script of *Dr Faustus* to Henslowe, there had been another incident. He had sought out Robert Greene, feeling for some reason he could not explain a need to see his rival; had persuaded him out of his bed and into his clothes and together they had spent the day in a Shoreditch tavern, drinking steadily and increasingly offensively.

Eventually the hostess had enough. When he called the drawer demanding more wine, she intervened.

'You've had more than enough. Now, if you please, take yourselves off.'

Greene narrowed his eyes in an attempt to focus them on her. 'What's that you say?'

'I said I want you out of here.'

'Do you realise, madam, who you are addressing?' Greene had responded with drunken dignity.

'A couple of swaggerers too drunk to know or care what they say, who are polluting my tavern with their foul language and disgusting ideas and offending my customers.'

'You repellant old whore, you pox-ridden tearsheet,' roared Greene. 'You seller of ale diluted with piss . . .'

At this point the hostess sent the boy for assistance and he soon returned with a sweating constable by the name of Alan Nicholls. Nicholls moved against Marlowe first, taking him by the collar and attempting to remove him by force. Marlowe, his quick temper exacerbated by drink, immediately punched him in the stomach, then followed it up with a crack across the head. Enraged, half-blinded and with his guts heaving, Allan summoned assistance and a brace of constables came to his aid and hauled Marlowe off to the local lock-up.

He had duly appeared before Sir Nicholas Bond,

Magistrate, the following morning, for being drunk and disorderly and assaulting a constable. Sir Nicholas had bound him over to keep the peace, adding a homily to the effect that he was weary of so-called gentlemen appearing before him in such circumstances and that he would be better employed down on his knees in God's house beseeching the Almighty to save himself and his fellows from the scourge of the Plague.

Now, once again, he was kicking his heels in London with nothing to do, unable to write and unable to rest. So it was that the chasm opened at his feet and he did not see it.

He had always managed, successfully, to keep the disparate parts of his life separate. There was the world of poetry, playwriting and the theatre; his acceptance in the intellectual world of the School of the Night and its well-born circle. Finally, there was his involvement in that dark world of espionage; that activity he still found addictive. Only Tom Walsingham had moved within all these circles, although, since Cecil had taken over the reins, he seemed to have lost interest in secret matters.

Informed by Henslowe that if the Plague continued to diminish, then he would re-open the Rose and his spirits raised at the prospect of seeing *Faustus* on stage, he set off once more in search of Greene. Greene had again taken to his bed which was covered in pages written in an almost unreadable scrawl.

'What's this? A new play? A satirical pamphlet?'

Greene snatched them up. 'A mere groatsworth of wit.'

'Well, when you get to your deathbed repentance, remember me,' Marlowe mocked.

There was a flash of the old spirit. 'Oh I will, Kit, I will.'

As he left his bed to dress, Marlowe realised how much he had deteriorated since the previous May. There was nothing left of the upper part of his body, whereas his legs and ankles were grotesquely swollen.

When they reached the fresh air it was obvious Greene could not walk far, so they made their way to the Mermaid in the hope that some of the actors might be there, but they found no one they knew. Both, for their different reasons, once again set about drinking heavily and on neither did it have a good effect. Robert Greene was consumed with black anger against everybody and everything: Emma for her lack of sympathy, Henslowe for refusing to advance him any money to write a new play, Will Shakespeare (especially Will Shakespeare) and, most of all, the disease that was rotting him.

'Will Shakespeare, he's a cosener, an upstart, a . . . a piece of country shit, pig-ignorant, slow in his wits, yet he sweeps all before him. The other day someone asked me, asked *me*, if I didn't think I had much to learn from him!'

'That's more or less what Henslowe said to me last year,' Marlowe replied, 'or something like it. He wondered I did not write similar plays on the lives of kings, which annoyed me so much that I went away and wrote him *Edward II*. I trust he's learned his lesson.'

Greene laughed, then coughed and continued until it seemed his chest would break. Marlowe watched him dispassionately. 'You're a living warning of the fate awaiting those who lust after women, Robin.'

Greene wiped his mouth. 'Oh I have the pox, for sure, but many live for years with it. Last week my landlady was so concerned that she brought the great Dr Foreman to see me and he tells me that it's the consumption that will take me to the grave, that is if the Plague doesn't get there first.'

They both resumed drinking in silence and the effect on Marlowe was that instead of becoming elated by drink, he was first bad tempered, then morose and, finally, plain evil. His talents, he said loudly, were insufficiently appreciated not only in the theatre, but also by those in high places who owed him so much. 'I could tell you things, if I wanted to. About all of them. Essex, Burleigh, Cecil, the Bacons . . .' He laughed. 'Especially the Bacons.' The few drinkers in the Mermaid paid him no heed; self-pitying, bragging drunks were hardly uncommon. But finally his words attracted the attention of a fair-haired, rabbit-faced man in a corner. There was mutual recognition.

'Well,' called out Marlowe, 'if it isn't Nick Skeres! Meet an old friend of mine, Robin: Nick Skeres, Robin Greene, and vice versa. Order me a drink, Nick, then come and join us.' Skeres gave Marlowe a tight smile then, after ordering three pints of ale from the drawer, came and joined them.

'Nick and I've worked together many times,' Marlowe added. 'Good ol' Nick. Not all that bright, but then we can't all be, can we?'

'Which company do you belong to?' enquired Greene.

Skeres looked nonplussed.

'No, no, Robin, it's not *that* kind of work. Nick doesn't act out parts or practise deception in the *playhouses*, do you my ol' friend. No, we appear together on a bigger stage, Nick and I. We deal in mighty matters, affairs of state, the defence of the realm!' He giggled, foolishly. 'D'you know,' he continued, looking around the room at his uninterested audience, 'd'you know, you'll soon be bowing the knee to Scots Jamie? And it won't be treason. "For if it prosper, none dare call it treason . . ." All those guttings at Tyburn, only to end up with a Stuart King. Think of it next time you cross London Bridge and gawp at the rotting skulls. Not that it matters a fart to me, who's on the English throne.' He hiccupped and stood up. 'I say there shall be no more Princes.'

It was unlikely that by the next morning Greene remembered anything that had been said, but Marlowe's outburst caused Skeres to swallow down his drink as if the Plague were after him, sending him hotfoot in search of Poley.

9

Still climbing after knowledge infinite,
And always moving as the restless spheres,
Will us to wear ourselves and never rest . . .

Tamburlaine Part 1   Marlowe

FOR A WHILE IT seemed almost as if the Plague had satiated itself. The burial carts no longer made their endless nightly rounds, the streets began to fill as those who had sought refuge in the country returned to their homes. Among these were the weary, dispirited and penurious actors, remnants of the companies which had set out on the roads so bravely months before.

Richard, calling at the home of the Popes for the first time in months, found that not only had Simon returned but Jenny as well. He was welcomed with open arms.

'Where are the boys?' he asked, for the big kitchen was unnaturally quiet.

'We thought it best to leave them with my father and my old nurse, Mollie, until we saw how matters were. It's very hard for me.' She smiled at Richard and patted his shoulder. She was not a pretty woman, not even striking like Emma, but the bones of her face and her large eyes made her attractive. Now, her unusually unruly hair was closely confined in a linen cap and she was wrapped around with sacking apron. The house had been locked up for six months and she had spent the last two days scrubbing and cleaning. It still smelled of damp and neglect but now a fire burned in the grate and savoury smells came from a large pot hanging above it.

Jenny brought him a mug of ale and invited him to join them in their meal. As she ladled a portion of stew out of the pot and on to a platter, which she had set down in front of him, she continued, 'Father says he'll teach Daniel to read and Sam his letters. Molly is kind and loves them dearly, but I miss them already. If we think it better they stay in Oxford, then I'll return though, as that will part me again from Simon, I am made unhappy either way.' She reached her hand over the table and Simon picked it up and kissed the palm; Richard felt a pang of envy at such contented domesticity.

Where women were concerned his own life seemed far from satisfactory; sometimes, he thought, he would have fared better with the country girls back home in Warwickshire. Like any personable actor he had become used to the discreet propositions from female members of the audiences, mostly the younger wives of merchants and artisans, and on several occasions of late he had spent energetic hours on the large ornate bedstead of an unknowing silversmith; but such tumbling was, of its very nature, fraught with hazard and led nowhere.

Talk then turned to Robert Greene. Did they know, asked Richard, that he was now mortally ill?

'We heard rumours,' Simon told him.

'As soon as we have finished our dinner, I will go to Emma,' said Jenny. 'She might well need help with the nursing and without the boys I am not tied.'

'But he's no longer with Emma,' said Richard. 'I've been sharing a workroom over the river with Tom Kyd. Robin took lodgings nearby some months ago, with a shoemaker and his wife. Emma told me he had said she and the child drove him to distraction.'

'She must love him dearly,' mused Jenny. 'I would never put up with his behaviour.'

Simon went over and put his arm round her. 'Nor would I expect it, my love.'

'And poor little Fortunatus,' asked Jenny, 'does he still live?'

'So far as I know. It's strange so frail and sickly a child survives when so many who are strong perish.'

'The old women say it's often the way with the Plague. It takes the hale and hearty and leaves the weak.' She began to clear away, saying that when she had finished she would walk over London Bridge to Emma's house to see what news there was. 'I must own I've never been easy with him. But even such a one as he, can't be allowed to die without the comfort of a friendly face.'

* * * *

'He's done *what?*' exploded Marlowe.

Tom Walsingham laughed. 'Surely you must have had wind of it, you who are so close in his circle?'

But the news of Raleigh's secret marriage had come as a complete shock. Marlowe had recently returned to Scadbury from Holland. For reasons he could not explain even to himself, he did not confide to Tom that he still worked, from time to time, for the secret world and Tom, naturally, had assumed he had spent the last two weeks in London.

'No, I had not. Lusts of the flesh are not discussed at meetings of the School of the Night. There are better topics. What now then, since you're new come from Court?'

'The Queen has sent him and Bess Throckmorton to cool their heels in the Tower until her rage abates. You can imagine it – one of her prime favourites and a Maid of Honour, who should ask her Sovereign's permission to wed. The royal wrath has rocked the Court. The main beneficiary will, of course, be Essex since now he has no other strong rival; and those who found Raleigh nothing but an arrogant, Devonian upstart, are crowing at his disgrace.'

The news made Marlowe feel uneasy. Of late he had sometimes felt that it might be useful to have a friend at Court, apart from Tom, and Raleigh had seemed so secure, so strongly placed. His imprisonment had many implications.

'And what now of the School of the Night?' he wondered. 'In the interests of discretion, it will, no doubt, cease it's meetings. Don't look so glum, Elizabeth will get over this as she has done on many occasions before. He'll be home before the year's out, you'll see. But I'm still amazed you didn't know of it. I thought you must have heard the famous story about the two of them.'

'What's that?'

Tom told him of the incident that Cecil had passed on to Poley the year before. 'So her cries of "Oh, Sir Walter", as he unlaced her bodice and threw up her petticoats, turned to "Switter, Swatter", in a rhythmic fashion until, at the point of pleasure, she called for all to hear "Ooooh, Sir Walter!" '

But Marlowe did not seem to find it amusing.

* * * *

At eight in the morning, a few days later, the actors assembled on the stage of the Rose. A long period out of London had taken its toll and there were some new faces. Will Hunt, the clown, had returned as had Dick Hoope, who could still play the roles of older women at nearly thirty. Of the apprentices, three had had their voices break and only one had returned, in the hope he might be given a chance to try his hand in other parts. Jamie, alone, was left to play the leading women's roles, a Jamie with more confidence. Among the new adult actors there was a personable fellow with a marked West Country accent, Henry Brodribb from Cornwall; and a thin, colourless young man who was reticent about his recent engagements.

The news from Henslowe was that they would now be known officially as the Lord Admiral's Men and had been registered as such. There would be six sharers in the expenses and profits of the company, and he had no plans to increase the number. The rest of the company would, as usual, be hired on a seasonal, monthly or weekly basis.

This caused Simon, later, to complain forthrightly to Richard and Will Hunt that he was unhappy with the way the company was organised. 'I'd thought to be a sharer by now. I've spent five years with Henslowe, proved my worth beyond doubt, yet I am still only a hired man. At my time of life I deserve something better.

'You should know by now how tight a hold Phillip and Ned like to keep on everything,' responded Will. 'You are unlikely to change matters.'

'Not at the Rose, certainly,' said Simon, then added, 'but since coming back to London, I've talked to Dick Burbage and Hemmings. Their company too is reforming and will become the Lord Chamberlain's Men. There are to be eight sharers and it's possible I'll be offered a share, along with Will Shakespeare.'

'I was at school with him,' said Richard, wondering what life would be like if Simon left the Rose.

'Were you indeed? You've never said.'

'He was a senior boy when I first went to the grammar school in Stratford. His father and mine are friends. When he was eighteen, Will got a woman much older than him with child and had to marry her. Some time later he ran away to London to be a player and when I left he'd not been heard of since. He was held up to me as an Awful Warning.'

'What a fund of knowledge we've had here all along,' marvelled Hunt. 'Who'd have thought quiet Will Shakespeare should have been such a lad!' Ah well, they say still waters run deep. I wonder you've not sought out his acquaintance in all this time.'

'I tried several times, but he's either been busy, and so will not come out, or away.'

'You must send a message with Ralph Wilkins next time we see him,' said Simon, 'inviting Will Shakespeare to supper. Do you recall your first night in London?'

'Hazily. I remember disgracing myself by vomiting in the street.'

'And how all laughed when you told Greene you came from Warwickshire? It was because of Will and how much Robin detests him.'

'I realised that afterwards. I think Robin was more offended, though, by my taking him, as I recall, for Kit Marlowe.'

At the mention of Robert Greene they fell silent. Will said, 'They say he's close to death.'

'Very, if rumour is to be believed,' responded Simon. 'And what of Kit? Who has seen him of late?'

It seemed nobody had but, said Hunt, 'I am told he's drinking hard and in a poisonous mood. Let's hope he keeps it to himself.'

The Lord Admiral's Men rehearsed long and hard, ready for the opening the following Monday. There was much to do as even some of the old company members had a change of roles, while the newcomers, like Richard long ago, had to learn as many as they could as quickly as possible. The first two plays would be the sure-fire favourites, Kyd's *Spanish Tragedy* and the anonymous *Arden of Faversham*. They were also given their parts for *Dr Faustus*. Its notoriety had preceded it.

'Did you hear,' asked Dick Hoope, always a prime gossip, 'what happened in Exeter? Well, my dears, I have it on the best authority that during the scene where Faustus raises the devils by necromancy, there seemed to be more devils on stage than there were actors to play them, devils unknown to anyone. This so terrified the company and the audience that the show had to be stopped, people rushed screaming from the hall where it was being performed, while Pembroke's Men spent the entire night down on their knees in prayer in Exeter Cathedral!'

On the first day of performance the company was gripped by excitement; it had been so long since they had performed together in a real playhouse. As the flag was run up on the flagpole and the trumpeter sounded the half-hour, the actors jostled each other before the mirrors, as they painted their faces and checked their personal props. Alleyn put aside the small bladder of pig's blood and piece of red felt, both of which he would insert in his mouth before the final scene, in which Hieronimo tears out his tongue to prevent his speaking under torture. It never failed to thrill the audience.

Now he knew Kyd so well, it never ceased to amaze Richard how so gentle and peaceable a man could have written a play so full of torture, murder and carnage; indeed he had asked him that question.

Kyd had smiled and shaken his head. 'My imagination can picture these things all too vividly, without need to experience them. And I am, from time to time, haunted by bad dreams.'

Before the play began, Henslowe wished his company luck, then went to see if all was well in the Rose. The theatre was packed to capacity, the gatherer so overwhelmed with collecting money that he had called in an apprentice to assist him. In the galleries there were a good many merchants and their families, even a sprinkling of young gallants. After months of fear and seclusion behind locked doors, there was a heartfelt need for entertainment.

From backstage the actors took it in turns to squint through a crack as the house filled up. The groundlings chatted, spat and drank their ale, the fruit and pie sellers were doing a brisk trade, as was a sober-suited fellow offering Plague remedies. Wafting backstage came the familiar smells of the playhouse, of sweaty close-packed bodies, oranges, strong perfumes (from the better off), smoke from the flares burning at the corners of the stage. The trumpet sounded a third time, and the new young actor, Gregory Sly, stepped forward as the ghost of Andrea to open the play. He was dressed in a white sheet, his face caked with make-up, his hair with flour.

The ghost's role was also to act as prologue and give the audience a resumé of the plot.

'When this eternal substance of my soul ...' he began, in a leaden monotone:

> Did live imprisoned in my mortal flesh,
> Each in their function serving other's need,

I was a courtier in the Spanish Court.
My name was Don Andrea . . .

He soon lost his audience, to cries of 'Hurry it along, man!' and 'Enough, Enough!', until he could scarcely make himself heard above the chatter; this made the first scene that followed very difficult, and it was not until Ned Alleyn strode on, hardly able to contain his rage, that the house finally quietened down and began to listen. After that, all went well, and the company took their bows to hearty applause.

'What possessed you to take on such an untalented dolt, Phillip?' thundered Alleyn, as soon as the actors returned backstage.

'We're very shorthanded, as you well know, and he claimed to have had a good deal of experience.'

Alleyn drew himself up to his full height. 'Either he goes or I do,' he said, grandly. Neither Henslowe nor anyone else took him seriously, but the newcomer was taken aside and told that unless he showed considerably more promise, he would have to find work elsewhere. In the meantime he would be better assisting the stage staff and learning the secrets of the special powders which made coloured smoke.

Gregory Sly took it uncomplainingly. After all, acting was not his prime purpose in taking employment at the Rose and Master Poley had promised to pay him well for the information he required on the behaviour of Christopher Marlowe. He applied himself to the coloured smoke.

10

This word damnation terrifies not him,
For he confounds Hell in Elysium . . .

Dr Faustus   Marlowe

ELATED BY THEIR SUCCESS, relieved to be back in
London and working together again, the actors spilled
out of the theatre, making their way, for the first time in
many months, to the Anchor Tavern. As usual they were
accompanied by a crowd of friends, well-wishers and
hangers-on; the latter included Ralph Wilkins, fresh from
his own rehearsals with the Lord Chamberlain's Men.
There was also Kit Marlowe.

For those who had not seen him for several months,
there was a noticeable change in his appearance. The fine
lines of his face seemed coarser and there were deep, purple
smudges under his eyes. His clothes, usually so elegant and
pristine, were soiled and creased, his doublet stained with
wine, his shirt collar grey. It was also apparent he was in a
foul mood. Adder-tongued, he put down with crushing
effect anyone with the temerity to speak to him uninvited.
He must, it was thought, have been drinking hard for
several days.

The Anchor's plump hostess welcomed back old
company members like long-lost relatives, giving and
returning hearty kisses. Yes, as they could see, she'd
survived the Plague so far – God be praised! – though
Hugh, her best drawer, had died of it along with his
mother and sisters, God rest their souls.

Drink flowed freely as news was exchanged, outrageous
stories swapped of their time on the road, as they pondered
on whether the Plague was now dead or only sleeping. The

86

drawers were run off their feet with orders for ale, sack and canary wine, as the noise level rose higher and higher. Groups formed around tables and Richard found himself with Simon, Tom Kyd (persuaded to come only with reluctance), Marlowe, with his arm round Jamie, Will Hunt and Ralph Wilkins.

The latter, borne aloft on a tide of strong ale, was booming out to the whole room the superiority of his own company and how the Burbages would have the best season in town. After opening with *Richard III*, they had another comedy, *Two Gentlemen of Verona*, which had a role for their own clown, Will Kempe, and a dog, which would have the audience splitting their sides. When Simon intervened to say they would soon be presenting Kit's new play, he capped that too. Will had written a fine tragedy, also set in Italy, about a pair of star-crossed lovers. It was all good, rough stuff, familiar to those used to thespian bragging. Tongues were loosened in drink and even poor Gregory Sly was talking animatedly to some fellow sitting beside him.

Then, in one of those sudden lulls that can happen in a noisy room, Marlowe shouted loudly, 'Get in some more drinks, for Christ's sake!' and looked directly at Tom Kyd.

'Isn't it about time you bought a round yourself?' asked Will Hunt. There had never been any love lost between them.

Marlowe held up his purse, untied it, then tipped it upside down. 'Gone, gone, all gone. I'll have to make shift to earn some more.' He laughed, foolishly. He must indeed be drunk, thought Richard, for usually he held his liquor better than this. Marlowe leaned across to Kyd and said, with deliberate offence, 'Tom here'll pay, won't you Tom. The little scrivener always keeps himself in funds by scrivening away, don't you?'

There was a chorus of disapproval from all who heard and, for once, even Kyd was stung to anger. 'Why should I? You haven't paid me what you owe me in rent for the room we shared last year.'

'You shared a room?' enquired Jamie, his voice high, his face flushed with wine.

Marlowe squeezed his shoulder. 'Only to work in, my dear. Never fancied Tom.' He smiled unpleasantly at Kyd. 'Go on, scrivener, I told you to get us some drinks.'

'I've had enough of this,' said Wilkins and, calling to a drawer, added 'if it'll keep you quiet, Marlowe, *I'll* buy the drinks, though I fail to understand why you can't pay for your own. You told us not ten minutes since that Henslowe had paid you four pounds for your new play.'

The drinks were brought and Marlowe, baulked of his prey, waved his tankard at the next table. 'Salutations! My money, Wilkins? My dear, it whistled in, then it whistled out.'

'And what about your precious patron, Tom Walsing-ham,' added Wilkins, 'has he tired of you?'

'Alas, the money he gave me has gone too. I fear I shall soon be reduced to working for the Crown yet again.' The unpleasant atmosphere he had engendered spread through the room, and his last remark drew the attention of both Gregory Sly and his weasel-faced companion.

'What do you mean?' asked Sly.

Marlowe ignored him and turned again to Wilkins. 'I trust Burbage pays you well for acting as trumpeter for Will Shakespeare, the Warwickshire Wantwit.'

'Will can look after himself without my help and since you've had such success with your *Tamburlaines* and *Jew*, you surely don't begrudge him his?'

'And Edward, please don't miss out poor Edward II,' returned Marlowe, 'even if he did end up with a poker up his arse. You,' he called over to Sly, 'whoever you are, I hope you realise you're sitting with the cream of London's artistic talent, if we leave out – and it's easy to do so – scrivener Kyd, author of . . . what's the piece called we saw today?'

'You poisonous bastard!' exclaimed Will Hunt.

'Nor must we forget young Jamie here. You know the exquisitely talented Jamie?'

'I play the girls' roles,' said Jamie nervously.

'To perfection,' added Marlowe.

Never a patient man at the best of times, Wilkins seemed set on pushing Marlowe further. 'Does your new play deal with buggery too?' he boomed.

'Sodomy, actually, if you mean Edward. No, this time my hero merely sells his soul to the Devil and is thus banished to eternal damnation. Haven't you heard of the *Faust Book*? Faustus is a brilliant scholar whose thirst for knowledge is all-consuming. So he trades his soul for twenty years of learning all the secrets of God and man, along with a few other toys such as wealth, power, miracle-working and the bedding of any woman he lusts after, even Helen of Troy. One must, after all, please the groundlings.'

'A terrible bargain!' said Kyd.

'Do you think so? Your soul for all the world's knowledge? I'd sell mine for that.'

The general level of noise had risen again. It was, after all, only Kit Marlowe showing off as usual. Taking advantage of attention shifting away, Simon leaned over to him and warned, 'You should watch what you say, Kit. Not everyone who hears will think you only jest.'

'But I don't.'

'I warned him when we worked together,' added Kyd, 'that these are perilous times. For God's sake, Kit, aren't you frightened of falling foul of those in authority when you say such things?'

'No one can touch me.'

'What did you mean when you said you might have to work for the Crown again?' broke in Jamie, who had nearly dozed off.

Marlowe gave him a look of drunken cunning. 'Let's just say I've done the state much service. What's more, I can prove it.'

'You can keep your views to yourself, Marlowe,' said Will Hunt, getting to his feet. While his was a very real talent for comedy and putting over bawdy rhymes, he was a devout man. 'I've had enough. I'm going home. He'll go to the Tower like his friend, Raleigh, and take us all with him, if he keeps shouting out such stuff to the whole world.'

'If you're going north, I'll join you,' said Wilkins, then was struck by a thought. 'Shouldn't Robin Greene be here?'

'Haven't you heard?' asked Richard. 'He's desperately ill, close to death.'

Marlowe took a swig from his glass. 'Indeed he is, and even now, so I understand, some missive is winging its way to me to tell me to mend my ways.' For a moment it looked as if Wilkins would respond but then, with a gesture, he followed Hunt out of the room.

'Would you really sell your soul to the Devil?' persisted Jamie.

'In the words of my Faustus, "this word, damnation, terrifies not me".'

This proved the final straw for Kyd. 'You'll answer to God for that on Judgement Day.'

'What God, what Judgement?' Marlowe roared back. 'I believe in neither. Only in the infinite capacity of man.' Kyd gave him one speaking look, and walked out.

Simon wrenched the glass out of Marlowe's hand and shook him. 'Dear Jesus, Kit, you know the penalties for this kind of talk. Doesn't the thought of the stake terrify you?'

'No, nor the hangman's rope or his disembowelling knife either.'

'Have you no fear of death?' asked Richard.

'Don't encourage him,' said Simon.

'The lad requires an answer. All men fear death, Richard, unless they are complete fools, which I am not. But for me, it's death that makes life worthwhile.' He drew out his dagger and ran his finger along its edge. 'Have you ever killed a man? It's very easy. A little, little thrust – and he's gone. Just carrion. There sits death, there sits imperious death, keeping his circuit by the slicing edge . . . The slicing edge of death . . . ' He slumped back, his head lolling.

'What in God's name's got into him?' asked Simon. 'He's like one driven by a daemon.'

Nearly everyone had left, among the last being Gregory Sly and his friend (whom he had introduced as 'Dick'), both of whom appeared to be so drunk they had to support each other. 'Come on, Richard,' said Simon. 'We'll leave the hostess to throw him out.'

As he spoke, Jenny came through the door, wrapped in a dark shawl. The two men stopped, in surprise, for she never joined the company at the Anchor.

Unsettled by the events of the night, and comforted by her dear familiar face, Simon asked gently, 'What is it love? We're just coming home.'

'It's Robert Greene. He's desperate to see you. I know how tired you must be, but I truly believe he may not last the night. I think it would give him comfort, Simon, if you came back with me.'

'Then I'll come at once. You too, Richard? Take us, then, Jenny.'

Jenny fumbled in her shawl and brought out a piece of paper, covered in Greene's scrawl.

'He sent this for Kit.' Marlowe, hearing his name, jerked himself awake and looked around. Wordlessly she handed him the paper and he squinted at it, trying to focus.

'Why, it's a diatribe on all my vices – drink, debauchery. That's rich, coming from him.'

'He's dying Kit,' said Simon. 'Won't you come with us to see him one last time.'

'Oh, he can die without me.' Marlowe's tone froze his listeners. He stared again at the paper. 'He's given me a final warning.' He staggered to his feet, clutching the paper. 'He says, and I quote, "I know the least of my demerits merit this miserable death, but wilful striving against known truth, exceeds all the terrors of the soul" – he always was an intellectual coward – "therefore, defer not with me, to this last point of extremity: for little knowest thou how, in

the end, thou shalt be visited." Now what can he possibly
mean by that?'

He was still laughing when they left the room.

*   *   *   *

It would seem that the fresh air cleared the heads of both
Gregory Sly and his companion, Dick Baines, amazingly
rapidly once they had left the Anchor. They crossed
London Bridge deep in conversation. Baines listened to
what Sly had to say then, on returning to his room,
despatched a note to Poley saying he had things to discuss.
Where and when might they meet?

Before replying, Poley presented himself again in Cecil's
office, making his report without preamble.

'I gather it will concern Kit's talking in drink,' he told
Cecil, 'which, of course, he's always done but never before
with such lack of discretion. Nor is it only that. My spy in
the theatre says he now makes no secret of his preference
for boys, going so far as to say that all those who love not
boys and tobacco are fools, thus drawing attention to
himself even more.'

Cecil considered this. 'His writings for the stage are also
beginning to cause concern. It hardly engenders respect for
the monarchy when the sick maunderings of a sodomite
King for his catamites, are paraded on the public stage as
entertainment. Now, I hear, we are to have a tale of a
scholar who sells his soul to the devil. So. What now?'

'You know my views on the Cambridge spies and this
man in particular, but I don't underestimate his intelligence
or the damage he might wreak if he chose. When sober,
he's a considerable adversary and learned much working
for Sir Francis.'

Cecil rapped the desk in irritation. 'Yet he is, as you say,
only a Cambridge spy. I have real matters of import to
concern myself with, not least the machinations of the Earl
of Essex and the contacts I know are being established
between Scotland and those who would be well placed

THE SLICING EDGE OF DEATH

when James comes to the throne.'

'With regard to information from Scotland, I suggest I send Marlowe to Edinburgh. No,' he added, seeing the look on Cecil's face, 'it is this kind of information gathering he does best. Also, I understand our somewhat unreliable source in the Essex household, Chomley, is also there. We can set them to watch each other.'

'You consider this a wise move?'

'Oh yes. For when we finally decide to bring Marlowe down, it will be useful to have apparently underhand dealings with the Scottish court as one of our reasons.'

Cecil rubbed his chin. 'It would seem you have already decided how his fall might be accomplished.'

Poley smiled and told him. Cecil listened carefully, then said, 'Yes. Yes, that might do very well. See to it for me, will you?'

11

Of this we will sup free, but moderately,
And we will have no Poley or Parrot by;
Nor shall our cups make any guilty men:
But at our parting we shall be as we innocently met . . .

'Inviting a Friend to Supper'   Jonson

O N A BEAUTIFUL SEPTEMBER morning, some days later, Robert Poley took a boat once again from St Paul's steps, but this time he did not go west to Westminster but east and downriver to Deptford. The tide was high and there was a good breeze, bringing with it the smell of the sea and so subsuming the stinks of effluent, especially those carried down by the Fleet River with its filthy cargo of turds, kitchen waste, dead rats, the carcasses of animals and, sometimes, those of nameless men.

The distance was such that he had had to hire a two-man wherry and the watermen took advantage of the turn of the tide, which carried them along at a brisk pace, as they picked their way through the forest of vessels at anchor in the Thames and the busy commercial traffic: barges carrying goods up to the City and Westminster, small coastal vessels from ports as far away as Fowey Haven in Cornwall and Lowestoft on the east coast, not to mention the dozens of ferries. In the countryside on the Surrey and Kent banks of the river, the trees were turning gold and the last of the apples were being harvested in the orchards.

The wherrymen brought him to one of the three sets of watersteps at Deptford Strand, a little above the busy dockyard from which came the sounds of hammering and sawing. Sir Francis Drake's *Golden Hind*, in which he had circumnavigated the world, was kept safe at Deptford, an attraction welcomed by the local taverns as it had become one of the sights to be seen in London for rural visitors to the capital.

Poley paid the men and ran up the steps. Ahead of him was Deptford Green and old St Nicholas' church, with its square tower and walled graveyard, where the graves were so close together that the tombstones almost tumbled over each other. But he was not bound for church. At the top of the watersteps he turned sharp right and made for the entrance to a large and finely timbered house with a tiled roof, which stood with its back to the river in the midst of a large garden, the whole enclosed by a high wall. He let himself in through the gate in the wall, then made his way to the main door of the dwelling and pulled on the bellrope hanging beside it. A mellifluous bell sounded somewhere inside and the door was opened to him by a pretty maid servant, dressed in a clean, blue stuff gown, with a spotless white apron and a cap on her head. She recognised him and curtsied to him, then held the door open for him to enter.

He gave her his hat, cloak and gloves. 'Good day to you, Jane, I trust you keep well?'

'Indeed I do, sir. We were fortunate here, for the Plague didn't set on us as fiercely as it did in the City.'

'Your mistress is expecting me,' he told her.

'Then if you'll just wait here a moment, sir, I'll tell her you've arrived.'

She bustled away up a fine carved staircase, leading out of the large square hall in which he stood. There were a number of doors opening off the hall itself, and the stairs led to a gallery, which ran round three sides of the house, obviously leading to many more chambers. He walked over to the window, which was slightly ajar, the morning being so fine, and looked out over the garden. Apple trees, some still with the last of their apples, were pleached against the soft red brick of the high wall and a gardener was working on a vegetable patch at the far end. Pleasant scents drifted in from the late roses, the pinks and stocks and from bushes of lavender. Bees buzzed in the herb garden.

'If you'll come up, sir . . . ' Jane called from the gallery above him and he went up the stairs and to the room into which she motioned him. It was very large, with two big windows overlooking the river on one wall and a third on that adjoining, which gave on to the garden. The owner was obviously someone of considerable means, for the walls were hung with fine tapestries telling the stories of classical lovers: Venus and Adonis, Hero and Leander, Dido and Aeneas. The highly polished floor was set here and there with choice rugs while the furniture, which included several splendidly carved oak chests, gave off a faint scent of beeswax which mingled with the sweet smell of great bowls of old roses, pink, crimson and white. At the other end of the room, opposite to the garden window, a fire burned in a small grate, near to which sat a lady at work on an embroidery frame. The room was, indeed, striking and beautiful.

So also was the lady.

The current fashion was for ladies to wear their hair frizzed and puffed – that is if they still had their own and so did not have to resort to wigs, like her Majesty the Queen; but Mistress Eleanor Bull wore her thick, dark-auburn hair simply, in a great coil, secured at the back of her head by jewelled pins. Her skin had a creamy pallor and her fine grey eyes looked out at the world from under level brows. She was fashionably dressed, her neck rising from a small, white ruff of the finest lace, her gown of dark grey silk worn over a small farthingale, which was embroidered most curiously with caterpillars, moths and spiders, all caught up in a web of silver thread. As Poley entered the room she stood up and came over to greet him, holding out her hand.

'Good day, Robert. What a pleasure to see you! You'll have some wine?' He assented, then kissed her hand. She went to the door and called to Jane to bring the wine, which must have been put ready, for the girl reappeared almost immediately with a silver tray, an opened bottle and two fine glasses which she set on a low table, then curtsied and went out. Mistress Eleanor poured two glasses and handed one to Poley.

'To your continuing good health, Robert!'

'And yours.'

They both drank and then she motioned him to be seated.

'You keep a good wine, Eleanor.'

She smiled. 'Well, I have few problems in importing it directly, as a result of our . . . arrangement, for which I am ever grateful.'

'Don't thank me, thank my paymasters.'

'Not to mention the upkeep of my house and garden.'

'It's most valuable for us to have such a discreet refuge right on the water steps; so convenient for those who need to come and go unremarked.'

She took another sip at her wine. 'You come and go more than most, Robert.'

'There's so much correspondence with the Low Countries these days. I seem to cross to Holland every few weeks which means I can't give sufficient time to my work here in London.'

They sat for a while in companionable silence. Eleanor Bull, if that was indeed her true name, was a mystery. He did not even know whether or not there had ever been a Master Bull, though she claimed to be the widow of a rich Suffolk merchant. It might well be true, of course, for many such had great wealth, yet she gave off an air of high breeding rather than trade. Nor did he know how she came to Deptford in the first place, or acquired the fine house and garden, only that she provided a safe haven for those such as he, who needed to slip in and out of the country unobserved, and that she also provided rooms where those who did not want to be seen publicly in each other's company could meet to discuss their affairs over a fine meal. She had first been employed in such work by Walsingham, and Cecil had continued the arrangement without demur; strangely, Eleanor Bull was the only person on his payroll about whom he refused to speak, even to Poley.

She broke into his thoughts. 'I meant to tell you before,

but it slipped my mind, that we now have a band of Puritans here in Deptford, some of whom have elected themselves to keep a watch over our morals. One of these worthies decided I must be keeping a bawdy house and so laid a complaint to the magistrates.'

Poley looked at her in some alarm. 'Has there been trouble then?'

'None at all. It seems the gentlemen felt that as I did not appear to have a husband, yet kept so large a house and was always well dressed, that I could not have acquired these things except by playing the bawd!'

'I thought it was accepted hereabouts that when your husband died he left you well set up.' Indeed, it was all Poley had ever been told about the lady and he had no way of knowing whether or not it was true.

'That is, indeed, the case and hitherto it's been believed. However, our upright citizen was so concerned for my soul that he took to watching of an evening to see if he was correct in his surmise and saw, from time to time, gentlemen coming in and out late at night, thus adding fuel to his suspicions.'

'I don't like it, Eleanor.'

'There's not the least need for you to concern yourself. Sir Edward, the magistrate, came to see me himself. He stood in my hall and admired my bowl of roses and then I took him into the garden – it being high summer – and gave him a little wine. He was already beginning to look foolish.'

'And what did you tell him?'

'Merely that when my late husband and I had lived in Suffolk, we had many friends who were fellow merchants and that when we bought this house, which is so convenient to the river, my husband's colleagues would often stay the night when they had to wait for the tide before taking ship, or had affairs to see to in the city; and that, after his death, I had continued this practice at his express wish. Also, that sometimes men of business needed to discuss these affairs or make bargains discreetly and so I would lend a room here, in which they could discuss such matters. I was able to assure him the business was of a pecuniary and not a venal nature. He apologised profusely as he left.'

'What happened to the layer of information.'

'Would you believe but that he was caught in a bed with one of his own serving wenches? Jane is my ears in this place and came to me one day full of merriment, having been told of his activities by one of his household, at which I . . . well, let us say it became common knowledge and that he had to stand at the church gate in a white sheet for three Sunday mornings with a notice around his neck, bearing the message, "Adulterer!" I do not think I shall be troubled in such a way again.'

There was a knock at the door and Jane came in to tell them that the first of the persons expected by Master Poley had arrived. Eleanor stood up. 'One of the small rooms downstairs has been made ready for you – Jane will show you to it. But what would you have me do with Kit Marlowe? It's an age since I've seen him, indeed, not since he became such a success in the playhouses. I had thought we might all three have a light repast up here.'

Poley considered for a moment. 'Yes, that might be a good notion in the circumstances.' He followed Jane downstairs, leaving Eleanor to her embroidery.

The man waiting in the hall below was moving from foot to foot, obviously ill at ease. Had there been anyone present who had been at the Anchor Tavern a few days earlier, they would have recognised him as the weasel-faced person who had spent his time in close conversation with the actor, Gregory, and had later supported him out through the door at the end of the evening. Jane showed the two men briskly into a small room furnished only with a table and several chairs and closed the door behind them. Wine and glasses stood on the table.

Poley picked up the bottle. 'Wine, Baines?' He poured a glass and handed it to the man who drank half of it in one gulp, then rubbed his mouth with the back of his hand.

JUDITH COOK

'It's a hellish way out of town. This house, I mean.'
'That's why it's so useful.'
'Is it an inn of some kind?'
'Of some kind. You might say that. You will never speak of having been here.'
'Not if you say so.'
'But I do say so and mark it well. You're known for saying too much.'
Baines looked uneasy. 'I also listen.'
'So let's sit down while you tell me what you've heard.'
Baines took another gulp of wine. 'Marlowe's drinking hard.'
'When did he not?'
'And talking loudly.'
'And says . . .?'
'Evil things. He blasphemes.'
'So do half the actors and playwrights in the playhouses. I hope you've more to tell me than this. And where did you learn of it, anyway?'
'By making a friend of a fool of an actor in the Lord Admiral's Company, a lamebrain that goes under the name of Gregory Sly. To get myself in with them I actually had to go and see one of their plays, *Spanish Tragedy* it was called or some such. The end was all right, though, when the old fellow tears his tongue out, almost as good as a hanging!'
'Spare me, if you will, your theatrical criticisms, and I put Sly there myself. What else?'
'Marlowe's written a play in which a man sells his soul to the devil to have everything he wants on earth.'
'If he has, then the idea isn't new. It is from a German story called the *Faust Book*.
'That's right. *Dr Faustus*, he's called it. I heard him say, though, that he would do the same himself if by so doing he could gain knowledge.'
Poley considered this then said, 'Typical of his arrogance but hardly a burning matter. What else?'
'In the Anchor Tavern on the same evening he said he

100

was so short of money he might need to work for the Crown again.'

Poley sat up. 'Did he now?'

'And when one of the actors asked what he meant, he said he'd done the state much service in his time.'

'I like that better. Yes, that's very good. Did he go on to confide what kind of service?'

'No, he stopped there.'

Poley stood up, felt in his pocket and took out a purse which he handed to Baines. 'Go back now to the Bankside. I need more yet, much more. Cultivate your friendship with your actor. I need to know if Marlowe says anything that might possibly be construed as treasonable and any real blasphemies. He could then be taken on either count.'

Baines put the purse in his pocket and stood up. 'He did say . . .'

'What?'

'That he was not frightened of death, either by burning or the executioner at Tyburn.'

'Others have said as much and died screaming and witless with fear and pain. Now go. I'm expecting another visitor.'

'It's a long way to come for so short a time,' grumbled Baines as Jane opened the front door for him.

'You've been well paid for it,' returned Poley. 'Hire a horse or, if you prefer, take a wherry from the steps.'

He went slowly back up the staircase to Mistress Eleanor's room. 'It was profitable?' she enquired.

'In part.'

'I will stay here to greet Kit Marlowe then leave you alone together while I see to the food. We can eat when you are ready.' Almost at once the bell rang below and they heard Jane letting someone into the house. Firm steps were heard running up the staircase, then the door opened and Marlowe came into the room. His face still showed signs of dissipation, but he had dressed carefully for the interview in his fine tobacco-coloured doublet and breeches. His riding boots were dusty for he had chosen to

hire a horse and ride to Deptford through the lanes and
fields. Eleanor turned at once to greet him.

'Kit! It's good to see you.'

'And you Eleanor; as beautiful as ever.' He bowed,
elaborately, kissed her hand and then, turning to Poley,
added, 'Who was that?'

'Who was who?'

'The man I saw leaving as I crossed the Green.'

'Are you sure he came from this house?'

'Yes, for he let himself out by the garden gate. He
looked somehow familiar, but I couldn't place him.'

'Well, I have no notion. He wasn't visiting me.'

'It is likely that he had business with my housekeeper,'
broke in Eleanor, 'we are presently having alterations made
to the kitchens. Now, you must have a glass of wine after
your journey.'

Like Baines, he drank deep. 'Excellent, Eleanor, but then
you always did keep a good cellar.'

She gave him a dazzling smile. 'You have had much
success since last we met and deservedly so. I've seen
Tamburlaine twice, also the *Jew of Malta* and next week
Jane and I, suitably squired, will visit the Rose to see your
new piece. I never thought of you as a man of the theatre
when you came here as a student.'

Marlowe smiled. 'That was a long time ago.'

'I remember it so clearly. When you set off for Rheims
you seemed lit from within with excitement.'

'I thought it a great game then, pitting myself against the
Jesuits, having to convince them I was a serious Catholic
student wishing to help bring down the Queen of England.
I did it too.'

'You were very accomplished. And now it's
playwriting.'

'Mostly.'

She made a slight curtsey. 'I'll leave you to your business
while I see to our lunch.'

As she left, Marlowe walked over to one of the long
windows and looked out over the busy river. 'I hear you've

written a play from the *Faust Book*,' said Poley.

'Yes, it's a wonderful subject.'

'Will it prove contentious?'

'I care little whether it will or not. I rather hope it might. The Faustian bargain – infinite knowledge, all man's desires, in exchange for that doubtful entity, the immortal soul.'

'Do you think your audiences will share your enthusiasm?'

'Some, those who are fascinated by such ideas, will see themselves in Faustus; the devout will feel happy when he receives his so-called just deserts, as Mephistopheles comes to claim his soul and the devils pull him down to Hell. Speaking of which, Phillip Henslowe's carpenters are even now building a fine Hell Mouth, through which will pour fire and red smoke. Then, for the groundlings, there's Faust's lust for Helen of Troy and a pageant of the Seven Deadly Sins. Yes, I think it might do well. But I hardly imagine you asked me here to discuss my latest play.'

'I asked you here because I have work for you, if you wish to undertake it, work best discussed out of town.'

'Your money's useful, certainly.'

'Doesn't Thomas Walsingham provide sufficient for your needs?'

'I can never have enough for my needs! Tom's very good to me, generous with his gold, loves my work ... the perfect patron in fact, which is why I don't like presuming on him too much.'

Poley poured Marlowe another glass of wine. 'They say he is being pressed to marry. At least that will be one marriage to which the Queen is unlikely to object.'

'It's expected of him, once a suitable bride has been found. He needs to secure the line,' replied Marlowe, ignoring the reference to Raleigh.

'That will surely affect you?'

'If you mean by that that we are unlikely to sleep three in a bed, then I agree, although Tom has always been both ways inclined. But what there is between us has long ceased to be passion, at least on my part, though so far as I'm capable of feeling true affection, then so I do for him. He's known since our Cambridge days my attraction to young boys, just on the cusp of manhood; fortunately the theatre's full of them as a constant supply is needed for the women's roles.'

Poley changed the subject abruptly. 'Times are changing, Marlowe. The rotting virgin presently at Nonesuch won't last forever and the Stuart faction no longer has need for Catholic plots. James is bound to succeed.'

Marlowe laughed gently. 'I like that, the "rotting virgin presently at Nonesuch", a phrase worthy of me, though not very kind to the monarch who has kept you fully employed and well remunerated for years.'

'It's the truth. That being the case, it's necessary to think ahead to what is to come. It were best to be forewarned when James assumes the crown.'

'You're being remarkably frank, Robert, so frank it makes me uneasy.'

'Why? Are we not old colleagues?'

'Because it's not your usual way to give opinions except, as I recall, in certain circumstances. You talked in just such a frank fashion to Antony Babbington and he was totally disarmed, believed in you until the disemboweller's knife slit into his stomach. Then you held free and frank discourse with poor Father Ballard over supper in this very house, as I recall, and look what happened to him . . . I fear that those who dine with you or walk with you in a garden, like Jesus Christ at Easter, do not fare well afterwards, Robert; they do not fare well at all.'

'It's not like you to be so cautious.'

'It's not like you to be so frank.'

Poley refused to be put down. 'Surely you agree, though? That being the case, it's necessary to make plans before the Queen dies. There are already those here who may well be making overtures to Scotland and I need to know who they are.'

'Well, it's all one to me whether I serve English Elizabeth or Scots Jamie'. Marlowe took more wine.

'Realistic as ever! What I want you to do, therefore, is to go to Edinburgh representing yourself as one who has Stuart interests at heart and find out, if you can, the names of those who have already done likewise. Can you do it?'

'It sounds simple enough and shouldn't take me away from London for too long. I'll see the first performances of *Faustus* next week then leave for Edinburgh. Yes, I can do that.'

'And there is one particular man I would have you watch. His name is Chomley and he is in the employ of the Earl of Essex.'

'I will seek him out.'

Poley stood up. 'I'll call Eleanor and tell her we've finished. You will be well paid for this.'

'And I'll need money on account.'

'Of course. That will be arranged.'

He stepped out and called over the gallery to Eleanor. As he came back in Marlowe was pouring out the last of the wine.'

'You drink too much.'

'We all drink too much.'

'So long as your tongue isn't loosened by it.'

'That's a risk you have to take.'

'Perhaps.' Poley changed the subject. 'These tapestries are fine, aren't they?'

Marlowe walked over to examine them closer. 'Very. Especially that of Hero and Leander. Coincidentally, I'm thinking of writing on that very subject next.'

'A new play.'

'No, a poem.' His face looked suddenly bleak. 'I finished *Faustus* months ago yet no new idea for a drama has come to me. That's never happened before. Sometimes I wake fearful that I've nowhere to go after such a subject as *Faustus*. So needs must I return to poetry.'

'Poetry?' said Eleanor, coming through the door. 'All London is singing your "Amorous Shepherd" to their

lutes – "Come live with me and be my love, And we will all
the pleasures prove . . . " Charming.'

Then the food was brought in and they sat and ate
together.

* * * *

It was early evening and almost dusk before Marlowe left.
He had drunk heavily but with care and at no time had he
been tempted into any indiscretion.

After he had gone, Eleanor and Poley walked together in
her garden. 'He's a strange one', she said. 'I wonder you
trust him.'

Poley stooped and picked a piece of lavender which he
rubbed between his fingers. 'I don't. He's becoming a
luxury we can no longer afford.'

'Yet you gave him more work.'

'For my own ends.' He felt suddenly exhultant. 'I've
spun them all into my web and now I can sit and wait for
Kit Marlowe to entrap himself, just like the rest.'

'Does what you do never concern you?'

'Do you mean, do I wake in the night racked with
remorse for my deeds? No, I sleep well.'

She smiled and looked across the garden. 'Why did you
choose such work?'

'I struggled up out of the gutter when many like me have
ended their days on a rope. I learned to act and speak like a
gentleman, even if I am not one. I studied hard to be the
best at my trade that there is and I can make them all dance
to my tune: rural Catholic gentlemen, recusant priests –
even that faded beauty Mary Stuart trusted me. I pit my
wits against them and I always win. Always. That's why
Cecil trusts me. We're two of a kind, he and I.'

A sudden chill wind blew across from the river. Eleanor
shivered. 'It grows cold. Let's go in. You'll stay the night?'

He assented, though he knew the invitation meant no
more than a pleasant supper, more talk and bed in a room
of his own. Not that he, or indeed any other man, would

not have enjoyed an invitation to something more, but Eleanor Bull was no hot-eyed Joan Yeomans. He found it impossible to believe that so beautiful and desirable a woman did not take a lover or lovers; but if she did then she kept it as much a mystery as she did everything else.

'And Kit Marlowe?' she asked as they went back into the house.

'A bastard, a clever arrogant bastard who's always patronised me. I shall enjoy the next few months.'

She put her hand on his arm. 'Shall we go in?'

12

... blot out my offences, and tread them
under feet, so as they may not be a
witnesse against me at the Day of Wrath.
Grant this, O Lord, I humbly beseech
thee for thy mercy's sake.'

The Repentance of Robert Greene

ROBERT GREENE LINGERED ON for several
days after the Rose Theatre had re-opened. There
were periods of lucidity when he had himself propped on
pillows and continued his frantic scribbling, after which he
would become comatose again. His mood swung between
bitterness and fear, bitterness over those he felt had
somehow conspired to deny him the recognition he felt
was due to his work, fear of what awaited him in the life to
come.

For his friends in the Lord Admiral's Company it was a
difficult time, for they were now playing every afternoon,
except for Sundays, while rehearsing *Dr Faustus* in the
mornings. Even so, Simon Pope elected to spend some
nights sitting beside him, in part to give the women a
chance to rest but also because, exasperating as he was,
Robert had been an integral part of that close-knit family
of actors, poets and playwrights which made up the new
society of the theatre. Also because Greene was terrified of
being left alone. The shoemaker's wife did what she could
for the 'poet and gentleman' who had taken up lodgings
with them, but he found her timorous presence irritating.
Jenny fared somewhat better although, as she told Tom,
she felt that at heart Robert simply did not like women,
seeing them only as necessary to satisfy sexual desire.

With Emma, who wished to nurse him, he was offhand to the point of being rude, making it clear her presence was something he only tolerated. She would arrive in the mornings, weary from a night seeking clients, usually bringing food and with little Fortunatus clinging to her. Like many sickly children his face looked older than that of a normal child of his years and, however fretful he might have been as a baby, he was now almost unnaturally quiet. He would sit in the corner of the sickroom playing with a few pieces of wood and an old rag doll, hardly making a sound. Eventually Jenny brought some wooden toys for him to play with which her own children had left behind in London.

To Simon, in the long hours of the night, he would spill out his bile towards his fellow poets and writers or, sweating with fear, cling to his hand imploring him to tell him what he thought would be his fate in the next world, and whether or not God would accept his repentance.

He reserved his most bitter words and savage writing for Will Shakespeare, as Simon saw when Greene gave him his last sheaf of papers to take to Chettle, the printer. 'Read it, Simon,' he said hoarsely, lying back on his pillow. 'Read what I say about him *there*,' and he pointed to a page.

Simon took the papers over to the window for there was little light in the attic room. After several passages of self pity, such as 'driven as myself to extreme shifts' and 'if by my misery you may be warned' (followed by a contemptuous dismissal of actors as 'those Puppets') Simon read: 'Yes trust them not: for there is an upstart Crow, beautified with our feathers, that with his *Tyger's heart wrapped in a player's hide*, supposes he is well able to bombast out a blank verse as the best of you: and being an absolute *Johannes factotum*, is, in his own conceit, the only Shakes-scene in the country.' After appending his strange warning to Marlowe, he then concluded:

> Well, my hand is tired, and I am forced to leave where I would begin: for a whole book cannot

contain their wrongs, which I am forced to knit up
in some few lines of words.
Desirous that you should live,
though himself be dying,
Robert Greene.

When she came in on the last morning of his life, Jenny
thought he had died in the night, he looked so white and
still. The early September sun shone through the window
lighting up the tumbled bed, the bleak room and the scatter
of books and papers which spilled on to the floor. The
room reeked of sickness. She found Simon asleep in a chair
by the bed and woke him gently. They exchanged greetings
in whispers, then Simon left for the final rehearsal of *Dr
Faustus* in which, fortunately, he was only playing a minor
role as one of the Seven Deadly Sins. A little while later
Emma arrived with the child, just as Robert opened his
eyes. Jenny raised him on her arm and held a cup to his
lips. He focused on the room and then on the two women.
'Why weep Emma? You'll soon be rid of me. You
always did bawl easily.' His voice was faint.
'Robin, will you at least give your son your name, write
on a paper that you are his father so that all the world
knows.'
Robert's mouth cracked in a smile. 'What use is that?
What value is it that he has a dead poet for a father?' Then
he turned to Jenny. 'You can read, can't you? See if this
makes sense.' He fumbled in the bed and brought out a
crumpled sheet. 'Read it so I can hear it, will you?'
It was a letter to the estranged wife, Dorothy, whom he
had not seen for six years.
'Sweet Wife,' he had written, 'as ever there was goodwill
or friendship between thee and me, see this bearer (my
Host) satisfied of his debt. I owe him ten pounds and but
for him I had perished in the streets. Forget and forgive my
wrongs done to you. Almighty God have mercy on my
soul until we meet in heaven, for on earth thou shalt ne'er
see me more. This second of September 1592. Written by

thy dying husband, Robert Greene.'

He listened carefully, then told them, 'I deserted her because she would try and reform me. They tell me she and my daughter are well and that she's sent good wishes for my recovery. I wish I might have seen her again for I fear I wronged her mightily.'

Then he whispered, 'Bring the shoemaker and his wife.' Jenny went and called them as Emma wiped his forehead. The couple crept into the room and Greene opened his eyes again. 'Davie,' he said to the shoemaker, 'will you go to Norwich to my wife? Her direction is written on this paper. Will you do it for me?' The shoemaker nodded his agreement.

Then he began a prayer in which they all joined. 'Oh Lord, forgive my manifold offences. Oh Lord, have mercy upon me. Oh Lord, forgive my secret sins and, in thy mercy, Lord, pardon them all. For thy mercy, Oh Lord, is above thy works.'

The shoemaker's wife began to cry, audibly. Robin turned to her with a flicker of the old mischief in his eyes. 'It was the pickled herrings you gave me last week that saw me off,' he said; and died.

The women wept and all crossed themselves, for although it was now officially frowned upon, old habits die hard. Fortunatus, aware that something had happened which he did not understand, broke suddenly into a loud wailing.

The next morning those of his friends and colleagues who were able to do so followed Robin's bier to the churchyard. He went to his grave as he would have wished, for his landlady had strewn him with garlands of bay.

* * * *

The following day the Lord Admiral's Company gave the first performance of *Dr Faustus*. The mood was very different from the elation that had gripped them before the performance of *The Spanish Tragedy*. Actors have ever

111

been superstitious and there was much in the new play that worried even those who did not pretend to any strong religious belief. It was said that the spell used by Faustus to raise devils, which began *Sint Mihi Dei Acherontis propitii*, was a real one, and that no one knew what speaking it might unleash. Marlowe, when appealed to, merely laughed. He had shown little interest in Greene's death, except to say that it seemed to have taken him a long time to shake off this mortal world, and he had not attended the funeral.

The play and the role had a definite effect on Ned Alleyn, who was by no means his usual self, his unease apparent in such passages as that when he has conjured up the demon, Mephistopheles, who tells him that he has appeared, not only because of the spell, but because he has 'racked the name of God', to which Faustus replies:

> So Faustus hath already done,
> And holds this principle:
> There is no chief only Beelzebub,
> To whom Faustus doth dedicate himself.
> This word 'damnation' terrifies not him,
> For he confounds hell in Elysium.

It was a truly terrible statement which brought shudders to all who heard it, as also when Faustus asks why Mephistopheles is not still in Hell, to be told 'Why, this is hell, nor am I out of it.' The feeling was that no good would come from dealing in such matters.

The Rose was crowded, so much so that nobody noticed the small, plainly dressed man, with one shoulder higher than the other, who watched the performance intently; then left, straight afterwards. However, in spite of the players' apprehensions, the play seemed to go down reasonably well, helped in the case of the groundlings by the appearance of Helen of Troy (Jamie in a long, fair wig and a small, white robe), the Seven Deadly Sins, especially Lust (Dick Hoope, dressed as a lascivious punk), and, most of all, the spectacular climax which ended the play. As Faustus began his last great speech, 'Ah Faustus, now hast thou but one bare hour to live', a vast wooden construction, the Hell Mouth, was trundled on by stage staff well hidden behind it. Soon clouds of red smoke issued from it (the actor, Gregory, vigorously applying the bellows) filling first the stage and then half the auditorium as well.

Then came the sound of a clock striking twelve, followed by the rattling of a thunder sheet and the flash of white fire representing lightning, whereupon all the actors who could be rounded up, led by the apprentices, appeared dressed as devils bearing pitchforks and burning torches; seizing Faustus, they dragged him through the Hell Mouth to his doom. It was the most spectacular effect ever seen on the stage of the Rose and thus enabled the performance to end to thunderous applause.

As Alleyn, down on his knees, had made his final speech expressing his fear and terror of what lay in store for him, Tom thought of poor Robert Greene and his sad and fearful death in the shoemaker's attic.

The stars move still, time runs, the clock will strike,
The devil will come and Faustus must be damned.
O, I'll leap up to my God! Who pulls me down?
See, see how Christ's blood streams in the firmament:
One drop would save my soul, half a drop. Ah my Christ!

It was wonderful verse, some of the finest Marlowe had ever written. Strange how, in an uncanny way, it echoed Greene's last desperate effort to make his peace with his God.

Robin had been a hard man to like, seemingly going out of his way to turn aside affection and continually insulting those who would be his friends. Yet he could turn his pen with skill from scurrilous pamphlets and such saucy works as *A Notable Discovery of Cosenage, Coniecatchers and*

113

Crossbiters, to gentle pastoral pieces like *George a Greene, Pinder of Wakefield* and the comic *Friar Bacon and Friar Bungay*. Infuriating and unpredictable, he would yet be sadly missed; his had been a considerable presence. However fearful he might have been that the sins of this world would bring about punishment in the next (thus leading to his very public repentance) Simon did not think he would share the fate of Faustus. If there was, indeed, a heaven, then there had to be a place in it for difficult poets.

* * * *

Henry Chettle, the printer, had handed Greene's final pamphlet over to his men after only a cursory glance. So it was that when he saw its content in print for the first time, he was appalled. In fact his conscience was to trouble him so much that three months later he sat down and wrote a play of his own, *A Kind Heart's Dream*, in which the ghost of Greene appeared and apologised to Will Shakespeare; for the printer had subsequently met the playwright, found him utterly unlike Greene's picture, and decided things must be put right. So he wrote in his preface, that 'myself hath seen his demeanour, no less civil than he is excellent in the quality he professes, besides divers of worship have reported his uprightness in dealing, which argues his honesty, and his facetious grace in writing that approves his art', which muddled verbiage caused Marlowe to say he would be better to stay with printing.

Will Shakespeare kept his views on Greene's notorious pamphlet to himself. Not so Marlowe. 'I don't give a fart at being described as an atheist,' he told all and sundry, 'but I consider the description "Machiavellian schemer" deeply offensive and I shall tell Chettle as much. He can write a second preface to his awful play.'

Chettle's response was that Marlowe was fortunate he had censored Greene's charge against him of homosexuality which 'had it been true, yet to publish it had been intolerable', adding that while neither of the rival playwrights, Shakespeare or Marlowe, had previously been known to him personally, he had no desire to remedy that defect with regard to Marlowe nor did he care what he thought. He then compounded it all by adding that he did, however, wish he had known Will before publication, because he would certainly have excised Greene's insults from the text.

Robert Poley bought a copy of the *Repentance* as soon as it appeared on the streets and filed it carefully away for possible future use. Then, as part of his careful plans, he sought out Nicholas Skeres once again. What he required, he told him, was a man who was not too fussy about what he did, so long as he was well paid for it. Someone who was not entirely without standing in his own community, and thus not merely a rogue or felon with past convictions, but who might well have successfully broken the law from time to time and could be lent on to do so again – if the price was right. It might be needful to set him up in such a way that he might require 'rescuing' from imprisonment, or worse, and so be even more amenable to what Poley had in mind. Did Nick, by any chance, know of such a one?

Nicholas Skeres replied without hesitation. He knew just the man.

13

... any person aforesaid, longing to
make a voyage in the Ship of Fools,
would venture all the wit his mother left
him to live in the country of the
Gulls . . .

The Gull's Horn Book Dekker

INGRAM FRIZER WAS NOT a happy man. His wife
had been nagging him; not that there was anything new
in this, for there was rarely a time when she did not. Even
though they had a decent house on the Scadbury estate, a
maidservant, kept a horse and lived in reasonable comfort,
she still felt she had somehow married beneath her (her
family hailed from Eltham) and never let him forget it. He
was feeling particularly aggrieved at present as he had
thought he had done all 'Her Majesty' had wanted him to
in the way of household improvements and new
furnishings. He had even had built on to the back of his
house – at his own expense mind, and not that of Master
Thomas Walsingham – a private privy so that they no
longer had to share the communal one with all those living
nearby. Next she had wanted new curtains for the parlour,
and he had provided those, a new dress for Sunday church,
and he had paid the dressmaker to have it made.

Then, what should it be, but that she wanted her portrait
painted! The husband of her best friend and gossip,
Margery Taylor, had taken pleasure in having *his* wife
portrayed on canvas, so why couldn't Ingram? At first he
had closed his ears to it, then, one day, he had struck up a
conversation with an affable kind of a fellow in a local
tavern, who had offered to paint a portrait in exchange for

a daily allowance of ale. The bargain had been struck and Mistress Frizer, her hair ferociously crimped and wearing her new mauve Sunday gown, had posed stiffly, as the artist applied his paint with a will; although it had to be admitted that his skill fell away in direct ratio to the amount of drink taken.

Came the day, awaited by Mistress Frizer with increasing impatience, when the picture was finally unveiled. There was a terrible silence. It had to be said that the painter had shown more enthusiasm than talent and that he had not flattered his subject. Indeed she was so enraged that when she recovered from her initial shock, she wrenched the painting from its stand and, after shouting that it looked like a cheap inn sign, smashed it over Ingram so that his head emerged from it as if from a ruff.

The artist had been unperturbed. Since he had been paid in ale, not money, he could hardly be asked for it back, so taking advantage of the subsequent noisy quarrel he picked up his damaged work of art and took it away; carefully repaired and retouched, it might indeed be sold to a tavern or inn. In fact the portrait might well be said to have brought him luck as he had a week of free drinks out of it on the strength of its history. Topers vied with each other to suggest suitable taverns it might adorn. For a while the Quiet Woman or the Ball and Chain were preferred, but the final victor was deemed to be the Nag's Head.

Now Her Majesty was on at Ingram morning, noon and night over the amount of money he allowed her for the household expenses.

Frizer's earnings fluctuated. He had a small stipend from Walsingham for general duties, and if he was able to bring off a particularly good deal for his master, he received extra remuneration as well. He was also usually able to squeeze himself a small commission out of the buying-in of goods of various kinds for the estate, a practice to which Walsingham obligingly turned a blind eye. All this was known to Mistress Frizer, but he was also prepared to do other things and these he did not discuss with his wife. She might complain every time he went to London, but she assumed it was on estate business and he did nothing to disabuse her.

These other earnings had improved considerably since he had gone into partnership with Nick Skeres. Good old Nick. He wasn't quite sure now how he had first come to meet up with him, something to do with a builders' merchant, he thought, but however it had come about it had proved profitable to both. All it required was a steady stream of idiots waiting to be 'gulled'.

So it was that being short of money he rode again towards London in the grey dawn of an April morning, having received the previous day a note from Nick that he had found a perfect victim for their now well-tried game. It had worked perfectly every time they set it up and there was no reason whatsoever to think anything might go wrong. Frizer clattered into London and picked his way across London Bridge through the early morning traders, then made certain arrangements, which included the collection from a friend of a large and rather heavy sack.

The meeting had been arranged for mid-morning, near to Tower Hill, a popular spot with visitors and, having allowed himself plenty of time, Frizer rode to an inn not too far away, which he had used on several occasions, and there stabled his horse. Still with the sack and also with the contents of his saddlebag, he ordered breakfast and asked for the use of a room in which to change his clothes. This he did, stuffing his doublet back in the saddlebag and putting on instead the kind of long black gown much favoured by respectable merchants. He then ate a hearty breakfast.

An hour later he walked out to keep his appointment. Just before he came in sight of the Tower he hid his sack behind the wall of a convenient garden, then pushed his way through the crowds of sightseers to where he could see Nick Skeres in earnest conversation with a young man, whose ruddy complexion spoke of the countryside. Tower Hill was always crowded and there were, as usual, a number of people standing about watching the world go by, including on this occasion a nondescript-looking fellow in a snuff-coloured doublet who was idly watching Skeres and his companion; but as Frizer joined them, he appeared to lose interest and turned away as if making for the river steps.

Frizer bustled up, nodding his head at Skeres slightly to confirm all was in hand. Frizer already knew the young man's problem – he was short of ready cash.

'Ingram!' called out Skeres as he reached them, 'this is Drew Woodleff, the young man I told you about.'

'Glad to meet you, sir!' said Woodleff, holding out his hand. What he saw was a respectable-looking man of early middle-age with something of the gentleman about him, wearing a decent long gown; such a one as you might see any day of the week in a place of business. There was something of a sharp look about his face, no doubt the result of years of City dealings. Woodleff felt reassured. Everything was going to be all right.

'Now, Master Woodleff,' said Skeres, 'tell my old friend Ingram what the problem is.'

The lad looked abashed. 'I've – er – got into a bit of debt and I daren't tell my mother, she's so strict . . .'

'Ah, women,' beamed Frizer, 'they don't understand these things can happen to anyone, do they?'

'That's right,' continued Woodleff, gratefully. 'So what I need is money just to tide me over for a few weeks.'

'You have expectations?'

'I was left some rents by my father, which I shall have collected in by the end of next month at the latest.'

Frizer clapped him on the shoulder. 'How much do you want then, lad?'

Woodleff gulped. 'Sixty pounds.'

'Hmm . . . ' Frizer appeared to give this serious thought. 'That's going it somewhat . . . Don't know that I could wait around for weeks for such a sum.'

'Oh please . . . ' Woodleff almost whimpered.

Frizer seemed suddenly to make up his mind. 'Don't

worry, lad, I reckon I can oblige you.' He was carrying over his shoulder a small satchel, which he put down on a nearby wall, promptly taking from it a small, carefully stoppered pot of ink and a piece of paper.

'Now,' he said, 'just write down here – you can write, can you? Not just make a cross?'

Woodleff assured him that he could, then added, 'What do you want me to write?'

'Put I.O.U. £60.' Woodleff laboriously wrote it. 'Now sign it.' Woodleff scratched his signature. 'Drew Wood-leff, there!'

'Right!' said Frizer, pocketing it carefully. 'I'll fetch the money. Don't go away!'

The man in the snuff-coloured doublet had reappeared and was now leaning against the wall opposite, engaged in casual conversation with a couple who looked as if they might be a farmer and his wife up to see the sights. After a few minutes, Frizer reappeared dragging behind him, to Woodleff's surprise, what seemed to be a large sack. He panted up and deposited the sack at Woodleff's feet. 'Here you are, lad.'

Woodleff looked mystified. 'What's that? Where's my money?'

Frizer gave him a huge, kind smile. 'Now, lad, don't you worry your head. As it happens, I found I couldn't just lay my hands on the cash, at least not the full amount . . . '

'But you said . . . ' Woodleff tried to intervene.

Skeres patted him on the shoulder. 'Don't worry, Drew. I told you Ingram'd see you all right.'

'I will indeed. In fact, you'll be better off. It's all in here.'

'In the sack? What is it then?' Woodleff's voice had risen an octave with anxiety.

'Old guns.'

'Old guns! Are you mad? What do I want with old guns?'

'You sell them, of course. They'll fetch far more than £60, but I'm not mean. You can keep the difference.'

Woodleff was close to tears. 'How can I? I've only been to London once before. I wouldn't know where to start.'

Frizer considered this for a moment then said, 'Look, I've taken a real fancy to you, Drew. I can call you Drew, can I? *I'll* sell the guns for you. Now, how's that? Just wait here again, I'll be back in five minutes.'

As soon as he had disappeared, Woodleff turned on Nick. 'Whatever have you got me into, Master Skeres? What's all this business with old guns?'

Nick put a reassuring arm round him. 'How many times do I have to tell you? Ingram'll sort it all out, you'll see. Don't worry. It's a fine day. If you look out there you can see right across the river. Take a look while I have a word with this gentleman here.' He crossed over to the man in the snuff-coloured doublet, leaving Woodleff gazing unhappily at the shipping in the Thames.

'Will he do?'

'For my purpose, yes,' said Poley. 'He'll need to be frightened, of course; but yes. I think he'll do.'

When Frizer returned again, without the sack, Poley had lost himself among the crowd and Skeres was once more standing with Woodleff. 'Did you sell them?' he asked Frizer, eagerly. 'Have you got my £60.'

'Not exactly.'

'What do you mean, not exactly? Have you or haven't you?'

'What I said, not exactly. I've got £30 actually. Guns were a bit slow to sell today but anyway, here you are lad, there's thirty sovereigns.'

An awful realisation began to dawn on Woodleff. 'So you've given me £30, but I signed an I.O.U. for £60!'

'So you have, son, so you have!'

'I'll . . . I'll have the law on you,' shouted Woodleff, looking around wildly, while Frizer said to no one in particular, 'There's one born every minute.' Hitherto when a victim threatened the law, nothing ever came of it, for by the time the gull had found an officer and fetched him to the spot, Frizer and Skeres had long since disappeared.

But this time it all went horribly wrong as the man in a snuff-coloured doublet rapidly intervened and caught him

121

by the arm, saying to Woodleff, 'If I were you, young man, I'd go straight and lay information against this fellow here with the nearest officer. If you go down the hill to that lane there, you will find in the corner house one William Hinde. Fetch him while I hold this man here.'

As he set off, Frizer tried to run away, only to find, to his amazement, that his way was blocked by Skeres.

'Here, what are you doing, Nick? Let me go.' Then, wildly, 'You brought me the gull in the first place!'

'Stop chattering,' said Poley, 'and listen. You've just committed a criminal offence. I'm a witness to it. A hanging matter, wouldn't you say, Skeres?'

Frizer looked from one to the other in bewilderment. 'You *know* each other? What is this?'

Skeres shook his head at Poley. 'Very probably. He might just get away with being branded and having his ears cropped, though. That is if someone can put in a good word for him.'

'Ears cropped?' squeaked Frizer, grey with fright. Branded?' Then, on a rising note, 'Hanged?' He was not a squeamish man. He could, if it was really necessary, inflict injury on others, he visited the Bear Pit regularly and enjoyed nothing more than a good hanging; but he was a complete coward when it came to withstanding pain. He fell on his knees.

'On the other hand,' continued Skeres, 'he might be released on bail if someone came up with sufficient money.'

'Perhaps his master, Thomas Walsingham, would do so,' suggested Poley, silkily.

Frizer's guts heaved. 'How do you know I'm Master Thomas's man?'

Poley smiled. 'I know everything. And all about you, from Skeres here. We're old acquaintances.'

'What are you going to do with me?'

'Why, hold you here of course, until that unfortunate young man returns with an officer to make an arrest.'

Frizer got to his feet again and turned on Nick. 'I'll say you knew all about it.'

'And I shall say he did not,' said Poley, 'and witnessed all that transpired. Which of us, do you think, will be believed?'

'Oh my God,' moaned Frizer. It was the stuff of nightmares.

'However,' continued Poley, 'if – and I mean *if* – you are quiet, say only that it was a misunderstanding or a jest of some kind and promise the young man you will give him the rest of his money and tear up his I.O.U., I will put up your bail money and have a word with the bench.'

'Thank you, sir, thank you,' Frizer grovelled. 'Master . . . who are you?'

'You don't need to know who I am – yet. If you do exactly as I say, I will see you are released. If you do not, then I shall ensure that a great many unpleasant things will happen to you. Quickly.'

Frizer was not a complete fool. 'Why are you doing this for me?' he asked.

'Because there is something I might need to have done and, if so, then I think you are the man to do it.'

* * * *

Back home in his lodgings that afternoon, Poley sat down and wrote a careful letter to Robert Cecil. In it he suggested that everything should now be put in hand for the arrest of Christopher Marlowe when the right moment came. He added, in a postscript, that if it were found it might be better Marlowe should not be brought to open court, then he had made the necessary arrangements.

14

Fond worldling, now his heart-blood dries with grief,
His conscience kills it, and his labouring brain
Begets a world of idle fantasies . . .

Dr Faustus   Marlowe

THE ACTORS' JOY AT returning to their theatre was
short lived. Usually, a severe epidemic of Plague raged
for several months until it burned itself out, after which it
might be years before it returned again with such
virulence; but the years of 1592 and 1593 proved the
exception to the rule. At the end of September, the number
of cases rose ominously, with the consequence that the
authorities again closed down all places of entertainment.

So most of the companies, the actors weary and
dispirited, packed their baskets, loaded up their carts and
took once more to the open road. But this time Henslowe
did not follow suit. One morning, at the end of September,
he called the Lord Admiral's Men together and told them
what he proposed. He was prepared to take a gamble. The
Plague could not possibly last forever and was certain, at
the very least, to die down again in the cold winter
weather. He was prepared to try and keep the company
together, paying those actors who chose to remain in
London a shilling or two a week until such time as it was
practicable to re-open the Rose. In that way he would be
well placed to take advantage of audiences again starved of
entertainment. The choice, however, lay with them: they
knew the risks they were taking.

After a certain amount of noisy discussion most of the
actors agreed to take a chance. There was no guarantee
they would escape the Plague even outside London, for the

epidemic had spread to most places they were likely to visit; indeed they had been refused entry to some towns during the previous spring and summer in case they brought it with them. What Henslowe then proposed was that they should meet regularly at the theatre to rehearse as wide a repertoire as possible for the re-opening. An immediate beneficiary of the situation was Thomas Kyd, who was given a chance not only to rework his *Prince Hamlet*, but was also handed a mishmash of a script, the work of many hands, on the life and death of Sir Thomas More and asked to put it into shape for performance.

The more cautious James Burbage had sent his son and the Lord Chamberlain's Men out of town, but on this occasion their star playwright did not accompany them. Shakespeare's excuse was that he needed time alone to write his next play, but in actual fact he was in an emotional turmoil, racked by a potent mixture of desire, jealousy and passion, feelings he had never experienced during his brief courtship of the woman who had become his wife.

He rarely spoke of his wife and children, even to his fellow actors and sharers in the Lord Chamberlain's company and he discouraged any probing. It was said his wife was older than he, that she had entrapped him into marriage with the oldest of tricks, and that he had fled from his responsibilities. No one knew for sure, nor did they know much of the dark lady who so obsessed him now and to whom he poured out golden rivers of verse. For the first time in his life, he was actually finding it difficult to get down to the practical business of writing a play.

* * * *

Marlowe was also in a state of turmoil, though for very different reasons. At first the disruption in the theatres had proved of use to him, enabling him to disappear to Scotland as planned, spend some weeks in Edinburgh ferretting out the names of those making overtures to James and to return without being missed. He had been extremely amused to discover that the rumours of Scots Jamie's sexual proclivities were in fact true: he might well have reluctantly agreed to marry to ensure the succession and give an appearance of respectability, but the Scottish Court was awash with pretty young gentlemen seeking to become royal favourites, to earn the lavish affection with which went financial reward. He reflected, somewhat ruefully, that he himself was far too old to take advantage of James' sexual tastes, but at least the dark mood, which he now found it almost impossible to shake off, lightened during his brief stay in the Scots capital. And he had found plenty of amusement; indeed, he had learned some of the information he had taken back to Poley in the bedchambers of attractive young court hopefuls.

He had also, as requested, sought out Richard Chomley and had found him only too eager for companionship. In the course of extracting from him details of Essex's mission he had succeeded, after a long night of drinking, to send the poor man to bed in a state of terror, having convinced him, by reasoned argument, that there was no God!

But the rise in his spirits did not survive his return to London. He had done his work well enough but it no longer gave him the old sense of satisfaction. He presented his report to Poley and Poley thanked him and paid him for it, but he seemed unusually withdrawn and cool, even for him. There was no sign of the apparent frankness he had shown in Deptford and their meeting left Marlowe with a strange feeling of unease, which he could not explain even to himself.

There were other, more personal, reasons for his feeling of malaise. The death of Robert Greene had apparently left him untouched, but he found he missed the presence of his old rival in the taverns and ordinaries, their verbal sparring, even the exchange of insults. Far worse, though, was the discovery, on his return to London, that Thomas Watson had died of the Plague in his absence; that loss went very deep. There was nothing he could do except to mourn the man who had been one of his closest and most tolerant friends.

Watson's death brought back a flood of memories of his early days in London, with the future shining; riding high on the unprecedented success of *Tamburlaine*, sought after, praised to the point of adulation and enjoying every minute of every day without need to turn the destructive side of his personality either outward on his friends and colleagues or inward on himself. He had poured out his ideas to Tom Watson, so sympathetic a listener; his plots for plays, for verse, the new scientific ideas discussed so avidly by the School of the Night which teemed through his head for days afterwards.

When had it all gone sour? It was hard to point to it exactly. Sometimes he felt the ominous signs were there from the time of that fatal duel in Hog Lane. Sometimes, in the dark watches of the night, he relived his bout with Bradley, the feel of the sweat running down his back, his exultation at the sure knowledge that he was by far the more superior swordsman. Then had come Tom's determined intervention and how, as Bradley had forced Tom relentlessly back towards the ditch, he had stood behind him, prepared and willing to deliver the fatal blow. Yet it was poor Tom, so unwilling to injure, let alone kill, who had spent five whole months in gaol while he had gone free. He wondered if Tom Watson had been permanently weakened by the wounds Bradley had inflicted and if this had contributed to his death.

Then there was the School of the Night. Elizabeth had relented sufficiently to allow Raleigh and his bride out of the Tower, but they were now virtually banished to his Dorset estate at Cerne Abbas and the School no longer met in London if, indeed, it met at all. Marlowe had, however, run into its most brilliant scholar one day, which had resulted in his spending a week with Harriot, discussing such enthralling matters as the use of the plain sphere in advanced mathematics. He was flattered that the scientist

127

had appeared to take his advice on what he considered to be its benefits. Harriot had wined and dined him well and had then crowned his generosity by making him a gift of a horse.

Before Harriot left to visit Cerne Abbas, Marlowe had sent word to Raleigh asking if he might accompany him on his visit but, to his chagrin, had received no reply. He was therefore in an even blacker mood than usual when he returned to his lodgings to find a rare letter awaiting him from his father. He was needed, wrote John Marlowe, to sign a document relating to the estate of one of his uncles, and while he was usually 'too busy', it seemed, to visit his family in Canterbury, would he now make shift to do so as soon as possible?

So, making good use of his new horse, he rode down through the Kent countryside, through woodlands where the leaves were now red and dropping fast, over the down-land and so into Canterbury with its soaring cathedral. From there he went on to the little timbered house in the town centre, close by the church of St George the Martyr where he had been baptised nearly thirty years before.

Time had put an almost impossible divide between himself and his shoemaker father, his busy, distracted mother, the pack of sisters and the one surviving brother, Thomas. At least there was one son to follow their father into the trade; the other two, dead as infants, lay buried in the nearby churchyard alongside two tiny sisters. All four girls, Margaret, Joan, Anne and Dorothy, were married to stout young tradesmen, Joan's wedding being a hurried affair a few weeks before her fourteenth birthday. She had been Marlowe's favourite, sharing something of his own reckless nature and sharp wit, which had given her a reputation as a shrew. For a little while Marlowe listened as patiently as he could to his father grumbling about the state of trade – he was still, and had perennially been, in debt – and to his mother, who regaled him with anecdotes and gossip about neighbours he had long forgotten or never known. His sisters displayed their children and brought

128

along husbands with whom he was supposed to make small talk about the cost of cloth or the price of leather, depending on which brother-in-law was holding forth at the time. Not surprisingly, he felt most sympathy for Dorothy's husband, who was a vintner.

He was asked repeatedly when he intended to marry and why he had not, questions he fended off as best he could. News of his success had spread to Canterbury, but his family were far more interested in who he knew, the lives of the actors and whether or not he had ever had a play performed before the Queen, than they were in his work. The main preoccupation of his sisters seemed to be the London fashions: was it true farthingales were becoming as big as cartwheels, that yellow starch was all the rage for ruffs?

The result was that after several days of this and of trying to keep his ill humour and caustic tongue in check, he had gone the rounds of the city's taverns, becoming ever more aggressive in drink until, at the Chequers Inn, he quarrelled with a local tailor, struck him, then picked him up and threw him bodily out of the taproom; whereupon the inn-keeper had promptly called the Watch. He then had the humiliation of spending the night in the town lock-up before appearing at the magistrates' court, a stone's throw away from the family home, where he was found guilty of being drunk and disorderly and of common assault, fined twenty shillings and bound over to keep the peace. This led to a furious argument with John Marlowe, after which he had ridden back to London with the recriminations of his family still ringing in his ears.

He was short of money, for he had soon run through what he had received from Poley, and was driven, though with some misgivings, to seek him out to see if there was further employment; but when he called at Poley's lodgings he was told that Master Poley had gone away and was not expected to return for some time.

He next applied to Phillip Henslowe, but the entrepreneur was struggling to pay his actors what small sums he could, unaided by box office receipts but augmented, from time to time, by occasional private performances at the houses of those of the wealthy, who had either not left town, or were temporarily back in London again. He might have been prepared to advance Marlowe money had he been able to offer him a plotline for a new play, but ideas for new plays simply would not come; and now the fear that had gripped him at the end of the summer, that he might never find such inspiration again, was rapidly turning into blind panic, in turn fuelling ever more feverish drinking.

Desperate for companionship, he even sought out Nick Skeres one evening, deciding boring company was better than none, to find to his surprise that he had Ingram Frizer staying under his roof; indeed the two men appeared to have become close friends. Frizer had been his usual unctuous self but had surprised Marlowe, when they had repaired to a nearby tavern, by telling him he had once run an inn himself, the Angel at Basingstoke, and indeed still owned it, but that his wife ('Her Majesty' as he was wont to refer to her) had not taken to the trade. What had brought him to London, and on what business he and Skeres were engaged, was left vague. Marlowe could hardly blame them whatever it was; times were hard and every man had to shift for himself.

It was about this time that he began to suffer from strange fancies. Sometimes, on his way home late at night, when the streets were silent, he could have sworn he heard soft footsteps padding behind him, yet when he stopped and looked round there was no one there. Or, even when fuddled with drink in a Bankside tavern, he would see among the drinkers a face that was somehow familiar, but that he could not place. He began to feel as if he were being watched and, on several occasions, he had pushed through the crowd to challenge the watcher, only to find that he had vanished.

In the dark watches of the night he lay wakeful, rehearsing who might be putting him under surveillance.

Not Spain, she had been too badly burned by the fiasco of the Armada and anyway, Spanish politics had never been his field. The Roman church and its emissaries in Rheims? He had ceased to be important to them: there were no longer any plots to put a Stuart on the English throne for that would happen anyway. Was Essex trying to discover through Poley, and therefore through him, what Cecil was plotting?

Which brought him to the obvious possibility, Cecil himself and his agent, Poley. So far as he knew, he had carried out all the tasks given to him satisfactorily, but had it been rumoured he could no longer be trusted? If so, what might Poley's next move be? In the cold light of day he would shrug off these as night fears, putting it down to a frustrated state of mind exacerbated by drink.

So, restless, depressed and haunted, he returned once again to Tom and Scadbury, pouring out his depression at his lack of creative inspiration, but not his secret anxieties. As ever, Tom listened courteously, waited until he had talked himself out, then asked, suddenly, 'Have you been working for Cecil?'

'Why?' answered Marlowe, in some surprise.

'It occurred to me from things you've let drop and your somewhat mysterious journeyings that you might have been.'

'I've recently been home to Canterbury, as you know.'

'I didn't mean Canterbury. I thought possibly the Low Countries? Further afield?'

'Why do you ask? You've led me to believe that since the death of Sir Francis, you'd no longer any interest in such matters.'

'I haven't. And I'd thought you'd left it behind you as well, as much as that's ever possible with a trade that can continue to stick to one.'

Marlowe thought for a moment, then said, 'Since you ask me, then yes, a little. Mainly through Poley who now seems to be Cecil's right-hand man. The money's useful.'

'You know you can come to me for anything you need.'

131

'I don't want to be always your debtor, Thomas.'

'I'd infinitely prefer that to your involving yourself with such as Cecil and Poley. Robert Cecil is no Francis Walsingham, nor do I have any such influence over him as I had over my uncle. Poley is . . . well, Poley. I don't have to tell you what kind of a man he is. Surely now with your success in the playhouses, my patronage and the place you've made for yourself in society, there's no need for you to grub around in that dirty world? Do Raleigh and Harriot and the like know of your activities?'

Marlowe was startled. 'Gracious Heavens, I trust not! No, I don't see how they can, unless one of them, unknown to me, has the ear of Cecil. If anything, it's rather the reverse, that Cecil has spies out to see who attends meetings of the School of the Night and what is discussed at them. Except that . . . ' he paused. 'Except that I sent word to Raleigh recently asking if I might visit him at Cerne Abbas but received no reply. But then, he has problems enough of his own. No, I think you worry over nothing.'

'I hope so.'

'You sound doubtful.'

Walsingham sighed then came and put his arm round his friend. 'I have a gut feeling – it's no more than that Kit – call it if you will a feeling of unease, of something not being quite right.' This so nearly matched Marlowe's own feelings that he was taken aback. For a moment he considered confiding his fears to Tom, then changed his mind.

'God's wounds, Tom,' he said, with an attempt at a laugh, 'what are you suggesting? That Cecil has me marked down for the rope or the assassin's knife. What harm have I done him?'

'I don't know, Kit. Indulge me, though, when I advise that you should stay close to Scadbury. Bend your mind again to poetry and leave that other world behind you.'

Marlowe smiled. 'I'll bear what you say in mind, Tom, but I'm restless, restless – you can't just summon up the muse at will. She has deserted me, it seems, and leaves me idle. As to the other . . . well, I've few illusions as to what can be the fate of agents who have outlived their usefulness, but I shall do my best to ensure nothing unpleasant befalls me. Besides which, if it ever came to it, then I would bring up the matter of . . . ' He stopped, abruptly.

'Of what?'

'Best you don't know, my dear.' Then, remembering something else, he said 'I saw your man Frizer in London last week.'

'He often goes to town, sometimes on my business, sometimes on his own account. I find it better not to enquire too closely as to what he does once he is outside my jurisdiction. I know you've never liked him.'

'Nor do I trust him. Did you know he was seeing Nick Skeres? Indeed he was lodging with him.'

'No. But then Skeres has had legitimate business with the estate of late, whatever his connection might have been in the past. He has been involved, with Frizer, in procuring materials for the repair of some of my properties. I shouldn't pay it any mind.'

The talk had then turned to more pleasant topics, but Tom's unexpected warning had shaken Marlowe more than he would admit even to himself, shadowing so closely, as they did, his own illogical misgivings.

* * * *

December brought in cold, dry weather, the frost sparkling on the trees and on the grass in the Paris Gardens. It was the least favourable climate for Plague. Without waiting to consult the authorities, Henslowe re-opened the Rose. Work was in short supply, money scarce and the population had been staring death in the face for months. It was a dangerous brew. London had always suffered outbursts of riotous behaviour by apprentices, especially on public holidays but now, with whole streets of shops and craft workshops shut, great gangs of young men roamed the streets, making mischief and terrorising people as they went about their business, smashing in the windows and doors of empty houses, overturning the stalls of street traders and causing mayhem in the taverns. Nor was that all, for their elders, desperate to blame their plight on something more concrete than God, Satan or the Plague, turned on the hard-working, sober colonies of immigrants who had escaped in successive waves from Catholic persecution on the Continent.

So it was that Flemish silk weavers and Dutch metalworkers suddenly found themselves at the receiving end of mindless prejudice, unfounded rumour and, increasingly, of violence; and that the authorities turned a blind eye to the re-opening of the Rose, thankful for anything that might offer a diversion.

Once again the flag with its red rose flew from the top of the tower and the trumpeter sounded his fanfare bravely. Wrapped in all the clothing they could lay their hands on to protect them from the cold, the groundlings stamped their feet, rubbed their hands and coughed, while the actors, their noses red and hands blue, gave of their best watched by their betters, comfortably wrapped in furs. Happy to take advantage of Burbage still being out of town, Henslowe wickedly revived the only Shakespeare play to which he had the rights, *Titus Andronicus*. This time it packed the house.

15

There sits Death; there sits imperious Death,
Keeping his circuit by the slicing edge.

Tamburlaine Part I   Marlowe

TOWARDS THE END OF April 1593, Phillip
Henslowe sat in his office adding up his accounts and
making notes in his diary. He had every reason to feel
satisfaction for he had managed to keep the Rose open
almost continually since Twelfth Night. There had been
over twenty performances in January, more than a dozen
in February, and although he had been forced to close
briefly in March, there had been performances throughout
April shared between the Lord Admiral's Men and the
company of my Lord of Sussex. Now a small tour had
been arranged, within easy reach of London, for the
beginning of May, during which time the theatre could be
thoroughly cleaned.

In the early part of the year, the audiences were rarely
large but they were reliable, and there was sufficient
income for Henslowe to pay his senior hired actors ten
shillings a week once more. By April people were
crowding in to see such pieces as *Friar Bacon*, *The Jew of
Malta*, Kyd's *Prince Hamlet of Denmark* (which he had
revised to Henslowe's satisfaction), and the old *King Lear
and His Three Daughters*. It amused Henslowe that once
Burbage had realised that the Rose was still open and,
despite the Plague, was attracting good audiences, he
brought the Lord Chamberlain's Men back to London for
a short season at the nearby playhouse at Newington
Butts.

Thus it was that the two companies were thrown

135

together in the Bankside taverns, a situation leading inevitably to much theatrical gossip and bragging as to the superiority of Henslowe over Burbage (and vice versa) and future prospects; not least whether they would be able to remain in London for the foreseeable future or be forced out on to the roads once again.

The last months had been a time for decisions. Jenny Pope had returned to Oxford and although Simon rode down to see her every time he had more than two days free, they were both tired of the situation and she had made him promise they would all be together again that summer, come what may. They also discussed, at length, whether Simon's future lay any longer with the Lord Admiral's Men.

Half-way through April, therefore, Simon went to see Henslowe and put his views to him forcibly. It was more than time he was offered a share in the company, as one of its most experienced actors with the best line of parts after Ned Alleyn. All together he had given Henslowe over six years of loyal service, yet here he was, still only a hired actor who, in theory, could be dispensed with at any time Henslowe or Alleyn chose. He was thirty-five years old and worthy of something better. Henslowe crouched behind his papers and busied himself with sharpening the nib of his pen, then took refuge in the vagueness he usually assumed when forced to deal with something he would prefer not to contemplate, resorting to anodyne comments such as 'Let's talk about it again when the Plague is past' and 'Come and see me at the turn of the year.'

Totally out of patience, Simon left his office and, after two days of thought, walked down to Newington Butts to spend several hours closeted with Dick Burbage, Master Hemminges, Henry Condell and Will Shakespeare. That night he sat down and wrote to Jenny that he had made his decision. The Lord Chamberlain's company had offered to admit him as a sharer when they re-organised in the summer and he had accepted. He would remain at the Rose for the rest of the remaining season, then join the company over the river at the Theatre. He hoped he might persuade Burbage to take Richard as well, that is if he wanted to make a move. Henslowe would soon fill their places as there were plenty of actors on whom he could call. The Cornishman, Henry Brodribb, was shaping up very well and would be quite adequate for some of his own roles.

For Richard, the last few months had been unhappy ones. A tentative romance with a pretty, red-haired servant girl had ended abruptly and tragically. Calling round to see her one morning, on his way to rehearsal, he had found the house marked with the dreaded red cross and the words 'God Have Mercy On Us!' A neighbour, her nose buried in a vinegar-soaked sponge in an effort to avoid infection, had told him that the entire family had been taken away in the night, and the girl along with them. 'It was bright moonlight and I saw her long red hair trailing over the side of the cart . . .'

Her untimely death had forced him to give serious consideration to his future. On the whole he had enjoyed those early years in London, but now he had grave doubts as to where his future lay. He knew he was a passable enough actor in the young men's roles which were given to him, but he also recognised, beyond all doubt, that he would never achieve the heights of the truly gifted, the Alleyns and the Burbages, nor even the all-round talent of Simon Pope. Nor had he ever completely got over his feeling of being an outsider, apart from when he was in the company of Tom Kyd or Simon. So it was that the hazards of the life, and the knowledge that while he might be a competent actor, he would never be a great one, made him wonder if it might not be better to put his theatrical career behind him and go home.

His doubts were reinforced when Simon broke the news that he was to leave the company at the Rose, making him feel even more depressed, although Simon had been hopeful of persuading Burbage to take him on. 'As a Sharer, I will be in a strong position to do this, especially if I point out that you're an old schoolfellow of Will's. It's

137

time you two met up again and I'll see if I can arrange it.'

So it was that a few days later, Simon brought Shakespeare back home with him for supper and Richard finally met him again after a gap of at least eight years. He had changed a good deal physically. The boy he had known had had a thick head of hair which flopped into his eyes, whereas this rather serious young man of nearly thirty was already balding, the loss of hair giving him a high, domed forehead, which altered the shape of his face. His personality was in direct contrast to that of his rival, Marlowe, for he was pleasant in his manner, soft spoken and modest as to his achievements, yet with a dry wit.

He was so sympathetic that Richard, made brave by wine, confided some of his doubts to him, adding 'perhaps, after all, I should go home and make peace with my family. If that's possible.'

Will looked thoughtful. 'I plan to go to Stratford myself in early June. My young brother, Edmund, writes to me that he wants to become a player. Why not come with me? Then I could accompany you when you return to your family to assure them you are highly regarded at the Rose. If my own experience is typical, they'll welcome you with open arms. Then you can decide your future.' Richard would have liked to have spoken further but, having finished his meal, Will rose and thanked Simon, saying he must now take his leave as he had an appointment which must be kept. As he spoke, a slight flush came over his face. It was obvious to Simon and Richard that he must have an assignation of some kind. Richard wondered what kind of reception he received from the wife he had deserted, when he paid one of his sporadic visits to Stratford.

* * * *

Years later, when his memories of those days at the Rose had, like something in a dream, become sufficiently faint and far off for him to dare recall them again, it seemed to Richard as if the events of that spring had been lit by a lurid glow, surpassing in their intensity any drama performed in a playhouse. Also, that although he had seen Kit Marlowe often enough in the mundane circumstances of the theatre or tavern, the most lasting and indelible impression he had made was of a man driven to an excess of extraordinary conduct by some daemon gnawing from within. He had seemed hellbent on his own destruction and, again and again, in the dark watches of the night, Richard would tell himself this, tell himself that the outcome would have been the same without the part he was to play in it. For indeed, while Marlowe's behaviour after the first night of *Dr Faustus* had been bad enough, it was as nothing to that at the great celebration given by Henslowe.

It was not Henslowe's style to ply his company with feasts and other such delights, but he had been prompted to do so on this occasion for a variety of good reasons. Most of the actors had remained loyal to the Lord Admiral's Men through the worst time the playhouses had ever experienced. He felt they deserved something for that, as did all those others so essential to the company, such as Peter the Bookkeeper, the Wardrobe Master, the Gatherer and the stage staff. Also, there had been no public festivities for the marriage of Ned Alleyn to Joan the Mouse, since the wedding had taken place at the height of the Plague, so now seemed a good opportunity to celebrate both the success of the company and the nuptials of its leading actor.

So, early in the evening, after a performance of *The Jew of Malta*, the stage was cleared of furniture and props and prepared for a feast. Long tables were put together in two rows towards the back of the stage, where the 'heavens' gave some protection from the open sky, benches were brought from the galleries and placed down each side, while chairs were brought and set at each end of the tables, for Master and Mistress Henslowe, and Ned and Joan Alleyn. Those actors who lived nearby went home after cleaning off their make-up to wash their faces and change their clothes. Each person had been told they could bring one guest and Simon, still without Jenny, had invited Ralph Wilkins, while Richard, unexpectedly meeting Emma in the street the previous day, had asked if she would like to come and she had readily accepted.

She was waiting for him outside the theatre when he returned from his lodgings. The double loss of brother and lover had taken its toll, and her thick, dark hair was now greying at the temples, her face gaunt. She could have passed for forty. Yet she had braided her hair bravely with sparkling beads and was wearing her best blue silk gown, the cast-off of some fine lady.

It seemed everyone was there, along with wives, sisters, daughters, sweethearts and friends. A scattering of playwrights included the Thomases Kyd and Nashe, and Kyd told Richard, with some relief, that he hoped to have the Thomas More play ready for rehearsal within the next two or three weeks. Such a comprehensive gathering brought back to them all memories of those who had died, causing Richard to wonder, fancifully, if the ghosts of Robin Greene and Tom Watson might not be hovering overhead.

There was, as yet, one notable omission. Although his own play had been performed that afternoon there was no sign of Marlowe. However, just as the servers began carrying in the food, he arrived, bringing with him a companion. He had spent little time of late either at the theatre or in the taverns frequented by actors, and so few present had seen him over the past months; therefore the change in him was most marked. He had lost weight and there was a strange, feverish look about him. He was dressed in the height of fashion in a lavishly slashed doublet of mulberry-coloured satin, over the puffed trunk hose favoured by Court gallants, and he wore a pearl in one ear. His companion, a weak-chinned, effeminate young man with thin ginger hair and a painted face, was even finer in a doublet and hose of finely worked brocade. He strode up on to the stage, greeted Henslowe, then pushed his way to the middle bench on one of the tables, insisting his companion be seated next to him, much to the chagrin of Jamie, who had not seen him for weeks. After a long period of neglect, he had gone to Marlowe's old lodgings in Hog Lane in search of him only to be told Master Marlowe had moved out some weeks earlier.

Emma told Simon in a low voice that she had seen Kit a number of times in the taverns of East Cheap and St Paul's, sometimes alone, sometimes in strange company, but always wildly drunk and increasingly vicious. Where he lodged, she no longer knew nor cared much. It was all she could do to see to her own life and that of her child.

'How is Fortunatus?' asked Simon.

'Much as ever.' She sighed. 'He doesn't thrive, you know. Nell cares for him most of the time. She never did take to whoring, so I earn the money for both of us and pay her to look after him. It's a fair bargain.'

For the next two or three hours all present applied themselves with gusto to the array of food set before them: great baskets of oysters, small salt fish, broiled carp, a haunch of venison, a side of beef, great raised pies, roasted capons and woodcocks all served with dishes of salad and vegetables. Then there were bowls of syllabub, fine cheeses, fruit and, the *pièce de résistance*, a model of the Rose Theatre made of sugar and marchpane. Barrels of ale and cider had been racked at the side of the stage from which the revellers could help themselves, and there was wine in abundance.

The company was lively, noisy but relatively well behaved; the presence of Henslowe and Alleyn and their wives ensured that. Then, as most of the dishes and platters were cleared away, and the nuts and sweetmeats were being handed around, Will Hunt produced his lute and struck up first some merry jigs, then popular songs such as 'Away to Twivver' and 'Greensleeves', after which he strummed the first few bars of the music to which Marlowe's own 'Amorous Shepherd' had been set. Soon they were all singing:

Come live with me and be my love,
And we will all the pleasures prove,
That valleys, groves, hills and fields,
Woods or steepy mountain yields

through to the last verse:

A belt of straw and ivy buds,
With coral clasps and amber studs,
And if these pleasures may thee move,
Come, live with me, and be my love.

The last notes died away to a round of applause. Even
Marlowe's mood seemed to have lightened, for he laughed
and then called across to Will Hunt, 'Did you know that
Raleigh had capped my verse?' and reaching over and
taking the lute from him, he accompanied himself and sang
in pleasant tenor voice:

But could youth last, and love still breed:
Had joys no date, nor age no need,
Then those delights my mind might move,
To live with thee, and be thy love.

There was further applause and laughter. Next came
Ralph Wilkins who sang unaccompanied in a light
baritone, 'Who is Sylvia, What is she?', from *Two
Gentlemen of Verona*. That went down well too. By now it
was almost dark in the theatre except for the stage area
which was illuminated by torches (as used in tragedies) and
candles stuck in bottles.

Finally, Henslowe drew the main part of the evening to a
close with a toast to the happy couple, and was duly
toasted himself as the founder of the feast. His party then
withdrew to their house, but not before Alleyn reminded
all present that they had a performance of *King Leir and
his Three Daughters* the following day and he wanted no
thick heads or forgotten lines. Their departure was a signal

for many others to leave as well; it had been a good night and they were now happy to go home to bed. Later, those who remained behind were to wish they had gone too.

It soon became obvious, to the dozen or so who were left, that Marlowe's mood had darkened again, once the laughing and singing were over. He had now reverted to his old habit of throwing out deliberately provocative statements in an effort to goad his listeners into some kind of response, and in this he was aided and abetted by his ginger-haired companion who, much to Jamie's misery and disgust, seemed to be on intimate terms with Marlowe.

It was then that Marlowe, lolling back and letting his eye wander around the faces at the tables, sat up suddenly and turned his attention to Dick Baines who was, as usual, accompanying Gregory Sly. This would, however, be the last time, for Sly had been discharged from the company, Henslowe telling him bluntly he should find another trade. Marlowe stared at Baines then said, 'My wits may be a shade addled but that fellow over there keeps watching me.'

'If he is, then you've brought it on yourself,' said Ralph, 'since you go out of your way to provoke attention.'

'Not only here and tonight,' continued Marlowe without taking any notice, 'but *everywhere*. I've seen you,' he called out, 'creeping round after me wherever I go. Don't think I haven't noticed.'

Everyone looked at Dick Baines, who shrugged his shoulders, shook his head and went back to his conversation. Marlowe drained his tankard. 'Who are you, pizzle-head?'

'You're drunk, Marlowe,' said the Bookkeeper, who had risen and was about to leave. 'Leave him be, for God's sake. He's doing you no harm.'

Marlowe continued his survey of those remaining until his eye next lit on Kyd, who had been studiously trying to avoid his gaze. 'Do you still dislike me, Tom?', he said, deliberately.

Kyd looked acutely embarrassed. 'No. I don't truly

dislike you, at least not you as you were. I admire your work immensely and I used to like you well enough, but now you frighten me.'

'Tell me in what way? I'm always ready to learn.'

'I hate all your blasphemous talk. It alarms me and I'm sure it alarms others.'

'Is that what you're here for, long ears?' Marlowe again called out to Baines. 'Have you been set on to take down my words and see if I blaspheme? If so, I'd hate to disappoint you.'

Will Hunt's wife, who had said little all evening, being so overawed by the company, promptly lent over and whispered something in her husband's ear. 'You're right, Betty, it's time to go,' he said. They got up and he put his wife's shawl round her shoulders then turned to Marlowe. 'You can never forebear to spoil an evening, can you? Why couldn't you leave us in peace and remain with your high and mighty friends? I'm told Master Raleigh and his circle practise necromancy. That should suit you.'

'You're a clown offstage as well as on, Will Hunt, and as bad as the Exeter actors who thought they saw the Devil on stage with them in *Faustus*, but then I could hardly expect a professional Fool to understand the intricacies of science and mathematics or the stupidities of the religious beliefs peddled by the Church; it would be way above your head'. But the Hunts were already half way out of the building. It was as if Marlowe could not stop, as if he had bound himself to a wheel which was now rolling away with him.

He again looked round the room. 'In fact, all that's lacking tonight to make up a parcel of Fools is the late poet and drunkard extraordinary, Robert Greene – at least that's one poxy playwright the less.' He swivelled round to Emma. She had been sitting half-asleep, content for once to be in congenial company with good food and drink in her belly, which she had not had to earn on her back or up against an alley wall: now she came fully awake. 'However,' continued Marlowe, 'I see we have his whore here, though looking somewhat the worse for wear. And how's the little brat, Fortunatus? Still living? It were surely better he joined his father, that is if Robin *was* his father!'

The ginger-haired young man brayed with laughter as Emma rose to her feet. Those who remembered her violent reaction to insults in the past fully expected her to smash a bottle over Marlowe's head and waited with bated breath as she made her way over to him. She looked deep into his dark, malicious eyes, then saw something which made her stop short. 'You're afraid, Kit Marlowe. That's what's the matter with you, you're afraid and God keep me from what it is you fear.' Then, in total silence, she returned to Richard, thanked him, and left. No one spoke.

Ralph Wilkins picked up the bottles left on the table one at a time. 'I think there's just about enough left in some of these for us all to have one last drink each, then I suggest we go home.' He walked round the table filling the glasses handed to him. If matters had been left there, then all might yet have been well, but the combination of Marlowe in so evil a mood, and Ralph, always truculent in drink, proved disastrous.

'How dare that punk say Kit's afraid,' said Marlowe's companion. 'He's not afraid of anything or anyone, are you Kit, not even Judgement Day.' He laughed, foolishly, 'Why, he told us all the other night that the Bible was full of nothing but fairytales and the resurrection but a story put out by credulous women with no truth in it.'

'I don't like this,' muttered Simon. 'That young wantwit seems determined to egg Kit on.'

'The truth, Marlowe?' Ralph responded, predictably. 'There's only the one and that's what the Church teaches us. Not that I go much myself,' he added, hastily, for he had recently been fined for his lack of attendance and everyone knew it, 'but I know what's right and what's wrong.'

'How touching,' sneered Marlowe.

Simon caught Ralph by the shoulder. 'For God's sake, don't pay him any mind.'

145

'You don't really mean what you said about not believing in what was in the Bible, do you?' asked the Cornishman, Henry Brodribb. 'What about the miracles and wonders Moses performed?'

Marlowe roared with laughter. 'What Moses did could as easily have been done by any competent conjuror travelling around the country fairs. And he must have been an exceptionally stupid man, since he led the Jews in the wilderness for four solid years before they reached the Promised Land. Any competent fellow could've done it in one. Be sure to make a note of that!'

Those that were left were now divided between the camp who wanted to see the scene out to its conclusion, and those who wanted to end it; noisy arguments broke out between the two camps.

'Surely even you must believe that Jesus Christ was the son of God,' said Ralph, finally, feeling it was time to finish the argument.

'Why? Those who knew him best said he was only a carpenter's son, and if those among whom he lived thought fit to crucify him as a meddler and a magician, why should we think them wrong? They knew his real origins better than we do, surely?' Carried away, Marlowe climbed on to the table and, apeing a parson holding the bands of his cassock intoned as if in church: 'I say to you his mother was merely a ba-wd, that he was himself a bas-tard, that the Angel Gabriel is but a pan-dar, acting for the Holy Gho-ost.'

'Please, please stop, Kit,' said Jamie, now almost tearful.

'There you are, Jamie, I didn't see you hiding away.' He motioned to the ginger-haired man. 'Hugh, meet my past lover; Jamie, meet my present one.'

'Tell them what you said, Kit, when you were told to think of the great love the first Apostles had for Jesus Christ, and most especially that between Him and St John,' said Hugh. Then, as Marlowe did not immediately respond, he continued, 'Kit said St John was Jesus' Alexis,' and looked triumphantly across at Dick Baines.

146

'Who's Alexis?' asked Henry Brodribb.

Marlowe leered across at Jamie. 'Why, his catamite, his bedfellow.' He looked at their faces blank with shock. 'Dear me, how very conventional you all are.' He got down from the table, knocking Richard aside as he did so and laughing at the expression on the actor's face.

'Taken over Robin's whore, have you, boy? Well, she should bring you a few shillings still.'

Released by much wine, all the antagonism Richard felt for Marlowe but had kept to himself, all the times he had been made to feel inadequate, suddenly exploded in a rush of words.

'We don't use each other in that fashion. That's all you can think of, can't you? How to use people. Emma was here tonight as of right. As one of us. But then, you wouldn't understand that. She's just someone else for you to despise, like Tom,' he gestured at Kyd, 'and like me. You don't care about anything or anyone, do you? Perhaps you should consider the warning Robin Greene sent you from his deathbed.'

'Deathbed repentances have never moved me. Robin drank and wenched his way through life, lived off Em like any ponce off his bawd and then, when death stared him in the face, rushed to settle his reckoning with God. It's common enough. You'll come to it, along with your friend the little scrivener, who seems to mean so much to you. Talking of which, are you of the inclination that loves them both? Men and women?'

Simon caught Richard's arm as he made to strike his tormentor. 'Steady, Richard. There's no point in arguing with him when he's in this mood.' He blew out the last of the candles and dowsed the remaining torches, then turning to Marlowe he added, 'If Robin had a reckoning to pay, then he'll have paid it now. Come on, all of you. I must lock up the theatre. You, too, Kit.'

Kyd led the way out, bade them all goodnight, and left for London Bridge. Marlowe watched him go then spat at Simon, 'Killjoy! Oh well, I suppose it must be the tavern.

147

Anyone want to join me?' Then he turned on Baines. 'Not even you, ratface? Go tell your paymasters Marlowe's misbehaving himself again.' Simon checked the door was properly locked then took Marlowe by the shoulder. 'I should go home, if I were you.'

'But you aren't me, are you?' He shook himself free and turned on the others, his face crimson, his eyes wild. 'I'll tell you all, Christianity's a myth, a myth to dull men's minds, to make them abase themselves for fear of Hell. "Why, this is Hell, and we are part of it." Every last one of us.' He came over to Baines and thrust his face against his. 'Tell your friends, spy, that if I fall, then they'll fall too. You can count on that. Oh, leave me, all of you, you're like children scared of the dark.' He hunched himself up, apeing some grotesque creature.

> From noise of scarefires rest ye free,
> From murders, Benedicite,
> From all mischances that may fright,
> Your pleasing slumbers in the night,
> Mercie secure you all and keep,
> The goblin from you, while you sleep . . . aaagh!

'I say the Apostles were a lot of base fellows, neither of worth nor wit. Only Paul had wit but he was a nervous man, telling others they should obey the magistrates. As to the Gospels, they are so badly written! And in filthy Greek!'

* * * *

They left him to it, to go their separate ways. Simon, concerned about the emotional state Richard was in, offered him a bed for the night, but Richard shrugged him off and stumbled away towards his own lodgings. Suddenly, he became aware of someone behind him and as he turned, a hand fell on his shoulder. He immediately reached for his dagger.

'Don't draw on me, I mean you no harm,' said Baines. 'I was concerned for I saw that Marlowe had angered you.'

In his hazy state, Richard could not remember clearly who Baines was and why he had been at the theatre in the first place, but his tone was sympathetic and Richard felt he needed sympathy, for the events of the evening, coupled with drink, had replaced the earlier enjoyment of the evening with intense depression. 'I'd just had enough of Marlowe and his viper's tongue, and the vile things he says about people and even God.'

'He is a dangerous man,' responded Baines, 'and says dangerous things.'

'And reads them, too,' Richard added.

'Does he? How do you know?'

'Last year I shared a workroom with Tom Kyd, that good, kind man he always mocks. Marlowe used to work there once and he'd left behind a heap of papers, some of which said terrible things. There was one which set out to prove there was no such thing as the Holy Trinity, that there was no God.' He shivered, for it had become chill. 'Tom says he was often frightened by Marlowe's talk.'

'I'm not surprised. Are the papers still there?'

'Where?'

'In the workroom of – who did you say, Thomas Kyd?'

'I suppose so. I haven't been there for months. Why?'

'No matter.' He clapped Richard on the shoulder. 'Well, I'm for my bed and I'm sure it's the best place for you too. You'll feel better in the morning.' And with that he strode away.

Richard felt anything but well in the morning. He remembered only the broad outline of the events of the evening and how he had turned on Kit Marlowe. Of his conversation with Baines he had only the faintest recollection, although for some reason it left him feeling uneasy.

16

Why, this is Hell, nor am I out of it.

Dr Faustus Marlowe

THEY OPERATED IN THE night, the nameless ones determined to use the refugees from religious persecution as scapegoats for all their troubles. For the Huguenots, the Flemish weavers and the Protestant Dutch, Plague had long ceased to be the only hazard facing them. Hostility in the streets had turned to arson, rags stuffed against their doors and set alight, attacks on their work-places and, increasingly, on their persons.

The covert campaign culminated at the end of April in a spate of pamphlets and bills distributed throughout London, many of which made no attempt to disguise open threats. The company from the Rose, gathering together to set off to play in Colchester and Chelmsford, found the walls outside the theatre flyposted with a particularly obnoxious verse:

> You strangers that inhabit in this land,
> Note this same writing, do it understand;
> Conceive it well for safeguard of your lives,
> Your goods, your children and your dearest wives.

The same doggerel could clearly be seen pasted on the doors of nearby immigrant homes, causing Simon Pope to remark that he wished he knew the author so that his work could be returned to him with the injunction that he use it to wipe his arse.

The posting of the verses finally provoked action from the Privy Council who, after a swiftly convened meeting, issued an Order to the effect that the publishing of such malicious libels must cease forthwith and that any found doing so would be punished with the utmost severity. In order to hunt such persons down and bring them to justice officers of the law would, from now on, be authorised to search the houses, lodgings or workplace of anyone suspected of this or similar crimes and should there be any cause, however slight, to think such a person had been discovered, then they must be arrested.

It ended on the chilling note: '. . . and after you shall have examined this person, if you shall find them to be suspected and they shall refuse to confess the truth, you shall, by the authority hereof, put them to the torture in Bridewell and by the extremity thereof, draw them to discover the knowledge they have. We pray you use your utmost travail and endeavour.'

Marlowe found a copy of the verse pasted to the door of the house across from his lodgings and, after reading it, removed it and tore it into small pieces. During the last few days he had undergone a dramatic change of mood. The daemon, which for months seemed to have been driving him to destruction, appeared suddenly to have left him and, what was more, he felt his old urge to write flooding back. Ideas, words, lines of verse filled his head as they used to in the old days. Consequently, he had woken on the morning of 30 April full of elation, his head clear and with a strange sense of peace. The night terrors had gone, he no longer felt the object of watching eyes. Best of all, the fitful Muse had finally returned and now all he wanted to do was write, write the long-planned poem of Hero and Leander. He decided there and then that he would take himself off to Scadbury so that he could work without interruption.

Indeed, why not go that very day and so take part in the May Day Festivities on the Scadbury estate? He left his bed, plunged his head into a bowl of cold water, dressed and made his way to a nearby Ordinary to find some breakfast. He walked down the street in the spring

151

sunshine in a state near to euphoria, taking himself to task for his recent fears. Looked at sensibly in the bright light of day, surely they had been nothing more than the product of a prolonged black mood coupled with an over-active imagination? He recollected too his behaviour at the Rose a few days earlier with some shame; it had been wild even for him and he determined he would send Henslowe a note from Scadbury apologising for the offence he must have caused. In spite of the overnight smells in the street he took a deep breath, filling his lungs with air and turned into the Ordinary with a light heart.

Thomas Kyd, on his way to his workroom, found a tearful Huguenot woman in the street with her small children, the remains of a fire smouldering in her porch and neighbours helping her clear away the mess as they comforted her. Ralph Wilkins, reading the copy of the verse that had been affixed to the door of the Newington Butts playhouse was accosted by a red-faced fellow with foodstains on his doublet, who ventured the opinion that indeed all such foreign scum, only here to take the bread out of the mouths of honest folk and spread the Plague, should be sent back whence they came and, he continued, looking Ralph up and down, they might do worse than take London's scurvy players with them. At which Ralph laid him flat in the gutter, calling out loudly as he did so, 'Lie there where you belong, shitbag,' before enquiring if there were any others with anything similar to say.

After breakfasting, Marlowe packed what he needed into a bag, paid his landlady, collected his horse from the stables and made for Scadbury in this most beautiful season of the year, riding through a countryside of woods and fields sporting every imaginable shade of green, where the birds sang in the trees and scent of blossom was heavy in the air. Scadbury was at its best, the beautifully proportioned timber-and-stone house reflected in the still waters of the wide moat. Swans were nesting in the reedbeds and a mallard proudly led a convoy of six small ducklings across the water to the far bank. He gave his horse to one of the stable lads and went in search of his friend. Tom Walsingham recognised his change of mood straight away.

'I hardly need to ask you if you're well, Kit.'

'Never better! It is as if I've come out at last from a long dark tunnel full of the figures of nightmare, into open land and fine weather. What's more, I must write again – which is why I am here.'

'That you shall do and uninterrupted, but first you must join with us in our celebration of the coming of summer!'

All England celebrated that great pagan festival which the Church had tried first to banish then to subsume but without effect. It was the great release of joy at the final end of winter and the coming of fine weather, cutting across all barriers from the highest in the land to the poorest labourer. From tiny village to the City of London there was maypole dancing, the choosing of May Queens and the ceremony of Bringing in the May. Late on the night of the last day of April, after much riotous drinking in the taverns and general horseplay in the streets, bands of young men and women went off to the nearest woods to cut down branches of May with which to return at dawn to decorate the outside of their houses and lodgings. As might be expected in such circumstances, May Day was followed inevitably by a rash of pregnancies but on the whole this was easily dealt with, for most young men were prepared to honour their obligations; not least because the extraction of maintenance for a bastard child, where the father was known, was pursued by the relevant authorities with vigour. Nor did most putative fathers fancy sitting in the stocks outside their local church for three consecutive Sundays, bearing round their necks legends such as 'John Smith has got Sara Cook with child.'

Tom Walsingham had taken a party of young ladies and gentlemen out to the estate woods that night for an alfresco supper of good food and wine, followed by singing and talk. As they rode back for breakfast they were soon surrounded by tired revellers bound for home: young

153

farmers or artisans on horseback; their girls, crowned with flowers and wearing the traditional spring colours of white and green, riding pillion behind them; labourers and honest workmen, walking hand-in-hand with red-faced wenches sporting green and white ribbons in their long hair, their petticoats dragging, their gowns creased and marked with leaves and grass stains, all clutching great boughs of may blossom. There were parties of gallants too, the ladies squired either by their husbands or those to whom they were betrothed or, in the case of the unmarried, under the wary eyes of a senior family member. There was much singing of traditional songs, 'Spring, the Sweet Spring', 'As I went out one May morning,' and 'Summer is icumen in'. In a mood of unusual tolerance, Marlowe breakfasted heartily, then, shutting himself away in his room, began to write.

On 2 May Ned Alleyn wrote to his 'good sweetheart and loving Mouse' from Chelmsford, where the company were playing, and after expressing his hope that all was well with her and that she was in good health, he informed her that news had already reached him of her own participation in the May revels. 'But I little thought to hear, Mouse', he wrote, 'that you were made by my Lord Mayor's officers to ride in a cart as May Queen and I wonder those strong supporters, your long legs, did not carry you away from such termagants, but Mouse, when I come home I'll be revenged on them! Till when, Mouse, I bid thee farewell and please send me word how thou dost.'

* * * *

On the morning of 12 May, Thomas Kyd sat writing in his workroom. He had finished his revisions on the script of the play of Sir Thomas More, doing his best to edit the various hands that had gone into its making into a cohesive whole. He had been much struck by the speech young William Shakespeare had written in to it during his brief sojourn with Henslowe, which begins:

Imagine that you see the wretched strangers,
Their babies on their backs, with their poor
    luggage,
Plodding to the ports and coasts for
    transportation . . .

then challenges the audience to examine their consciences
with regard to immigrants, asking what they might feel if
they, too, were the object of persecution:

Whither would you go?
What country, by the nature of your error,
Should give you harbour? Go to France or
    Flanders?
To any German province, Spain or Portugal?
Nay, anywhere that not adheres to England,
Why, you must needs be strangers.

He had delivered the script to Henslowe, pointing out
that it was the best he could do, so many hands having
been at work on it in the past. Henslowe had glanced at it
but had still seemed unhappy and had told Kyd that he
would put it by until Ned returned and could give his
opinion. The completion of the task now left Kyd free to
begin an original piece of his own. Thanks to the
continuing interest of his patron, he no longer had to dance
attendance on Henslowe, nor break off to copy legal
documents or write letters for the illiterate. He was content
with his modest good fortune.

Carefully he set out neatly everything he might need: a
small pile of clean paper, the ink pot newly filled, a
selection of quill pens, ready sharpened but with the knife
nearby. The number of Plague deaths had risen again and
he could hear the death-bell tolling, but this had become a
sound he did his best to ignore. Before him on his desk
were a number of supposed prophylactics against the
disease: a jar containing a posy of rue and mint, an orange
stuck with cloves and a sponge soaked in white vinegar

with which he wiped down his desk and chair every morning. He settled into his work.

The noise of tramping feet along the street outside did not unduly disturb him, nor did he take much notice when it stopped, but the sound of hammering and thumping on the front door did make him look up in surprise. He heard the door below opened to the shout of 'Open up in the name of the law!', followed by the whining tones of the old man from whom he rented the room. Then came the sound of loud footsteps on the wooden staircase and the door of his room was thrown open.

'You are Thomas Kyd?' asked the leading officer.

'Yes.' He stood up. 'Why are you here? What do you want?'

The leading officer produced a scroll and read out the terms of the Order of the Privy Council on the distribution of malicious libels, down to the paragraph which authorised them to search 'chambers, studies, chests or other like places for all manner of writings or papers that may give light for discovery of the libellers'.

Kyd was incredulous. 'You come seeking *here* for the author of this scurrilous stuff? Who has set you on? No one who knows me, and I can give you the names of many such, could possibly think me capable of spreading such poisonous rubbish.'

'That's as maybe,' replied the officer, 'but our orders are to search this room thoroughly.'

'Then do so,' said Kyd. 'By all means turn out my chests, go through my papers. You'll find nothing to your purpose,' at which he sat down again and folded his arms.

He had expected the searchers to go roughly through his books and papers, flinging them here and there, before admitting they had come on a fool's errand and departing, leaving him to clear up the mess. But this was not the case. One young man, who seemed to be some kind of official, sat at the table once used by Kit Marlowe and began sifting through the papers on it. 'Not all those over there are mine,' Kyd told him, 'some belong to a previous occupant.

I've kept telling him to come and collect them but he never bothers.'

It was near the bottom of the third pile, and after a search which had lasted well over an hour, that the young man apparently found what he wanted. He walked over to Kyd and flourished the paper in his face. 'What do you call this?' he said.

Kyd took the paper from him. At first he did not recognise it, then suddenly he realised what it must be. 'Why, it's one of Kit's papers, a treatise by someone called, if I recollect, Arrian, refuting some religious tract or other dedicated to the Queen's late sister, the Catholic Mary Tudor.'

'You are aware of its heretical nature?'

'No, for I never read beyond the first page. Such things are of no interest to me. Great Heavens, man, it must be all of fifty years old!'

'It is a vile and atheistical document; it's age is immaterial.'

For the first time an icy spasm of fear clutched Kyd's heart. 'But it isn't even mine,' he insisted, 'it belongs to Kit Marlowe. If you want to know its origins or argue over its contents, then go and see him. As I said, it's been here for months along with his other papers. It's well over a year, perhaps more, since he shared the room with me.'

'I think we have all the evidence we need,' said the leading officer. Then, with great formality, he continued: 'Thomas Kyd, on the Order of the Privy Council and in the name of Her Majesty, our Sovereign Lady Queen Elizabeth the First of England, I arrest you.'

'On what charge,' cried Kyd, wildly, 'you said you were looking for papers connected with the spreading of malicious lies about foreign immigrants and you have found none, nor will. What has that old paper of Marlowe's got to do with me?'

'That is for others to discover.' He turned to his men. 'Conduct him to Bridewell Prison.'

They tied his arms behind his back and hustled him

down the stairs, past the gaping landlord, eyes agog, through the now crowded streets, men with pikes going in front and behind, the leading officer and the searcher riding beside Kyd as he stumbled along on foot, slithering in and out of the kennel in the middle of the road.

Half an hour later he was standing in front of the Keeper of Bridewell Prison.

'The prisoner, Thomas Kyd, sir.'

The grave-faced man in the long dark gown looked at Kyd.

'You know why you've been brought here?'

'No, I do not. Only that one of the officers found some old paper in my workroom. I've told him again and again that it does not belong to me but to Christopher Marlowe and that if they want to know more of it, then they must apply to him.'

'You do not deny, do you, that these writings are vile and heretical conceits denying the very deity of Jesus Christ, our Saviour?'

'As heaven's my witness, I do not. I have never even read the paper through. I have said that many times already.'

'You do not share Marlowe's views then?'

'What views? If you are asking me to say I agree with the sentiments expressed in a pamphlet I have never properly read, but which you say deny that Christ is indeed our Risen Lord, then of course I don't believe that. On my living soul, I hate blasphemy.'

'And what of Marlowe's other interests?'

'I don't understand,' said Kyd, in growing desperation. 'What other interests, for God's sake?'

'Treasonable interests. Matters referring to James of Scotland. What has he discussed with you?'

'Treason? James of Scotland?' Kyd looked round, wildly, 'This is surely some nightmare from which I will wake with the morning. Or I am dead and gone straight to Hell. I know nothing of treason and the King of the Scots, I have never discussed such matters with him, never *would* discuss such matters.'

158

The Keeper frowned. 'I fear you know more of this than you are prepared to say.' Kyd shook his head, shouting 'No, no!' The Keeper looked at him coldly. 'Put him to the rack,' he said.

* * * *

Robert Poley, returning from yet another trip to Holland, found a messenger from Cecil waiting for him on the quayside as soon as he had disembarked from the vessel which had brought him back to England. He was to come to Cecil's office immediately; the messenger had a boat standing by waiting to row them both up river. No, he told Poley, he did not know what business was afoot that was so urgent, only that he had been told there was no time to lose.

They arrived in the anteroom to Cecil's office where, somewhat to Poley's surprise, he found Richard Baines already there before him. The messenger left them waiting while he went to inform John Dowling that Poley had arrived. The two men exchanged greetings and Poley asked why Baines had been summoned, but the informer did not know. He had had nothing to add to the report on Marlowe he had given to Poley three weeks earlier.

'And I made sure it reached Cecil before I left the country. Possibly something has happened since which has decided Cecil to make a move.'

They were interrupted by Dowling who showed them into Cecil's office. The Secretary was standing looking out of his window but, as they came in, he walked back to his desk. He looked first at the informer.

'Baines, is it?'

'Yes, sir.'

Cecil picked up a paper. 'I have your report here. Marlowe appears to have said enough to merit a charge of blasphemy ten times over.'

'There was never likely to be any trouble finding proof of that,' said Poley. 'It merely adds to what we already know.'

'I've been most assiduous in my duties,' Baines cut in,

159

crossly. 'I've hardly let Marlowe out of my sight for months.'

'To the point where he became aware of it,' said Poley, coldly.

Cecil looked at Baines. 'That hardly shows great skill on your part. Continue, Poley.'

'Fortunately, Marlowe being the type of man he is, it made him more reckless rather than less, but I agree. You're a shoddy tool, Baines.'

Cecil scanned Baines' report then regarded him. 'You can swear he said all this? Are there other witnesses?'

'I can certainly swear it, and much of what he has said has been before witnesses.' Cecil rang his small bell for Dowling and when his secretary appeared said: 'Take this man away and get him to swear an affidavit to this document. Then you may go, Baines.'

Baines looked from one to the other. 'What about my payments? Aren't you going . . . ' but Cecil merely motioned him to follow Dowling as Poley said, 'You heard the Secretary. Go and do as he says, the question of remuneration can be settled when this business has been concluded and we can gauge how useful you proved.' It seemed at first that he was prepared to argue but then, realising the futility of such a move, followed Dowling out of the room.

'I cannot think he is to be trusted,' said Cecil as the door closed behind Baines.

'He'll do for what we have in mind and afterwards . . . well he can easily be dispensed with if you so wish.'

'So, we can definitely proceed on blasphemy. That at least will stand.'

'Oh, it will stand, no question. As to the rest . . . my ploy of sending him to Edinburgh has worked exactly as I thought and given us some useful information on the Scots Court as well.'

'If he comes to trial he will say he did exactly as you set him on, that he presented himself to James on your orders.'

Poley smiled. 'I will naturally deny all knowledge of the

matter. What is of more concern is that if he felt his life were at stake, he would not hesitate to tell the Court of the Queen's secret work he has undertaken on our behalf, showing them perhaps the copy of the Privy Council Order signed by your predecessor.' He paused a moment then said 'Where is Marlowe, by the way?'

'Fast at Scadbury. I would know if he were to leave,' said Cecil, then added, 'You know we have been taking steps to find those who have been spreading malicious libels about foreign immigrants?'

'Yes,' said Poley, 'but I would not think either Marlowe or Thomas Walsingham are likely to be among them.'

Cecil rocked back on his chair. 'Among the places searched was the workroom of one Thomas Kyd.'

'Kyd the playwright?' said Poley, astonished. 'He who wrote *The Spanish Tragedy*? He's the meekest of men.'

'Maybe, but among his papers were found writings by the heretic, Arrian.'

Poley almost laughed. 'Surely Arrian died half a century ago? Anyway, I can't believe Tom Kyd either writes malicious libels or holds heretical views.'

'Whether he does or not is irrelevant,' snapped Cecil. 'The point is that he said the writing belonged to Marlowe and must have been left by him from the time they shared a room together.'

Poley considered this. 'That's true, they did. They shared a room in Hog Lane, close by where I live. There are many of their profession there.'

Cecil continued as if the other had not spoken. 'So, as our officers did not believe him, they took him to Bridewell.'

'But he was almost certainly speaking the truth!'

Cecil smiled to himself. 'I imagine he was.'

'So he is released?'

'He is to be put to the rack.'

Poley had not usually been one to care particularly about those innocently caught up in the nets of state intrigue, but for some reason on this occasion the plight of

161

Kyd seemed to him to be not only unnecessary and possibly counter-productive but grossly unfair. It was a feeling that was new to him. 'But why? If you know it was among Marlowe's papers, then why rack Kyd? These Arrian ramblings will merely help your case against Marlowe.'

'You seem unduly concerned over this man, Poley. I will continue. When Kyd said the paper belonged to Marlowe, he was next asked what he knew of his activities against the Crown. He took fright at once, saying he knew nothing of that either, excepting what Marlowe shouted to the world in drink.'

'That's also likely to be true.'

'You wish to take his part?'

'Look,' said Poley in exasperation, 'Kyd's a nobody, a little scrivener who has had some success in the playhouses. He wouldn't harm a fly. For once, possibly for the first time in my professional life, I actually feel sorry for a man. I do not believe that anything you can extract from him under torture will be of the least use. If you are determined to seek more evidence, then there are others of far more worth and importance than Kyd.'

'Perhaps,' said Cecil, quietly, 'you need reminding, Poley, that no one is too important to be dispensed with.'

'Is that a threat?'

'Make of it what you will. To return to the matter under discussion, when we bring Marlowe in, we must have as much evidence against him as possible should it be decided to proceed openly against him. You've told me on many occasions that he is a formidable adversary. I feel sure the rack might assist Master Kyd to remember more.'

'He can't tell you what he doesn't know.'

'Then,' said Cecil, signalling that the interview was at an end, 'no doubt he can be persuaded to embroider a little. I shall await the results of the interrogation before deciding on my next move, though I am rapidly coming to the conclusion that it were better Marlowe is never brought to trial. You may go, Poley. I'll send for you again when I have made my final decision.'

*   *   *   *

He lay amid filthy straw on the stone floor of the cell in pools of his own urine and vomit. His throat was raw with screaming and the pain in his limbs was such that he prayed only for death. At the last he had remembered how the young actor, Richard, had asked him how so gentle a man as he was able to write as he did of torture and murder, and how he had replied that it was easy, all he had had to do was to draw on his imagination. He was wrong. Nothing he had ever imagined could have prepared him for the pain of the reality, or the depths of his betrayal. 'God forgive me, Kit,' he moaned, then slid into oblivion.

17

It is always possible to find pretexts for confiscating a
person's property . . . On the other hand, pretexts for
executing someone are harder to find and they are less
easily sustained.

The Prince Machiavelli

ON THE MORNING OF 18 May, Marlowe woke
early. The poem of Hero and Leander was now
absorbing him day and night, driving him so hard that he
could scarcely break off to eat; he felt full of energy,
energy that needed to be burned away by exercise. The
house was quiet as he left it, the only sounds to be heard
coming from the kitchens, where the servants were seeing
to the fires and preparing breakfast. Outside, in the kitchen
gardens, the maidservants were spreading washing to dry
on the hedges and he had to wake a sleepy ostler to saddle a
horse. There was a light mist over the lake and in the
hollows of the meadows as he rode out of the stable yard.
It was obviously going to be another fine day. He trotted
briskly down the avenue then urged his horse to a gallop
across the parkland.

He cantered back full of vigour, lines of verse circling
through his head. From the woods came the 'hoo, hoo,
hoo – hoo, hoo' of wood pigeons, mingled with the songs
of thrush and blackbird. Across the fields dogs barked and
from the house came the noise of clattering pots and the
singing of a dairy-maid churning butter. Smoke rose from
the kitchen chimney and there was a good smell of bacon.
When he reached the stable yard he was surprised to see a
number of strange men, servants of some kind, talking
among themselves in a group, their horses tethered nearby.

He had not known Tom expected company. He dismounted and, still in his shirt sleeves, with his doublet draped around his shoulders, he ran lightly up the short flight of stairs and into the room normally used for morning meals.

From the look Tom gave him, he knew at once that something was very badly wrong. Beside Tom stood a tall, soldierly looking man of middle age. Marlowe looked from one to the other.

'This gentleman is Henry Maunder,' said Walsingham, 'a messenger of Her Majesty's Chamber.'

'Do you bring us bad news from Court, sir?' asked Marlowe.

'I take it, sir, you are Christopher Marlowe,' said Maunder in response.

'I am. What do you want of me?'

'Then I must inform you that you are under arrest.'

'Under arr . . .' He looked across at Tom. 'What does this mean?'

Maunder continued. 'My warrant expressly states that I am to repair to the house of Master Thomas Walsingham in Kent, or to any other place where I shall understand Christopher Marlowe to be remaining, and by virtue thereof to apprehend him, and bring him to the Court in my company. And in case of need to require aid.'

'On what charge?' asked Marlowe.

'That you will learn when you present yourself before the Star Chamber.'

The marvellous energy that had coursed through him during his ride drained suddenly away, leaving him cold. So he had been right after all. The footsteps in the night, the listeners in the taverns and at the playhouse had not been figments of a feverish imagination and he had indeed been under surveillance throughout the last long months. It was ironic that this should come now, when the black, vicious, destructive mood had finally left him.

'Well,' he said, 'it seems I have little choice but to accompany you to London.'

'Surely you will allow the man to break his fast?' asked Walsingham, peremptorily. 'Half an hour or twenty minutes cannot matter. I will arrange for your men to be given food and drink in the kitchen and you are welcome to my hospitality here. But I would ask you to excuse us, as I must consult my friend in private as he eats.'

Maunder appeared to think this over; he then said, somewhat grudgingly, 'He can eat then, but let it be quick.'

Marlowe sat white-faced as food and a tankard of ale was placed before him. He had been ravenously hungry when he returned from his ride but now his appetite had deserted him. He toyed with a small piece of bread and a little cheese. 'It would seem your presentiment was correct, Tom. What next, my dear, what next?'

'Being proved right in such circumstances is scarcely a matter for satisfaction, Kit. And I'd begun to think that perhaps, after all, it was mere fancy.'

'I will tell you now that although I couldn't bring myself to admit it to you at the time, I shared your unease. More than that, I felt I was continually being followed and watched; but then the feeling suddenly left me and, as it did and the desire to write poetry returned, I put it all down to womanish fears. It is obvious what had happened. They had decided there was no longer any need for surveillance.'

Walsingham slapped his hand on the table. 'I shall go to Cecil myself.'

'If they've decided to destroy me then there's precious little you can do about it, Tom. I do not, however, intend to go down without a fight or without bringing others down with me – that is, if they give me the chance. I would not be the first to disappear following the garotte in a quiet cell. I would that I had finished *Hero and Leander* though.'

'You talk as if you will not.'

'We shall see.'

He stood up and the two men embraced. Ten minutes later Marlowe was riding down the avenue he had cantered up so light-heartedly an hour before, this time guarded on all sides by armed men.

Just before noon he presented himself before a committee of the Star Chamber, presided over by no lesser personage than the Archbishop of Canterbury, made up of the Lord Keeper, the Lord Treasurer, Lord Derby, the Lord Chamberlain (who was patron of Burbage's company), Lord Buckhurst, Sir John Woolley and Sir John Fortescue. What followed was a formality. He had been called before them to answer various diverse charges and he must be prepared to 'scrape his conscience' and to do so with truth. However, the members had graciously agreed that after he had been examined by Acting Secretary to the Privy Council, Robert Cecil, he would be released so long as he undertook to appear before them daily until further notice.

Marlowe did his best not to show his astonishment. He had expected, at the very least, immediate imprisonment. The clerk to the proceedings flourished a parchment before him on which was written: 'This day Christopher Marlowe of London, gentleman, being sent for by warrant from their Lordships, hath entered his appearance accordingly for his Indemnity therein; and is commanded to give his daily attendance on their Lordships until he be licensed to the contrary.' He signed 'Christopher Marlowe' with a flourish, before being taken to the office of Robert Cecil.

The two men looked at each other with interest. In front of him Marlowe saw the small man with a humped shoulder, intelligent face and cold, dispassionate eyes he had seen, but not made the acquaintance of, when both had been up at Cambridge. Cecil, who had little or no recollection of the 'cobbler's son', found Marlowe's appearance very unlike that he had imagined. The man looked more like a wary scholar than the blaspheming trouble-maker he had been expecting. He inclined his head and asked Marlowe to be seated. They sat looking at each other for a while in silence, then Cecil said: 'Have you any notion why you are here?'

167

'No,' Marlowe replied, 'except that I imagine you must consider it of some importance since you sent an armed guard to bring me hither. The Lord Archbishop has informed me that there are a number of matters on which you want to examine me and that I must, as he put it, "scrape my conscience", to assist you.'

Cecil stood up and commenced his familiar pacing up and down, speaking as he did so. 'There are at least three serious charges against you, Marlowe. First, it is said you have made overtures to the Scots King and have been seen in his court in Edinburgh.'

Marlowe had been expecting this. 'That is, of course, true nor would I seek to deny it – or that such overtures were made on your express wish, as detailed to me by Robert Poley. You must have had my report. I find it hard to believe you've chosen to call "treason" and use that against me; you are not known to lack wit. Am I to presume that Poley would become star witness and with one hand on his heart and the other on the Bible, though lacking a third to hold a purse, swear he knew nothing of my venture over the border? I am no Anthony Babington to throw up my hands and resign myself to the rope. Much would come to light in the ensuing public proceedings.'

'Then,' continued Cecil, 'there is the question of blasphemy. You have had much to say on matters of religion and in public places too and before witnesses.'

'If you want to arraign me for blasphemy then there is little I can say except that witnesses could also be brought to swear I will say anything in my cups. How is your standing at Court, by the by? As I can recall I have said nothing that has not been discussed by some of the highest in the land. This would not, of course, be considered a defence but might prove difficult politically. I merely mention it.'

Cecil ceased his pacing, came back to his desk and sat down. He placed his hands on the desk, resting them together almost as if in prayer.

'Then there is the question of sodomy.'

'I see.'

'It is a most heinous offence.'

'So it is said.'

'It is a burning matter.'

It was then Marlowe chose to play his only ace. 'Indeed it is. How fortunate it was, therefore, that your cousin had such powerful friends to intervene for him, otherwise I fear he would have gone to the stake in Montauban some . . . let me think . . . is it six or seven years ago? I'm sure you must recall the date, for they burned a priest at Cahors for a similar offence at about the same time.'

Cecil had been totally unprepared for this. He gripped his hands together as if he would squeeze the blood out of them. 'I fear I do not understand you, Marlowe.'

Marlowe smiled. 'Oh, but I'm sure you do. Surely, you have not forgotten? Then, let me remind you. It was common knowledge in the Catholic Seminary in Rheims when I was there, sent, you will recollect, by your predecessor. You will recall that your cousin, Antony Bacon – brother to the noble Sir Francis – was living in Montaubon though loosely attached to our embassy in Paris. He was himself a gatherer of intelligence but he had a fatal flaw, did he not? Although he lived with his lover, Thomas Lawson, this did not prevent him from desiring young boys, very young boys. I have every sympathy with him. I am, as you must know from your records, so inclined myself. But I digress . . .

'So he filled his household with pretty pages and soon it became rumoured among the local population – unsophisticated as they were – that unnatural practices were taking place in the Bacon household. The news was greeted with relish at the Rheims Seminary where they laughed heartily at what they refer to as the "English Vice", though I can assure you, if you are interested, that it is equally prevalent among the French. However, it seems that some of the older boys preyed on the younger, until one lad ran away and reported, with much corroborative physical detail, that he had been sexually abused, not only by the

169

older boys, but also by Antony Bacon. You stare! Did you not know of this?'

'Go on,' said Cecil.

'In this way word got about that Antony Bacon seduced and abused his pages, persuading them into the performance of unnatural acts. He only escaped prosecution and burning on the direct intervention of Henry of Navarre and only then after powerful representations had been made to him by our own government, reminding him how much he continued to owe to England's support for his cause.'

Cecil was shocked to the core. It had been a scandal of devastating proportions, of almost limitless potential. His cousin Antony's arrest and the subsequent frantic diplomacy which had gone on to prevent the matter being brought out into the open had been known only to a handful and those all members of the Privy Council. The matter had been kept so secret that the decision had been taken to destroy all papers referring to it, and this had been done long before Sir Francis Walsingham's death. Cecil, himself, only knew the bones of the matter. Yet now, it appeared, it had been common gossip among the seminarists in Rheims.

'You look taken aback, Master Cecil,' said Marlowe. 'I can understand you might be reluctant to have this matter discussed in open court, but should it be decided to send me to the stake, then I would have little to lose in publishing it abroad that there are others who might well stand beside me in the flames.'

'I will admit you have surprised me,' said Cecil, with an effort. 'However, at present there is no need to think in such dramatic terms as the stake or the rope. You have been given leave to go your way, so long as you remain in London and report daily at Westminster. Be sure I will give due consideration to what you have said.'

Marlowe smiled again. 'Oh, I'm sure you will. After all, you have little choice, have you?'

* * * *

An hour after Marlowe had walked free into the street, Thomas Walsingham called for his riding boots and his cloak and attended only by his groom, set off at a gallop for London. After taking a boat over the river to Westminster steps, he made his way to Cecil's office and demanded peremptorily of Dowling that he be admitted at once to the Acting Secretary.

'You mean Secretary Cecil, do you not?' said Dowling.

'No, I do not. So far as I'm aware, Her Majesty has *still* not confirmed the appointment.' Then, as Dowling hesitated, he shouted, 'Well, go on, man. Tell him I'm here or do I have to break open the door?'

The noise brought Cecil out to see what was the matter.

'So,' boomed Tom, 'you *are* skulking in there, Robert. Will you let me in, or shall we hold our discussion out here?'

For once, Cecil did not stand on his dignity, in fact, he seemed in an unusually good humour. 'Leave this to me,' he said to his secretary then, clapping Walsingham on the shoulder, led the way into his office. 'Sit down, Thomas, we do not need to stand and bawl at each other like Thames' watermen.' He gave an expansive smile. 'You can relax. Christopher Marlowe has come to no harm.'

Walsingham dropped into a chair. 'Then where is he?'

Cecil shrugged. 'I have no idea. Try his lodgings. Or the playhouse. He left here some time ago. I've told you, there's no need for alarm, he's at liberty.'

'You've set him free then?'

'Not exactly. There are questions he must answer, but, after I had intervened with them, their lordships saw no reason why he should not be released, so long as he signed an indemnity to appear before the Council when required, and presents himself on bail every morning.'

'But what is he supposed to have done?'

'There have been allegations . . . representations have been made to me, the Privy Council was alerted . . . these

171

matters need to be cleared up. I was finally persuaded it was necessary to bring him here.'

Walsingham banged his fist on the desk, making the ink pot jump in its ornate silver inkstand. 'Don't think to gull me, Robert, into believing that all this has been imposed on you by the Privy Council. I don't believe it.'

'I'm sorry you feel that way since I assure you it's true. It's very tiresome, I agree, but I'm sure the matter can soon be resolved. Meanwhile there are steps that could be taken which might assist this affair to blow over.' He leaned across to Walsingham. 'If you could put to him that it might be a good idea if he went abroad for a little while, Thomas . . . possibly to the Low Countries? Until these allegations have been satisfactorily looked into?'

Walsingham considered this. 'The Low Countries? I suppose that might well do . . . and I can see he is properly provided for until he returns. When would this be?'

'The sooner the better, don't you agree? There will be a Dutch ship at Deptford at the end of the month, one of the vessels which regularly runs our couriers to and from the continent. I suggest that, in his own best interests and as his closest friend, you persuade Marlowe of the good sense of such a plan.'

'If it is the only way his safety can be assured, then I'll do my best. He is the dearest friend I have ever had. It goes back a long way.'

'Indeed. To Cambridge, I understand. Very touching.'

'I can rely on you, Cecil?'

'In what way?'

'To ensure that he will be neither imprisoned or brought to trial between now and the end of the month?'

'Most certainly. I will give you my solemn promise that will not happen.'

18

The Devil will come and Faustus must be
damned.

Dr Faustus   Marlowe

THERE WAS NOTHING A man would not do, he
had now learned, to bring about the cessation of pain.
He had never considered himself a particularly brave man
but he had withstood with stoicism the commonplace
ailments and hurts of life. This was in an altogether
different dimension. At first, whatever they did, he had
been unable to answer the questions put to him by his
torturers: he simply did not know the answers. But as time
went on and they began to suggest ideas to him he had
done his best to tell them what it seemed they wanted to
hear and, in his final extremity, dredged from the far
recesses of his mind every irreligious remark he had ever
heard Marlowe express, either privately in the workroom
or publicly when drunk in the taverns, including that final
manic outburst at the Rose Theatre a few weeks earlier.

After he had been dragged back from the rack and
thrown into his cell Kyd had, for a blessed period, fainted
away but soon consciousness returned and with it the
realisation that every movement was agonising. He could
hardly raise himself from the floor and wondered if he
would ever walk again. One gaoler, slightly more
sympathetic than most, had held a cup of water to his lips
on several occasions as his arms were too weak to lift it.

Three days after his ordeal he was visited by the Keeper,
Sir John Puckering, who required written confirmation of
what he had had to say and when Kyd had said he did not
see how he could hold a pen, his arms were so injured,

Puckering replied brusquely that if he did not agree to it, he would once more be put to the torture. So, laboriously holding his right hand with his left to steady it, he who had been so proud of his beautiful script, scrawled as well as he could a list of Marlowe's supposed sins.

> Pleaseth your honourable lordship, he wrote, touching Marlowe's monstrous opinions as I cannot but with an aggrieved conscience think on him or them, so can I but particularise a few of them that kept him greater company. Howbeit, in discharge of duty both towards good your lordship and the world, thus much have I thought good briefly to discover in all humbleness.
>
> It was his custom when I knew him first and, as I hear say he continued it at tabletalk or otherwise, to jest at the divine scriptures, jibe at prayers and strive in arguments to frustrate and confute what have been spoken and written by prophets and other such holy men.
>
> 1. He would report St John to be our Saviour Christ's Alexis. I cover it with reverence and trembling: that is that Christ did love him with an extraordinary love.
>
> 2. That for me to write a poem of St Paul's conversion, as I was determined, he said would be as if I should go write a book of fast and loose cosenage, esteeming Paul to be nothing but juggler.
>
> 3. That the prodigal Child's portion was but four nobles, as he held his purse so near the bottom in all pictures, and that it either was a jest or else four nobles was thought to be a great patrimony, not thinking it a parable.
>
> 4. That things esteemed to be done by divine power, might as well have been done by observation of men; all of which he would so suddenly take slight occasion to slip out, as I and many others in regard of his other rashnesses, in

attempting sudden privy injuries to men, did overlook; though often reprehending him for it. And for which, God is my witness, as well as my lord's commandment, as in hatred of his life and thoughts, I often left and did refrain his company.

It was a pathetic little document for so much agony.

Robert Cecil, reading it in the privacy of his office, was under few illusions as to how it would stand, offered in open court, as part of a prosecution case for blasphemy. It would not be difficult for a man like Marlowe to dismiss it as the frantic ramblings of a man put to the Question.

He then pulled over Baines' report and read through it once again. With one or two exceptions it was only marginally better than that of Kyd, consisting largely of a somewhat haphazard list of overheard remarks and hearsay. Baines had headed it, grandiosely, 'A note containing the opinions of one Christopher Marlowe concerning his Damnable Judgement of Religion and Scorn of God's Word.'

He had begun by claiming that Marlowe had said that the Indians and many ancients of antiquity seemed to have been writing at least 16,000 years back yet, according to the Bible, Adam had lived only 6000 years ago. Then, that Moses made the Jews travel four years in the wilderness to reach the Promised Land, when it could have easily been done in a year, possibly because he hoped that those who knew his plottings might perish during the journey, so ensuring that everlasting superstition remained in the hearts of the people, and that anyway the first beginning of religion was only to keep men in awe.

Cecil yawned and read on, 'that Christ was a bastard and his mother dishonest.' That was slightly better, as was 'that Christ deserved better to die than Barabbas and that the Jews made a good choice, even though Barabbas was a thief and a murderer; that if there be any God or good religion, then it is in the papists because the service of God is performed with more ceremonies by singing men with

175

shaven crowns', and, 'all Protestants are hypocritical asses!' The last sounded like the authentic Marlowe.

Baines had made no effort to list his charges in order of importance – he claimed Marlowe had said that if he were put to invent a new religion, he would undertake better methods to promote it and that the Gospels were badly translated, to which he tacked on as an afterthought, 'the woman of Samaria and her sister were but whores and Christ knew them dishonestly'.

The claim that one Richard Chomley had been persuaded by Marlowe to become an atheist caused Cecil to pause and underline the paragraph concerned. In view of Chomley's particular position, that was unlikely to be pressed, although the information might come in useful should it be decided to proceed against the School of the Night.

Most damaging by far was the section dealing with what Cecil described to himself as 'unnatural vice', but in view of Marlowe's devastating revelation that he knew about the Bacon affair, one might well ask damaging to whom? According to Baines, Marlowe had said, 'that St John the Evangelist was bedfellow to Christ and leaned always in his bosom and that he used him as the sinners of Sodom', and that, at least, had been unknowingly confirmed by Kyd, although he had found himself unable to be so explicit. Then came Marlowe's well-known view, that 'all those who love not tobacco and boys are fools.'

For good measure, Baines had thrown in that Marlowe had been overheard by someone unspecified to say that he had as 'good right to coin as the Queen of England and was acquainted with a prisoner in Newgate, one John Poole, who had great skills in the mixture of metals and having learned some things of him he meant, through the help of a cunning stampmaker, to coin French crowns and pistolets and English shillings'. It seemed a most unlikely statement to attribute to Marlowe, leaving Cecil to wonder whether Baines had added to his note any remarks made by anyone which might help to pad it out.

He ended as he had begun with boot-licking piety, that
the above had been given on his own oath and on the
testimony of many honest men (unnamed) and that it was
widely known that Marlowe spent most of his time trying
to persuade men to atheism, telling them not to be afraid of
hobgoblins and scorning both God and his ministers; for
which sins, 'I, Richard Baines, think all men in Christianity
ought to endeavour that the mouth of so dangerous a
member be stopped.'

Apart from the alleged remarks about Christ's sodomy
and his own predeliction for boys, there was nothing in
either statement that could not have been cobbled up in an
hour by some fellow with a keen imagination, thought
Cecil, wearily. However, suitably presented and, hopefully
with the prisoner effectively cowed, it would just be
possible to condemn him for blasphemy. Next came
treason. There was no question but that Poley, standing
firm as a witness, would be believed, but there was also no
doubt that in his own defence, Marlowe would do his best
to open up to public scrutiny areas of a secret world which
must be kept hidden. As for unnatural vice, Cecil's blood
ran cold at the mere notion of Antony Bacon's prosecution
in France for sodomy, not only becoming common
knowledge but finally reaching the ears of the Queen. So
far he had kept Marlowe's threat to himself. He had not
even told his father, let alone Antony's brother, Francis.
His very position, so coveted, so assiduously worked at,
would be in jeopardy: a position the confirmation of which
remained as elusive as ever. No, he was now more sure
than ever that his own instinct as to the best way to deal
with the matter was the right one. Dipping his pen in the
silver inkpot, he wrote a careful and explicit letter to
Eleanor Bull, sealing it with his own signet ring, before
handing it to a messenger to be taken at once to Deptford
Strand. He then sent word for Poley to present himself
before noon the following day, without fail.

* * * *

Rumours that Kit Marlowe was under arrest and brought before the Star Chamber ran like wildfire around the Rose, as the actors unpacked their baskets on their return to London from Essex.

No one knew who started the story; first one had heard it, then another. When Henslowe came into the playhouse to discuss the new repertoire, he was besieged with questions on the subject. Was it true Marlowe was under arrest? That he had been brought to London from Scadbury under armed guard? That he was to appear before the terrible Star Chamber? If so, on what charges? And where was he? Henslowe knew no more than they did. He was trying to ascertain the truth, he told them, and if he learned anything more, then he would see they were informed. In the meantime, they would rehearse as usual even though it was beginning to look as if he might be refused permission to open the theatre again because of the Plague.

He was interrupted at this point by the arrival of Jamie, white-faced and breathing as if he had been running.

'What time do you call this?' shouted Ned Alleyn. 'Do you consider yourself so high, boy, that you can come in as you choose?'

'I'm very sorry, Ned,' he apologised, 'but I have been seeking information regarding Kit.' There was an immediate babble of noise as questions came from all quarters, but it seemed the boy could add little to what they knew already. 'I heard the rumour last night and went at once to Kit's lodgings. His landlady seemed surprised at my concern. She told me he'd left for Scadbury three weeks ago telling her he wouldn't be returning until the beginning of June at the earliest, as he had work to do. Then he paid her his rent. She'd heard nothing since, nor expected to. I searched frantically all night for anyone else who might tell me more, but I could find no one.'

'How about that red-headed court dandy Kit brought to the celebration?' Simon asked.

'I could find neither him nor anyone who knew of him. He seems to have vanished into thin air.'

178

'Do any of you know any reason or cause why Marlowe should be in such straits, supposing this story to be true?' asked Henslowe.

'He's been wild in drink and getting wilder,' said Will Hunt.

'He's been pretty foolish in the taverns, certainly,' Simon conceded, 'but I can't believe the Star Chamber would concern themselves overmuch with a man merely because he enjoys provoking and shocking people when he's had too much wine. I warned him myself once or twice that he was asking for trouble, but I didn't seriously think matters would come to this.'

'If he was at Scadbury, how is it that his patron, Thomas Walsingham, allowed his arrest?' asked Ned Alleyn, 'he has much influence in Government circles.'

Henslowe knitted his heavy brows. It was obviously in his own interests to find out as much as he could. It would not do to be seen promoting the interests of one who might soon feature in a highly scandalous public trial. In the meantime, he reminded them, life must go on and theatrical life in particular. His intention had been to revive *Dr Faustus*, largely because the audiences so adored all the special effects, which led Alleyn to ask him what he now wished them to do about it? Henslowe heaved a sigh. 'You'd better rehearse as planned, but if I find there is due cause for concern then we will play something else. As it is, it may well all come to nought, if I am kept from opening the Rose.' On which glum note he departed.

So the actors set up the stage for *Faustus* and began rehearsing, starting at the point in the play where Mephistopholes (played by Simon) first negotiates the deadly bargain with Faustus (played by Ned Alleyn) and Faustus asks if Lucifer was not once an angel, and, on hearing that this was so, questions why he is now the Prince of Devils.

All eyes were turned on Mephistopheles to hear his response when a voice answered 'Oh, by aspiring pride and insolence!'

179

'Kit!' shrieked Jamie. Marlowe was immediately surrounded by the company, all asking questions at the same time.

'I'm flattered you're all so concerned.'

'So you weren't arrested yesterday, Kit?' asked Jamie, clutching him by the arm as if to make sure he was real.

'Oh, it's quite true, I assure you.'

They all fell silent, then Simon asked, 'So they realised their mistake as soon as you were brought to London?'

'No!'

'Come, man,' said Ned Alleyn, testily, 'then how is it that you walk free?'

'It seems their lordships decided, in their wisdom, that I might be released on my own cognizance, so long as I present myself to them daily. In actual fact that means I report to the clerk to the Chamber. I doubt their lordships would wish to go to the trouble of assembling daily just for me to pay my respects to them.' In many ways he sounded much like his old self, had he not looked so strained and pale.

'But that's unheard of!' exclaimed Will Hunt. 'It must be unprecedented that one brought before the Chamber is allowed to walk free again. Did Thomas Walsingham intervene?'

Of a sudden, Marlowe's energy seemed to leave him and he sat down suddenly on a bench before answering quietly, 'I don't know. But I think not, since I must have been released before he arrived at Westminster to plead on my behalf.'

'And why the Star Chamber, why not an ordinary court?' asked Richard.

'Perhaps because I'm no ordinary man,' replied Marlowe, with something of his old spirit.

'More to the point,' said Ned Alleyn, 'with what are you charged? I presume you know?'

'Oh yes, I know. There are three counts – treason, blasphemy and . . . unnatural vice.'

'And they let you go?'

'They let me go.' He looked down at Jamie who was clinging to him again. 'Don't look so dismal, Jamie, I'm not dead yet. Look at you all! Any moment now you'll be putting your heads together to write my epitaph!'

'I think it best if I go and tell Phillip what has transpired,' said Ned Alleyn in his most pompous tones. 'He will need to be fully informed. Shall I tell him you will see him yourself shortly, Marlowe?'

'By all means. I only wish I knew myself what was going on.'

Alleyn prepared to leave. 'Pray continue the rehearsal until I return. Peter!' he called to the Bookkeeper, as the actors once again assembled on the stage. 'Read in my part for me, will you? Enough time has been wasted already.'

* * * *

Marlowe made no immediate effort to leave the Rose. After all, where could he go? He had not told the actors the entire truth regarding Tom Walsingham, for reasons of his own. As the rehearsal progressed, he went back in his mind over their last conversation.

After hours of searching, Tom had run him down in a quiet tavern, then taken him back to his own London lodgings close to the Strand, where, he told him, he must remain during the next few days. Anything he needed could be brought to him from Scadbury by messenger.

They had talked long into the night, trying to make sense of what had occurred. In answer to Tom's penetrating questions, Marlowe had repeated what he had said in answer to the spurious charge of treason and the accusation of blasphemy. 'With regard to treason, Poley himself sent me to Edinburgh to gather information on those making overtures to King James, most especially those of the Essex faction. I've no doubt Poley would happily betray me in court, but Cecil must reckon that I might find friends to support me and the services I have undertaken for the state.'

'That I will do and willingly,' said Tom. 'Let's pray it never comes to that. And blasphemy?'

'I imagine that comes from the time my black mood was on me and my ramblings in taverns when drunk. I am certain now that one fellow, who seemed to be about everywhere and to whom I took a particular dislike, must have been a professional informer. He attached himself to one of the Rose actors. So, you see, the evidence on the first charge can be contested and that on the second is heavily based on hearsay. Of course, men have faced death for less . . .'

'It is still remarkable that you have been granted relative freedom.'

'Wasn't that your doing?' Marlowe asked in surprise.

'No. By the time I reached Westminster you were already free. I was much amazed myself.'

'There was one other charge: that of sodomy.'

'And what did you reply?'

'With a story I had heard when I was in Rheims. I will tell you no more other than it closely touches not only one of the most powerful men in England but also Cecil's own family. And it is quite, quite true. I think it best you know no more than that; at least, not yet.'

'How did Cecil react to this . . . story?'

'He was amazed and knew not what to say . . . Indeed, he went sheet white and gaped at me with his mouth open. He resembled nothing so much as a codfish!'

'He is utterly ruthless. You do realise that?'

'Yes. I do realise that.'

Then Walsingham had relayed to him Cecil's suggestion. 'Hopefully, it would only be for a short time, Kit. Then, when this has all died down, as I'm sure it will once you are no longer around to remind people, you can come home and live your life normally.'

'Did Cecil say how he would explain my disappearance to the Star Chamber after giving my cognizance I would not run? I fail to see how I can ever return safely so long as these charges are still outstanding.'

'No, he did not. But I presume he has something in mind.'

'So, I am to wait here until I am told otherwise, then go to Deptford and take ship for Holland. I don't know.'

'But you surely must prefer that to what might well befall you if you remain in the country? God's wounds,' Walsingham almost shouted, 'you can't want to risk Tyburn or the stake? However brilliantly you might defend yourself, if it is decided you are to die, then die you will. This is the one chance you have of ensuring your survival.'

Marlowe clutched his head. 'Let me think about it, Thomas.'

Walsingham could hardly contain his exasperation. 'Then think and think fast. I have until tomorrow to bring word to Cecil as to what you have decided. In the meantime, stay quiet and stay close to home. If you must go out then go only where you are among those you know.'

'That won't protect me from the assassin's knife in an alleyway, Tom.'

'Nothing will protect you from that, but I don't believe it's what Cecil has in mind. Just why he's going to these lengths I don't understand; but please, for God's sake Kit, take up his offer.'

Marlowe had done his best to reassure him. He promised to consider it during the next twenty-four hours and let Tom know his decision when he returned again from Scadbury, bringing with him the uncompleted *Hero and Leander*. As he was leaving, Marlowe posed a question. 'Suppose the next time I call in to report, their Lordships decided I must be imprisoned? Or rushed to trial before the end of the month?'

On this point, Walsingham could offer reasurance. 'Cecil has given me his most solemn promise that won't happen.'

* * * *

The frantic knocking at the door of the Rose both roused Kit from his reverie and made his heart pound, so overwhelming now was his sense of insecurity. The noise took longer to rouse the Gatherer, who had been sitting in his usual seat, snoring quietly. The old man awoke with a start and, amid much loud complaining, opened the door to let in the youngest of the apprentices, who had been sent earlier that morning on an errand for the Wardrobe Master. The rehearsal halted again as they looked at the boy. His face was flushed with running and he could scarcely get his words out.

'What is it now?' asked the Bookkeeper, crossly. 'Are we never to get through this piece?'

'It's Tom,' gasped the boy, 'Tom Kyd. He was taken to Bridewell six nights ago.'

Scandal was piled on scandal. The actors climbed down off the stage to hear more. There was no reason why Kyd should have been waiting at the Rose to greet them on their return and he had not been expected to appear before rehearsals began for *Thomas More*.

'I can't believe it,' said Richard. 'Not Tom Kyd! Whatever can he possibly have done to merit that? You've misheard some story, lad.' There was a general murmer of assent.

'No, I haven't. It's true. While we've been away the officers have been searching houses and lodgings for those people who were writing and putting up the verses about foreigners.'

'But Kyd would never put his name to anything like that,' protested the Bookkeeper.

'No, but my brother says that among his papers was found part of an atheistical pamphlet.' Then for the first time he noticed Marlowe, who had not moved from his place by the stage. 'He said it was not his, but belonged to you, Master Marlowe.'

Richard was struck as if by a knife. He felt cold, his mouth went dry, bile rose in his throat. A pamphlet? And in Tom Kyd's workroom? No, he told himself, surely not. The hand in the dark, the sympathetic stranger. Not me. They couldn't have found it through me. Oh God, don't let it be because of me.

184

'Go on,' said Marlowe.

'How does your brother come to know all this?' asked Simon.

'Surely you know he's a turnkey at Bridewell, Master Pope?' said the boy. 'I just saw him in the street. He says . . . he says Thomas Kyd has twice been put to the rack and has signed a confession.'

Marlowe sat down suddenly on the floor, then recited:

> The stars move still, time runs, the clock will strike.
> The devil will come and Faustus must be damned!

They all stared at him, appalled.

... for little knowest thou how in the
end thou might be visited.

The Repentance of Robert Greene

THERE FOLLOWED A TIME which would not be
forgotten by any who lived through it; a time of
uncertainty, of not knowing from day to day what might
happen next, a time of terror, played out against a
background of increasing Plague deaths and persecution of
immigrants. It was all a long way from those early days of
Elizabeth, when she had been hailed as Gloriana.

For Marlowe the uncertainty had lasted only until he
heard of Kyd's arrest and subsequent torture. It was
manifestly clear that whatever the reasoning behind his
being allowed relative freedom, evidence was steadily
being compiled against him, using any means available.
Poor Tom Kyd! To some extent it was fruitless wondering
what they might have drawn from him – certainly some of
his own more offensive and provocative remarks when he
was either drunk, at his most vicious, or both. Very likely
too, by the time they had finished, Kyd would have said
anything, sworn to anything they wanted him to that
might incriminate their real quarry, whether it was true or
not. It took a great martyr to a fine cause to stay silent in
such circumstances and Kyd was, God help him, an
ordinary man.

So it was that he told Tom Walsingham that, given the
circumstances, he had no choice but to take up Cecil's offer
of sanctuary in Holland, even though he still mistrusted his
motives. Consequent upon this, Walsingham brought
Poley to his lodgings to discuss the arrangements. Poley

was smooth, affable, apparently sympathetic yet, thought Marlowe, he *must* know what is behind all this; he *must* have been party to the informing, the steady collection of damning evidence, the footsteps in the dark. He had been tempted to ask him outright if he would have been the chief witness should the Star Chamber have decided he be brought to court for treason; but what was the use? Poley would only lie and the result of such pressure might well be his persuading Cecil to change his mind and prosecute; either that or that he would not survive long enough to board the Dutch ship.

Therefore he kept his counsel, accepting the arrangements made for him. The Dutch vessel was due to anchor off Deptford within the next three or four days and expected to sail again for Holland on the thirtieth of the month. In the meantime Marlowe should report daily to the Star Chamber, exactly as he had been doing and in no way act as to arouse suspicion. Then, after reporting on the morning of the thirtieth, he must take a boat from Westminster straight to Deptford, where Poley would be waiting for him at Eleanor Bull's house. As it would obviously look strange if he were to be seen embarking carrying large bundles of possessions, Nicholas Skeres would call on him first thing that morning to collect what Marlowe needed to take for his immediate use; after which he too would make his way, by boat, to Deptford. Once Marlowe had found lodgings in Holland, anything else he needed could easily be brought over for him by a courier, possibly even by Poley himself. It all sounded very sensible and well thought out, which left Marlowe wondering why, if that was the case, he should feel so uneasy; though that might well be because the fears he had shaken off so successfully only a few weeks previously had returned in full force.

Meanwhile outright fear, bordering on panic, gripped the Lord Admiral's Men. First Marlowe brought before the Star Chamber, then Tom Kyd put to the rack. What next? *Who* next? Was no one safe? And most of all – *why*?

The progress of the Plague, and doubt over whether or not the theatre would re-open, took second place to the awful realisation that somehow, through no fault of their own, they had become inadvertently caught up in some sinister, unknown business, reaching up to the highest in the land.

No one was more aware of the implications than Phillip Henslowe. Visions of the Rose being closed permanently, the Lord Chamberlain refusing to licence any play submitted by him, and his never achieving the post of Royal Bear Warden, paled into insignificance beside nightmares in which he was woken before dawn by a hammering on his door, taken from his bed to Bridewell to be put to the rack or, worse still, dragged before the Star Chamber and immediately sentenced to death – for what? For some criminal stupidity of Kit Marlowe's which had now involved them all?

With such notions seething around in his head, he called all the company together. In view of the combination of the Plague, and what he described euphemistically as 'current uncertainties', he was sending the company out on the road from the first week of June. As he reasoned to himself, it would be out of sight out of mind so far as those in authority were concerned. Any actors who did not want to take part in the tour would have to do as best they could; he offered no alternative. In the meantime, during the remaining days in May, there would be intensive rehearsals. All Marlowe's pieces – *Tamburlaine, The Jew of Malta, Edward II* and *Dr Faustus* – would be dropped from the repertoire forthwith, along with Kyd's *Spanish Tragedy* and *Prince Hamlet of Denmark*. A new repertoire was to be discussed with the Bookkeeper immediately, and the company would start work on it as soon as it was finalised. He also made one more proviso. In the circumstances, Christopher Marlowe would not be allowed into the Rose and he must be informed of this if he presented himself at the theatre.

It was all very sensible, of course, but it only added to the actors' feeling of being under siege. Henslowe's change of plan also faced Simon Pope with a dilemma. He had thought to remain with the Lord Admiral's Men into June, when Henslowe had been expected to decide whether or not to tour. Now, out of fairness to his fellow-actors, he would have to tell him that he would shortly be leaving the company. He would, he told Richard, offer to remain until the company left, in order to coach the actors taking over his parts.

That night he invited the young actor back with him for supper, intending to discuss with him whether or not he had decided where his future lay. As they reached the small house near the Paris Gardens, they were surprised to see windows open and cloths hanging out to dry. The reason for this soon became apparent: Jenny had returned. 'I decided not to tell you,' she told Simon, 'as I was sure you would tell me it wasn't safe, but I needed to know how things were with you and if you had yet told Master Henslowe you would be leaving. I thought you might like to have me with you to talk over what we do next.'

Simon caught her in his arms in a great surge of affection. 'The boys are well?' he asked between kisses. 'They grow like flowers,' she responded, as well as she could. He released her, then said, 'I'm happier to see you than I can say, my love, but you come at an ill time. There's more to fear than Plague'; and, so saying, he sat her down and retailed the events of the last two weeks. She listened in silence before replying,

'I can scarcely bear to think what poor Tom Kyd must have suffered. And for what? Surely they can't think him capable of treason and as for blasphemy, he always made it plain he found any such talk abhorrent – don't you recall how he would take Kit to task for it?'

'Indeed I do,' replied her husband, grimly, 'and I fear he will have had wrenched out of him all that Kit has ever said, and more, and who can blame him?'

'Kit must have powerful enemies,' she said, gravely. 'There must be serious matters behind all this; matters of state, don't you think? But why should Kit be involved?

He's a poet, not a politician. Unless it is something to do with Raleigh's disgrace; but then, Raleigh is now a free man again.'

'He's given the impression sometimes that he had knowledge of mysterious affairs,' said Richard. 'But until now I've always put it down to attention-seeking or his liking to feel superior to us. Perhaps there was truth in it after all.'

Jenny released herself from the shelter of Simon's arm and firmly waved them towards the table. 'There is something more pressing than all of this. I've been cooking all afternoon and now you must sit down and eat with appetite. We can talk again later; and on the table, Simon, you will find a letter written to you by our son, Daniel, to show what great progress he has made with his letters.'

* * * *

Nothing could possibly go wrong now, thought Poley. He had briefed them all carefully. He had no worries about Nick Skeres, of course, and anyway, his role was straightforward; merely to collect Marlowe's essential belongings from Walsingham's lodgings and bring them to Deptford. Ingram Frizer was more of a problem, cunning and sharp enough certainly, but there was an underlying weakness there. However, the threat of prosecution over the Woodleff affair was still hanging over him and this, coupled with the promise of reward if he carried out his part satisfactorily, should ensure he did what was required of him, even if he was not the best of tools. He had been told to arrive in Deptford on horseback half-way through the morning with money for Marlowe, apparently sent by Walsingham for his immediate needs; there had to be some reason for his being there and even if Walsingham had already given Marlowe funds, it would merely look as if he had decided, at the very last minute, to increase them.

Poley had then talked the whole plan through in detail with Eleanor Bull on the evening of 29 May.

'Very professional,' she had said when she had heard him out. 'Quite Machiavellian – but are you sure he will come?'

'Oh yes, he'll come.'

'But you told me yourself he was suspicious of you even before this. Why should he trust you now?'

'Because, dear Nell, he knows it's his only hope. What is the alternative? To be broken by torture before a trial which can only have one possible outcome – either the stake for blasphemy or to be hanged, drawn and quartered at Tyburn for treason? There's also a more pressing reason why Cecil wants him removed as soon as possible.'

'And what is that?'

He paused, looking thoughtful. 'I honestly don't know. All I do know is that it's so serious, it's even frightened Secretary Cecil. It must be some piece of information known only to Marlowe. But Cecil would tell me nothing of it.'

'And you have no idea what it might be?'

'I have to admit, much as it galls me, that I haven't. But, to return to tomorrow. Nick Skeres will arrive first, followed soon after by Marlowe. Frizer will come last.'

'Surely it must seem strange to Kit that he's been allowed such licence – that the Star Chamber has still not sent for him for questioning and that he's free to come and go almost at will?'

'Obviously. The man's no fool. At first I think he thought the "evidence" against him was slight, though now he must know we hold Thomas Kyd. Possibly he imagines his continued freedom has been due to the intervention of Tom Walsingham, and latterly because Cecil has thought it best he leaves the country.'

'And what does Walsingham say to all this?'

'Oh, he agrees that it's best for Marlowe to go until the matter has died down.'

'And afterwards?' she asked.

He smiled. 'Afterwards?'

191

* * * *

The sky was a clear blue and the sun already warm as Marlowe made his way to the dusty office of the clerk to the Star Chamber that Wednesday morning. The man blinked and peered at him as if to assure himself it really was the right man, then pushed the big, leather-bound book towards him, nodding towards the inkpot and pen. The routine was the same every day. Marlowe dipped the pen in the ink and wrote 'Christopher Marlowe' under the previous day's signature, then dated it 30 May 1593. Next, as instructed, he made his way to the watersteps and hailed a boat from one of the many watermen competing to make the journey 'Eastward Ho!'

Since first he woke he had been suffering from a feeling of dissociation which was becoming stronger with every hour that passed. The tide was on the turn and progress downriver swift.

It seemed quite unreal that he should be leaving the country, God only knew for how long, but then the events of the past two weeks had seemed increasingly so. Now, at least for the time being, he had to try and make a life for himself in Holland, forced against his will into exile. He loved London, every stinking back alley of it. He loved the noise, the clamour, the excitement that coursed through it and the dangers and perils that could so easily turn to bloodshed.

He recalled the familiar smells of the playhouse, that of burning rope, which lit the stage, mingling with those of the oversweet scent of the face paint used by the actors, the juice of oranges, stale bottle ale and, overall, the sweaty, musty smell of the crowds. He remembered the nights he had spent in taverns, the wit, and the crack of minds, bent like his to poetry and the plots of plays, ever more plays, long evenings followed by nights of lovemaking with . . . oh, so many sly young lads apprenticed to honest artisans, sharp young cutpurses, pretty Jamie from the Rose . . . the Rose . . . that brought back the memory of Robin Greene who, like him, had tempted fate, until the pox and the wasting disease had driven him to public repentance; of clever, sympathetic Tom Watson, and the pathetic little scrivener now lying broken on the floor of a Bridewell cell. Robin and Tom had now been rotting in their graves for months, Tom Kyd was most like wishing he was. Marlowe shivered.

He brought himself back to the present with a jolt, as London unrolled itself along the banks of the Thames like some giant tapestry. Behind the houses of the rich and wealthy on the Middlesex Bank and the gardens of the Inns of Court, he could see the spire of St Clement's church at the east end of the Strand and, further back still, the low hills with their windmills. Next came the substantial Blackfriars homes of the city merchants and, facing them on the Surrey side, the close-packed terraces of Lambeth and Bankside. It all seemed as clear cut and unreal as a landscape in a dream. Past Baynard's Castle, once London home of Crookback Richard. Richard Plantagenet . . . perhaps, after all, he should have taken the trouble to see Will Shakespeare's piece, it now almost equalled *Tamburlaine* in popularity. Well, Shakespeare at least would benefit from his exile, he had no rival now.

St Paul's mighty bulk loomed of a sudden on his left, while over to the right he could just see the topmost tier of the Rose and its tower, but there was no performance flag flying from the flagstaff. Would he ever see another of his plays there? More, would he ever even visit it again? With a loud shout and a string of foul oaths, the waterman guided his craft adroitly under London Bridge with its twenty solid piers and nineteen arches. It took real skill, especially when the water was flowing fast, to avoid the 'starlings', the large, flat, boat-like structures built around the piers to protect them from the tide race. It was said London Bridge had been there since the time of that Crookback Richard; some said, even longer.

Looking at it reminded him of how he had once come across young Richard Crawley gazing up in horrified

193

fascination at the decaying heads and how he had joked about treason – 'for if it prosper, none dare call it treason'. Yet he had not even plotted it. The heads brought back other images of dead men; Bradley dying in the gutter in a gush of blood, Cutting Ball Jack's gallant death at Tyburn. Tyburn! If Cecil had pressed charges then, that would have been his likely end. His own words came back to him, how he had scoffed at the scaffold and the disemboweller's knife, the death decreed for a traitor who could not boast aristocratic blood. How he had said, so carelessly, that he trusted he would have been as witty as Jack at the last. It was dark now in the shadows.

Once under the Bridge they ran easily down to Deptford Strand and, as he ran up the steps after paying off the waterman, he noted that the clock on St Nicholas' church tower stood at a little before ten. All had gone exactly according to plan.

The strange dreamlike sense of unreality continued when Jane, having opened the door of Eleanor Bull's house to him with a curtsey, took him through into the more private garden which ran at the side of the dwelling, and was separated from that at the front by a high wall. Inside that wall it was so sheltered it felt hot enough for midsummer rather than the end of May, and the garden was full of flowers; flowers of late spring cheek by jowl with those of early summer. Bees buzzed and the air was full of scent. The scene was arcadian.

Under a spreading elm there sat a picturesque group. Eleanor Bull was wearing a gown of soft pink, embroidered with the whites, lavenders and pale blues of summer flowers, over a kirtle of heavy white silk. As usual her thick auburn hair was piled on top of her head but this time she had chosen not to wear a ruff; instead, a high starched collar of the finest and most transparent lace framed her fine face. Beside her sat Poley, his doublet thrown off, his shirt open at the neck. They were laughing together while, at their feet, Nick Skeres lay flat on his back on the grass gazing up at the sky. Marlowe had already noted that his baggage had arrived, for it was safely stacked away in the hall.

Eleanor rose to greet him and gave him her hand to kiss. 'Bring us some more wine, Jane, and tell cook we shall eat our lunch out here. It's far too good a day to go indoors until we have to.' Marlowe kissed her hand. Even he, who was not moved by women, had to recognise that she was remarkably beautiful, with a beauty he felt was now at its peak and could not last. How old was she? Probably near to him in age; if so, then time had been kind to leave her so untouched.

She led him to a seat and, as the wine was brought, Poley rehearsed the details of the day again. Marlowe no doubt had noticed the large Dutch vessel anchored in midstream almost opposite the watersteps? Good, then he could see for himself that everything had been put in hand. Captain Schmidt would sail on the turn of the tide which would be about eleven at night. They would all stay secure, therefore, at Eleanor's, then take a little supper together in the middle part of the evening before Poley saw Marlowe safely aboard. A ship's boat would be sent to the watersteps on the point of ten to collect them.

Certainly everything seemed to have been thought of, which left Marlowe wondering why, if that were the case, he still felt so sick at heart; but the talk was good and the wine flowed freely, of which he took full advantage, having been unusually abstemious in recent days. Then, just as the servants were carrying out the food, Jane trotted into the garden to say to her mistress that there was a Master Ingram Frizer in the hall, come from Master Thomas Walsingham with a message for Master Marlowe.

'Are you expecting this man?' enquired Poley, irritably. 'I thought we had agreed we would all say nothing of your coming here to Deptford today.'

'Nor have I. But you know Tom Walsingham is as deep in this business as any of us. This man Frizer, who I hardly know, lives on the Scadbury estate and sometimes undertakes tasks for him. I cannot imagine why Tom

195

should have sent him here unless he has some dealings with Nick, as they are acquaintances.'

Skeres sat up, shrugged and shook his head.

'Perhaps it's best we find out,' said Eleanor. 'Fetch him to us, Jane.'

The girl went back into the house to appear, within minutes, with Ingram Frizer. Frizer did not look quite his usual bouncy self but he nodded his head to Nick Skeres, then addressed himself to 'Mistress Bull', before making an elaborate bow. 'What's your business with us, Master Frizer?' she enquired. 'Oh – er – madame, mistress . . .', he stammered nervously, 'my master, Thomas Walsingham, had sent me with this purse to give to Master Marlowe. He gave no message except that he wished him well and hoped he'd find it useful.'

'That's very generous of him,' said Marlowe in some surprise, 'he's already given me ample for my immediate needs. But it's very like him.' He took the purse and pocketed it.

'Perhaps you would like to eat with us?' suggested Eleanor. 'There's plenty for all, as you can see.'

Frizer huffed and puffed and spluttered that he would be honoured indeed. Marlowe had never seen the man so ill at ease, but then Eleanor was somewhat overwhelming to those who had not met her before. 'Do you know Master Robert Poley?' she asked, 'an old friend of mine and of Kit?'

No, Ingram Frizer had never had that pleasure. The two men bowed to each other and exchanged civilities, after which they all fell to with hearty appetites.

The long warm afternoon passed with conversation and more wine, Marlowe feeling more and more removed from what was happening with every hour that passed. It was almost as if he were sitting in the gallery of a playhouse watching himself taking part in a play. It was very odd. It was odd, too, that Frizer seemed in no hurry to return, in fact he and Nick Skeres were talking away ten to the dozen. With the early evening there came a sudden change in the weather, the clear sky was overcast with dark clouds, while the incoming tide brought with it a sharp and chilly wind, driving the party back into the house. Ingram Frizer said at once that he really must take his leave if he was to reach Scadbury for supper, at which Nick Skeres remarked he too ought to be going; but Eleanor suggested that as it was now so late they might just as well stay for supper. She had horses enough in her stables and if Nick wished she could lend him one so that he and Frizer could keep each other company, at least part of the way.

From the tall windows of her long room Marlowe could see the Dutch vessel riding at her moorings, the little figures moving about the decks in the fast-fading light making ready for sea. Then he sat down at Eleanor's beautiful table to be served with an array of fine food, oysters, lampreys and fillets of salmon, quails in aspic, woodcock resting on beds of salad, venison basted with red wine; wine, there was apparently a never-ending supply of it, white wines sharp or honey-sweet, thick, dark reds, smelling of must and tasting of the south.

Marlowe was aware he was drinking too much. His head was swimming. It was kind of Tom to have sent the extra money. Odd, though, that he had sent Frizer. He had always been attracted to low-life rogues, so why was it he had never taken to Frizer. Still the man had proved quite amusing. He shook his head and took another gulp of wine. A fine, white dessert wine this, but with rather a cloying taste. Jesus, but it was hot in the room, why did Eleanor keep her house so warm with summer nearly here? He wondered when he would see Tom Walsingham again, Tom who had been so much part of his life since they became lovers, fresh up at Cambridge. The previous day Tom had told him what he had already heard rumoured at Scadbury, that he was soon likely to be betrothed as the pressure to wed and found a family was now overwhelming. Kit had met the lady at those May Day celebrations which now seemed a world away and an age ago; Audrey Shelton, daughter of Sir Ralph Shelton, High

Sheriff of Norfolk, a witty young woman with a clever, monkey face.

Marriage would mean far-reaching changes at Scadbury when he came back, when . . . it must be 'when' and not 'if', surely? God, the look on Cecil's face when he'd told him he knew about Antony Bacon's sodomy and the French scandal!

The party at the dinner table had now become small and far off, as if he were looking at them through the wrong end of a telescope; Eleanor, in her pink dress, leaning forward to say something light to Poley, at which they both looked at him and smiled, Nick and Frizer loudly laying odds on a favourite hawk. Their words sounded far off too. The maid had lit the candles, causing shadows to dip and dance in their flickering light but the curtains remained open. Through the window the lights of anchored ships could be seen bobbing on the tide. The tide? Wasn't there something he should remember about the tide? He shook his head again.

The dancing ships' lanterns and the candle flames all merged together into a spiral of light behind which he could vaguely make out a blur of watching faces. He thought he heard the rustle of Eleanor's silk dress but it was so far away and he was tired. He must have some fresh air. Yes, that's what he needed. He tried to get to his feet but found he could not, for his limbs were like lead and his legs would not obey him.

His head flopped over the back of his chair and when he tried to move it, it felt as if someone or something was holding it there. 'Oh, I'll leap up to my God, who pulls me down?' he said, but it emerged only as a meaningless noise. Voices came to him, indistinct and from a long way away. First a man's:

'Is he gone?'

Then a woman's voice. 'Quite. It was a strong draught.'

There was some kind of movement and now it felt as if his arms were being held behind the chair. The man spoke again. 'Right, you know what to do.' A pause. 'Go on, then. Do it!' Another pause. 'God in Heaven, Frizer, *now*, or I'll cut your throat myself.' Who was Frizer and what was he supposed to do?

With enormous effort Marlowe opened his leaden eyelids and found he was staring at the ceiling. 'See, see where Christ's blood streams in the firmament; one drop would save my soul, half a drop. Ah, my Christ!' The candlelight threw grotesque shadows on the white plasterwork, shadows which came together into one enormous one, a black shapeless figure with its arm raised holding what looked like . . . a knife?

It was the last thing he was to see on earth before the dagger was driven through his eyesocket, deep into his brain.

20

Second Clown: But is this the law?
First Clown: Ay, marry, is't. Crowner's Quest Law.

Hamlet   Shakespeare

RICHARD WAS AGAIN SHARING the apprentices' room at the Popes' house, as he had on that very first night in London. Before he finally fell into a wretched sleep, he contrasted that first evening, with its gaiety, the sparring between Marlowe and Greene, and his seemingly glowing future, with the desperate present. His sense of isolation was now complete, he was quite unable to tell the Popes of his betrayal of Tom Kyd, for that's what it was. Somehow what he had spluttered out, half-drunk, on the night of the Rose party to the man who had befriended him in the street must have got back to the authorities. Why, why, had he not curbed his tongue? But there seemed no danger. Marlowe had called the man a spy, but then he had been just as offensive to everyone else. But it must have been true. Why else would they have searched Kyd's room? How else could they have known? It was his fault, all his fault, that one of the few people for whom he truly felt affection in this terrible city was now suffering horribly for having done him a kindness.

Much of the previous evening had been taken up with discussing how best Simon might present his resignation to Henslowe the following day and whether Richard wanted to continue as a player and go with him to Burbage's company, or turn his back on the theatre for good. In his present state of mind he had been unable to say anything sensible. Before what had happened, he had still been no nearer a decision, knowing he could not make up his mind

200

until he had once again seen his family, now . . .

He was woken by the banging on the door. At first it was all part of unpleasant dreams of pursuit and unknown perils, but finally he realised that there really was someone outside, knocking with desperate urgency.

He hastily pulled on his breeches and stumbled along the passageway to the stairs, as the Popes appeared at their chamber door, Jenny in her nightshift with her hair in a plait, Simon draped around with a blanket. Richard reached the door first and threw it open to reveal Emma Bell clutching little Fortunatus by the hand. It was pouring with rain and they were both soaked. As Richard asked what was the matter, Jenny pushed past him and pulled Emma and the child indoors. 'Whatever it is, let them come in out of the rain.'

She led Emma into the big kitchen and sat her down by the remnants of the fire. 'Wait there a moment while I fetch you a dry gown and some clothes for Fortunatus. There are some my younger son has outgrown which should fit him.'

'No . . . that is before you go, I must tell you what brought me here. Kit Marlowe's dead.'

Simon looked at her in astonishment. 'You're sure of that?'

Let it be an accident, prayed Richard silently, or in a fight. He was always one for a fight. Don't let it be to do with the other . . . first Tom, then Kit Marlowe, and all because of me. Please God, not this too.

'How did he die?' he asked.

'I know very little, only what I was told by one of my customers, who knew I was acquainted with Kit. He's a seaman and had newly landed at Deptford. He was in a tavern near the river when suddenly there was a great to-do in the street outside and a crying out for the constables. He took little notice, there's often trouble when ships arrive back in port, but some time later one of the constables came into the tavern and he was asked what had caused the commotion. He said there'd been a fight and that a fellow

201

called Christopher Marlowe had been killed.'

'Did he say what the fight was about?' asked Jenny.

'He said the constable told him it was to do with who paid the reckoning for the supper. It seems he was with some friends at the time.'

'Come now, Emma, and change your clothes, and those of Fortunatus too,' said Jenny, firmly, 'we can discuss this further afterwards.' The knocking, followed by raised voices below, had succeeded in rousing the two young apprentices, who now crept down, wide eyed, to find out what was happening. As Jenny shepherded Emma and Fortunatus up the stairs, she told them to sit quietly and say nothing. The child stumbled on the bottom step and she stopped and picked him up. He was worryingly light for a child of his age. His hair was now auburn, several shades darker than his father's had been, but the dark eyes which looked back at her from his solemn little face were very much those of Robin Greene.

'What in God's name was he doing in Deptford?' exclaimed Richard when the women had gone upstairs. 'He said he had to report every day to the office of the Star Chamber.'

'Heaven knows . . . unless . . .'

'Yes?'

'Unless he had decided to leave the country while he was still able.'

They were still considering this when the women returned, Emma in one of Jenny's gowns and Fortunatus in a clean, dry pair of breeches and a shirt, his hair newly dried. The rubbing of the towel caused it to stand upright on his head and for an instant he looked like a little pale ghost of his father. Jenny immediately set about putting out bread, cheese and ale, then poured out a beaker of milk for the little boy.

'You're quite sure your fellow was right about this, Emma?' asked Simon.

'Oh yes. He came straight to me from Deptford, knocking on my door after midnight when I was already abed. He has used me many times before. But he was urgent from his weeks at sea and didn't tell me about Kit's death until afterwards. He had no cause to lie.'

They sat down to eat their bread and cheese, the apprentices aware that something momentous had occurred, but not of its implications, eating theirs, for once, in silence. They were half-way through the meal when they had another visitor, a white-faced and distraught Jamie, bringing the same news. His story was similar to Emma's. Kit had been drinking and dining with friends in Deptford, had then picked a quarrel when it came to paying the bill and in the subsequent struggle had been stabbed, dying almost at once. 'They say there's to be a Crowner's Quest there tomorrow; I shall go myself and if that upsets Ned Alleyn then he can go hang himself!'

'I think Richard and I had better come with you to Deptford tomorrow,' said Simon. 'Even Phillip Henslowe might like to know what really did occur, rather than rely on rumours which will only grow in the retelling, and I have to see him this morning anyway.' It was not a cheering prospect to be the bearer of the news to Henslowe that his leading playwright had been murdered and that one of his leading actors was about to leave him. Jenny put her hand on his arm. 'I will also come with you to the inquest, unless you object. Will you come, too, Emma?'

Emma shook her head. 'It's no place for me. I'll leave you to tell me all about it. What's happened is a terrible thing, but surely not surprising to any of us, knowing the man. I wouldn't have wished him such a fate, God help us, but I can't pretend to have had any love for him.' Then she stopped suddenly. 'Do you not recall what my Robin said to him? "... for little knowest though how, in the end, thou shalt be visited". It was as if he had known.'

* * * *

It was not raining when the four passengers took the two-man wherry from the Bankside steps the next morning, but it was cold and grey for the first of June. 'More like February,' grumbled Simon. The meeting with Henslowe had been profoundly unpleasant, as the news of Marlowe's death had reached the entrepreneur the previous night. Simon was left with the impression, however, that a playwright killed in a drunken brawl was infinitely preferable to one dragged through the highest courts in the land. The news that he himself was to become a sharer in a rival company had prompted only, 'well, you must do as you must', followed by only the most grudging of thanks for the years of work. He would leave therefore at the end of the following week, at which time Richard would ride to Stratford with Shakespeare.

By the time Simon had reached the subject of the inquest and their proposed attendance at it, Henslowe had buried himself in his papers again, dismissing him with a wave of the hand. They had already decided to go anyway. Neither Simon nor Richard had anything to lose, and nothing would have kept Jamie from it. Kit had been the great love of his short life and at present he could see no path out of the darkness that enveloped him.

Also rumour, as Simon had rightly suspected, was now rife in the company. Dick Hoope had heard that Marlowe and his killer had been playing cards for money, that each had accused the other of cheating, and that in the subsequent fight, with poignards, Marlowe had been killed. The innocent Henry Brodribb raised a grim laugh when he said he'd been told, my someone who really knew, that Marlowe had been stabbed by a bawdy serving man, a rival of his in lewd love for a high-class whore. Ralph Wilkins, arriving hot foot at the Rose to see what gossip he could pick up, had been accosted in the street by a clergyman who had asked him if he knew of the death of Marlowe, 'the Cambridge scholar, poet and Filthy Playmaker'. The cleric's version was that Marlowe had set on some innocent passer-by, forced a quarrel on him, and that the other, 'perceiving his villainy', had caught his hand, turning his dagger back into his own brains (which came out on the dagger's point) and thus, 'still blaspheming, he yielded up his stinking breath'. 'Colourful, don't you think?' asked Ralph. 'He then said, "mark this well, player, you who live by making fools laugh at sin and wickedness." '

There was, therefore, much on all their minds as they took their seats in the wherry. The two watermen had grumbled loudly at having to take four passengers, demanding a higher fee as they had to row against a strong incoming tide. They kept up a steady stream of complaints, which they broke off only to shout abuse or oaths at other passing craft. It was nearly eleven by the time the boat put in at Deptford, leaving its small party little time to find out where the inquest was being held. After several fruitless enquiries, they were pointed in the direction of a large inn facing on to the green. The landlord was standing outside, full of self-importance, directing people to an upstairs room. Yes, he told them, this was the right place. In fact, he added with ghoulish relish, the body of the deceased was lying even now in his stable, 'with a great 'ole in 'is eye'. No, they couldn't see it, it was being viewed by the jurors.

They climbed the stairs to the room, which had been set out with two tables at the front for the coroner and the clerk of the court, a large number of chairs on one side for the jurors, and a smaller number for the witnesses. There were rows of benches for the public but these were only half occupied. Fights, especially those involving knives, were commonplace in a small dockside place like Deptford, where there were always many seamen, either seeking work or returning from voyages; the name of Christopher Marlowe meant little in Deptford.

There were a number of elderly people who, from their conversations, obviously found a good inquest provided entertainment: several women were commenting loudly that they did not know what things were coming to these days, street brawlers should be made examples of, and a sour Puritan all in black clutched his Bible. They made their way towards the back of the room and sat down.

Sharp on eleven o'clock the door opened and two constables appeared, proceeding solemnly before a distinguished, elderly man wearing the fine long gown of a prosperous lawyer. Behind him came the clerk of the court carrying rolls of parchment, an inkpot and several pens. These he proceeded to put down at a smaller table beside that of the coroner.

'You will all rise,' he said to those assembled in front of him and there was much scuffling and coughing as they all rose to their feet. 'This Inquisition,' he continued, 'is held today to enquire into the circumstances surrounding the death of Christopher Marlowe, the proceedings being before William Danby, Coroner of the Household of our Sovereign Lady, Queen Elizabeth I.' 'Why the Queen's own coroner?' whispered Jamie, 'why not the ordinary Deptford man?' The clerk looked over at him. 'There will be silence throughout these proceedings.'

Sir William Danby settled himself behind the larger table then, in a dry and cultured voice, told them they might be seated.

The clerk rose again and read out: 'This Inquisition is called at Deptford Strand in the County of Kent, within the verge, on the first day of June in the thirty-fifth year of the reign of Elizabeth by the grace of God, Queen of England, France and Ireland, Queen Defender of the Faith, in the presence of William Danby, Coroner of the Household of our said lady the Queen, upon the view of the body of Christopher Marlowe there lying dead and slain. The jury will now take the oath.'

There was a great noise of feet as the sixteen members of the jury tramped into the room, each one in turn swearing the oath on the Bible placed before them by the clerk; William Draper, Wolstan Randall, William Curry, Adrian Walker, John Barber, Robert Baldwyn, Giles Field, George Halfpenny, Henry Awger, James Batt, Henry Bendyn, Thomas Batt senior, John Baldwyn, Alexander Burrage, Edmund Goodcheepe and Henry Dabyns, all good solid citizens.

'You have viewed the body?' asked Danby.

'We have, your honour,' they chorused.

'Have you elected one among you to be foreman?'

'We have decided it shall be Giles Field,' replied William Draper.

'Thank you. You may all be seated. Will you read the indictment, Master Clerk?'

The clerk stood up and unrolled another parchment from which he read; 'It is stated upon oath that a certain Ingram Frizer, gentleman of London, and Robert Poley of London aforesaid, gentlemen, and one Nicholas Skeres did on the thirtieth day of May meet at Deptford Strand at the house of Eleanor Bull, widow.'

'I thought this was supposed to have taken place in a tavern, not a private house,' Jamie whispered again, drawing on himself another furious glower from the clerk.

'And there passed time and dined and were in quiet sort and walked in the garden until the sixth hour of the afternoon, then returned from the garden to the house aforesaid and there together, in company, supped and that after supper the said Christopher Marlowe uttered malicious words for the reason that he could not agree as to the payment of the reckoning and that he, Christopher Marlowe, did move against Ingram Frizer in anger and drew his dagger on him, giving him two wounds in the head, whereupon the said Ingram, for fear of being slain and for the saving of his life, struggled with the said Marlowe, in which affray – and in his own defence – with the dagger aforesaid (value twelve pence) gave the said Christopher there and then a mortal wound over his eye to the depth of two inches, of which mortal wound the said Christopher Marlowe instantly died.'

'Thank you,' said the coroner, 'call the first witness.'

Ingram Frizer had dressed for his performance in the long merchant's gown he had last worn that unhappy morning on Tower Hill, the morning which had promised so well but had been the start of all this. His face was pale and his forehead was dramatically swathed with a large bandage. He took the oath in unctuous tones and smiled obsequiously at the coroner.

'You have taken the oath – you know what it means?'

'Yes, your grace.'

' "Sir" or "your honour" will be quite adequate, Frizer. I am not a royal Duke. Now, I am unclear as to how this mishap occurred. Enlighten me.'

'Well, it was like he said, your . . . sir. We'd had a good day, the four of us, first with lunch, then sitting out in the lady's garden and it was at supper . . .'

'This Marlowe was a friend of yours?' Danby interrupted.

'Well, not to say a *friend*, more of an acquaintance really. He is – was – a friend of my master, Thomas Walsingham. I hadn't known he'd be there. It was my friend, Nick Skeres, who invited me. He said *his* friend, Mr Poley there, was getting up a little party in Deptford and would I like to come?'

'I see. Proceed.'

'We had our supper, it was a good one too with plenty of wine and I suppose we were all a little merry, begging your pardon, but Marlowe, he just kept on drinking till he got quite wild. He was lying on this bed . . .'

'Bed? In a supper room? What manner of house is this?'

'Most respectable, your honour, sir. I should have said couch. He said he felt giddy – not surprising really seeing how much he had to drink, so he got up from the supper table and went and lay down. The three of us, that is Mr Poley, Nick and myself, were finishing our supper, me sitting between the two of them on the same bench, when Mr Poley calls out to Marlowe how much he would have to put towards the reckoning. What should Marlowe do then but sit up and bawl that he had thought it was all supposed to be on Mr Poley and then *I* said I didn't like a man who wouldn't stand his shout, at which point,' he paused, dramatically, 'Marlowe got up and snatched my own dagger out of my belt and cut me twice on the head – here' He pointed theatrically to the bandage.

'And what did your companions do while this was taking place?'

'They kept on eating. They didn't realise what was happening at first and they couldn't do anything because of the way we were all three seated on the one bench, and I couldn't get out of Marlowe's way because I was stuck between them.' Simon, aware that Jamie was about to erupt at this, pulled him down on the seat and hissed for him to be quiet.

'Continue,' said Danby.

'Marlowe looked wild, his eyes were staring. I thought my last day had come, so I sort of . . . twisted round and got my hand over his, the one holding the dagger and tried to get it off him, but somehow he . . . well he fell forward and next thing I knew he was down on the floor. Mr Poley said he must have died straight away, and so he drew the dagger out. That's the truth, so help me God.'

Danby looked at him thoughtfully. 'Thank you. You may sit over there. Call the next witness, please.'

Robert Poley was neatly dressed in a grey doublet and breeches with a clean white ruff. He looked like any respectable gentleman of moderate means. 'Robert Poley,' said Danby, 'can you support the account given by Ingram Frizer?'

'Indeed I can, sir. I hadn't seen Marlowe for some months and I had forgotten how seriously drink now affected him, although I was aware it had brought him trouble in the past. Throughout the morning and afternoon, however, he had been in good spirits but then, when we were putting our money together after supper to pay for the day's entertainment, he suddenly flew into this mad rage and attacked Mr Frizer in the manner he describes. It was all over before I realised what had occurred.'

'You knew this Marlowe well?'

'Not well, but we were once neighbours and remained on friendly terms.'

'Why did you invite him to Deptford?'

209

'I thought it might distract him. I had had business to discuss at Mistress Bull's house the previous evening and she had already invited Nicholas Skeres for lunch the next day, along with his friend, Master Frizer, as well as myself. On my way to take the boat to Deptford, I came across Marlowe in the street and as he seemed in poor spirits and in need of distraction, I invited him to join us, knowing Mistress Bull's hospitable nature.'

'Thank you, Mr Poley. That will be all. You may be seated. Now, can I see this other man, Nicholas Skeres?'

Skeres, although considerably shabbier than the other two, was reasonably clean and decent. He took the oath in a low mumble.

'Have you anything to add to what we have already heard, Skeres?' asked Danby.

'Nothing, sir. Ingram and Robert have told you exactly what happened. It was just as they said, one minute Marlowe was contented and pleasant, the next he was like a madman. Had Ingram not sought to take the knife from him, I truly believe Marlowe would have killed him.'

'Thank you. You may stand down.'

The clerk moved over to Danby and said something to him in a low voice. 'Ah yes,' Danby responded. 'Mistress Eleanor Bull. Is she present?'

There was a rustle of silk at the door at the back of the room, followed by the scraping of benches and chairs as everyone turned to see the next witness enter. If Ingram Frizer had taken pains to present himself as a man of solid worth, Eleanor had dressed for her part to perfection. She wore no grey silk embroidered with creeping insects, or pink satin smothered in summer flowers, but a straight, black gown with a wide white collar, worn without a farthingale. Her hair was almost completely concealed under a neat lace cap and she carried a large handkerchief and a pomander stuck with cloves.

Danby smiled at her. 'Will you take the oath, Mistress Bull?'

'Certainly. What must I do?'

210

The clerk went over to her with the Bible. 'You must lay your hand on this book and say after me . . .' She took the oath in a soft, clear voice.

'Now, Mistress Bull, you are a widow?'

'Yes, sir, my husband has been dead these eight years.'

'You have lived long in Deptford?'

'Some ten years, sir.'

'You are in business?'

'My late husband purchased our house two years before his death – he also had property in Suffolk. When in London he would often entertain his friends and business acquaintances on their way to and from the Continent. When he died it occurred to me that I might make a respectable living offering accommodation to such as they, who might need to take ship from the river or inspect cargo, and this has indeed been the case.'

'Did your husband not leave you adequately provided for?'

'Not as well as he thought, sir, which is why I decided to run my house as I have described. It has proved most useful both to those I have accommodated and indeed, to me, not just in terms of gain but for the company it has given me. Unhappily, my husband and I were childless, and life for a widow can be very lonely.'

'You would not describe your establishment as an inn or tavern then?'

Eleanor looked shocked. 'Oh no. I provide bed and board only for very particular guests. I also hire out rooms where gentlemen can discuss business affairs in private and on such occasions I offer food and drink.'

'There is no question of your providing rooms for other purposes?'

'I don't understand your meaning, sir.'

'To put it in plain terms, your house is not used as a place of assignation?'

'A place of . . .' Mistress Bull looked as if she were about to faint. A tear trickled down her cheek. 'I keep a most, a most . . . *respectable* house.'

'Thank you,' said Danby. 'I did not wish to distress you. Now can you tell us what you saw and heard.'

'Master Poley had arrived the night before. He has often taken rooms with me for business meetings and also when making journeys abroad. Master Skeres was seeing to the purchase of wood for my new kitchens. When I invited him for lunch, he asked if he might bring his friend, Master Frizer. I had not met Master Marlowe until Master Poley invited him, though I was very pleased to meet him as I have so much enjoyed his plays of *Tamburlaine* and *The Jew of Malta* and I told him so.

'After lunch we sat in the garden and he told me about the playhouses and the actors and the different plays, while the other gentlemen played cards. He was most entertaining.

'Then we all went into the house and my servants brought the gentlemen their supper. I took my own in the downstairs parlour with my maid, Jane, who is also a companion to me. She was with me when we heard raised voices from the room above. At first I thought it merely the noisy talk of gentlemen who have drunk a fair amount of wine, but then I heard one shout out about the payment of the reckoning. Later I was told this was Master Marlowe. Then I heard a scuffling noise above followed by the sound of breaking glass.'

Danby leaned forward. 'Did you not seek to discover what this meant?'

'Indeed I did. I had already left my supper to go upstairs when suddenly there was a loud crash. I ran at once into the room above and found the table in disarray, that gentleman there, with the bandage, with blood trickling down his face from cuts on his forehead and Marlowe lying on the floor. Master Poley was trying to revive him but . . .' She began to weep quietly into her handkerchief. 'It was very unpleasant sir. I never could stand the sight of blood . . . his eyes . . .' She sniffed her pomander.

'It must have been very distressing for you, Mistress Bull. You have been very helpful. I don't think I need detain you any longer.'

THE SLICING EDGE OF DEATH

'Thank you, sir,' she replied, in a failing voice, dabbing her eyes with her handkerchief. She looked on the point of collapse.

'Members of the jury,' said Danby, 'you must now consider your verdict, whether you find Ingram Frizer guilty of wilful murder or whether he acted in self-defence. The inquest will now adjourn briefly.'

There was a buzz of conversation as the sixteen jurors filed out. 'You should hire her for the playhouse!' said Jenny as soon as the last man had disappeared. 'Rarely have I seen such a performance.' 'Yet the coroner appeared to accept she was telling the truth,' said Richard. 'The truth, is it?' Jenny's voice rose, 'That one would not recognise the truth if it passed her by in a cart at the Lord Mayor's Show!'

Simon looked at his indignant wife and smiled. 'I agree, love. It did tend to put me in mind of an actor in a play. But if that's so, what is her true role in all this?'

'None of it makes sense,' said Jamie. 'Oh, I know Kit could quarrel easily, even turn to violence, but this? Here in Deptford? And he in such straits already?'

'And why,' added Richard, 'did the other two men just sit there like stocks, while the third, sitting between them, fought for his life?'

They could say no more as the door opened again to admit Danby, followed by the jurors.

'Members of the jury,' said Danby, 'you have heard the statements of the witnesses. What judgement have you reached?'

The foreman, Giles Field, stepped forward. 'It would seem to us, sir, that Mr Frizer acted solely in self-defence in order to protect his own life from an unprovoked attack by the said Christopher Marlowe.'

'Thank you,' said Danby. 'I am in agreement with your conclusion. Ingram Frizer, be pleased to stand before me.'

Frizer rose from his seat and stood in front of Danby with an ingratiating smile.

'For now you must be returned to Newgate Prison,

213

Frizer, but I can see no reason why you should remain there for long. I shall today recommend that you be granted a Free Pardon by her Majesty on the grounds that you acted solely to save your own life.'

Frizer was still bowing and smiling and thanking him when Sir William Danby, special Coroner to her Queen's own Majesty, rose and swept out of the room.

21

And had I but escaped this stratagem,
I would have brought confusion on you all.

The Jew of Malta   Marlowe

HARDLY HAD SIR WILLIAM Danby confirmed
the verdict, collected up his papers and taken himself
off, before the carpenter was nailing down the coffin in the
stable at the back of the inn. The four companions had
been somewhat delayed leaving the room, first because the
doorway was blocked by jury members congratulating
themselves on the outcome, and then by a noisy argument
between a maidservant and a potboy, which was taking
place on the stairs.

Indeed the carpenter, watched in a desultory fashion by
four large and shabby fellows, was about to put the last few
nails into the cheap deal box when they reached the stable
door. Simon, seeing the stage matters had reached, shouted
out to him to stop.

The man looked up with a surly expression. 'What for?
It's all over, isn't it? And who are you?'

'Friends of the man who was killed. We wish to pay our
last respects to him before his burial.'

'I don't see as how you can. A couple more nails and
he'll be fastened down snug. They're waiting for him in the
churchyard and I've orders to see he's taken there without
delay. These lads here are going to carry him over the road,
then it'll be a few quarts of ale and a piece of pie in the
Ordinary for all of us.' He put two nails in his mouth and
picked up his hammer.

'Can't you prise up the lid again, just for a moment?'
begged Jamie.

215

'A minute or two can't harm surely, man,' said Richard, 'for God's sake, anyone would think he was a Plague victim that he must needs be hustled into his grave with such haste.'

The carpenter removed the nails from his mouth. 'What ceremony would you have then for a drunk killed in a tavern brawl?'

Simon turned to Richard and said in a low voice, 'I imagine we'll have to pay the fellow.' They all felt in their purses and provided Simon with what they could. 'Here's half a guinea, carpenter, it's the best we can do. You can see we aren't wealthy folk.' The carpenter took the coins, bit each one in turn then, with a shrug, prised open the lid.

The body inside was wrapped in a coarse hessian shroud. The face had been cleaned, but was disfigured by the empty socket of the right eye which was clotted with congealed dark brown blood. Death had smoothed away the lines and blemishes on Marlowe's face, giving it a look of peace it had never worn in life; with its fine bones, firmly marked black eyebrows and fringe of dark beard it looked almost like a mask. Looking at that dead face, Richard knew he could now never tell anyone of his part in it; that one incautious statement had led to Kyd's torture and Marlowe's death. For it must have been because of him. Why else would all this have happened.

The sight of his dead lover provoked Jamie to renewed tears.

Richard put his arm round the boy. 'Come on now, Jamie, you know he would have mocked your grief.'

Jamie lent over and kissed Marlowe goodbye, then drew back. 'They said in there that he was stabbed *above* the eye, yet it must have been obvious to all the jury members that he wasn't. Nor,' he added, thoughtfully, 'would it have been easy to drive a dagger home through the skull. And to reach the brain, it must needs have been driven inwards and upwards. It's very strange.'

'There's much that's very strange.'

'Satisfied?' enquired the carpenter, and promptly

replacing the lid, he quickly nailed it back into place.

'This business is beyond me,' said Simon. 'He had friends with influence and wealth, a faithful patron, not to mention the company of the Lord Admiral's Men of the Rose Theatre. There was no need to shroud him in sackcloth and bury him in such a fashion.' The man did not respond and, with a final tap, drove the last nail home. The four waiting men came forward to take the coffin.

'Can't we even help perform this last task for him?' asked Jamie in anguish. The carpenter gave a weary sigh. 'My orders were to nail him down and then hand him over to these four fellows. They've already been paid to take him to St Nicholas' churchyard. That's what I was told to do and that's what I'm doing. I've pandered to you long enough.' He straightened up and spat on his hands. 'Right, lads, off you go.'

The men hoisted the coffin on to their shoulders and marched out through the inn courtyard into the street outside, the four friends following behind. The church stood a little way apart from the main bustle of the town and the road outside was quiet. The few bystanders there watched the small cortege pass by with little interest, pauper funerals being commonplace; only a handful of the devout crossed themselves in the old-fashioned manner.

The atmosphere of haste was equally apparent at the churchyard gate where an elderly curate, his cassock soiled and covered in clumsy darns, was standing prayer book in hand and already open at the appropriate place. 'I am the Resurrection and the Life, saith the Lord,' he began in a low mutter, trotting smartly ahead of the coffin, 'he that believeth in me though he were dead, yet he shall live . . .' The rest of the words were lost to those at the back.

'Merciful heavens, Simon,' said Jenny, 'even Robin Greene was carried to his grave by his friends with a crown of bays on his coffin!'

'At home only those who are thought to have taken their own lives would be treated in so shabby a way,' said Richard.

It seemed there was to be no ceremony of any kind inside the church as the curate and bearers stopped before a newly dug grave beside the north wall. 'Who decided the grave should be dug even while the Crowner's Quest was still sitting?' asked Jamie, 'and all things in such haste?'

The four men put down the coffin. The sky was still dark and grey and a chilly wind blew across the churchyard from the river, bringing with it an unpleasant smell of mud and sewage. There was one other person at the graveside, the man in the grey doublet who had given evidence at the inquest as the person who had set up the ill-fated excursion to Deptford – Robert Poley.

'What did he say his name was?' whispered Richard. 'Pooley? Pole? I couldn't help but think I'd seen him before, but can't recollect where. But then, he's an ordinary-enough looking fellow, hardly one to stand out. There must be many like him.' As if aware of his gaze, the man glanced across at them with a level look, then signalled to the curate to proceed.

The curate rattled on: 'Man that is born of woman hath but a short time to live and is full of misery. He cometh up and is cut down like a flower . . .', gabble, gabble, '. . . in the midst of life we are in death . . .' It was a strange scene, the old churchyard with its packed and twisted gravestones under the leaden sky, the cheap coffin and threadbare churchman, the three actors in their bright but shabby clothes and Jenny, the only woman, wrapped in her dark cloak; and the solitary figure of the man in grey.

The curate stumbled on. 'For as much as it hath pleased God of his great mercy to take unto himself the soul of our dear brother . . . er.' He ground to a halt.

'Christopher!' called out Jamie, 'can't you even get that right!'

'Christopher, here departed. We therefore commit his body to the ground: earth to earth, ashes to ashes, dust to dust.' Poley bent and picked up a handful of earth which he dropped on the coffin, at which Jenny pushed in front of the bearers, closely followed by the other three. They too threw earth on the coffin and Jamie, seeing a straggling rose growing on a bush nearby, picked it and threw it down as well.

'In sure and certain hope of the resurrection to eternal life,' continued the curate, fearful of becoming hopelessly lost, 'through our Lord Jesus Christ . . .' his voice trailed away into an inaudible murmur. Then with a brief nod to the watchers, he turned and trotted smartly into the church, clanging the door shut behind him. This being the signal that it was all over, the four bearers began to make their way purposefully towards the church gate as Simon nodded his head towards Poley. 'I think I'll have a word with that one,' but was diverted as the bearers, in their haste, collided with the sexton who had just appeared to fill in the grave, his spade over his shoulder. By the time Simon turned back to Poley he had vanished as if he had never been.

'Well,' he said, 'there seems no more to be done. Shall we find food and drink here or return to Bankside?'

'Speaking for myself,' said Richard, 'this place chills my blood. I'd prefer we went home.'

This being the general mood, they left the churchyard and made again for the watersteps. 'That must be Mistress Bull's house behind that high wall,' commented Richard. 'It looks very grand.'

'Merchant's widow, indeed,' scoffed Jenny, 'and left ill provided! One who believes that would believe in the philosopher's stone! I wonder who she really is and what she really does.'

A two-man wherry was making for the steps, a fare aboard. The incoming tide, now almost at the flood, was rapidly covering the mud flats, damping down the unpleasant smells. Ships anchored in mid-channel swung at their moorings and a substantial number of merchantmen were making ready for sea on the high tide. Shouted orders could be heard above the noise of screaming gulls. The mainsail of a large Dutch vessel, close at hand, was loosened suddenly and billowed out in the freshening wind.

The watermen ran their boat alongside the steps and one

jumped out to hold the boat steady while the passenger, a stout elderly fellow in a merchant's gown, stepped ashore and paid him his fee. Simon hailed the watermen.

'Where to?' asked one.

'Bankside.'

'Get in, then.' They did so and the waterman pushed off and jumped in after them. It would be an easy journey on the top of the tide. 'Then Westward Ho it is,' he said, and bent to his oars.

* * * *

As soon as he had seen the coffin safely into the grave, Poley took horse and made at full gallop for Greenwich Palace, carrying with him a note from Sir William Danby as to the finding of the inquest. It was useful that the Queen had been at Greenwich, thus allowing her own coroner to preside, Deptford being 'within the verge' of her presence and her court. There were unlikely to be any repercussions or questions asked and any talk would soon die down. The dead man's propensity for hard drinking and resort to violence were well enough known and could – and would – be helped by rumour. Presumably, he thought, the four strangers were friends or acquaintances of Marlowe. The three men were almost certainly players and the girlish younger one probably one of his catamites; presumably the woman was wife or mistress to one of the other two.

A servant came to tell Cecil that Poley had arrived as he was at lunch; he immediately excused himself and hurried to meet his messenger. He read Danby's note with a smile. 'You've done well, Poley, very well. It's been a long and tedious business. He's now safely in his grave?'

'Well and truly buried, sir. There were four strangers at the graveside, three men and a woman, so word must have got round of his death. The men looked like players. There is little to fear from them.'

'Excellent! I shall ensure that everything is put in hand

immediately for Frizer's pardon and remuneration. In view of his association with Thomas Walsingham, he's more valuable alive than dead. I will give you money for Skeres.'

'And Eleanor Bull?'

'I shall see to that personally. Oh, and Poley, I took the opportunity of having this drawn up in advance.' It was a substantial payment to Robert Poley authorised 'upon a warrant signed by the Vice Chamberlain to the Court 9 June 1593 for the carrying of letters for her Majesty's special and secret affairs of great importance from the Court at Croydon on 8 May 1593 to the Low Countries of the town of The Hague in Holland and for returning back again with letters of answer to the court at Nonesuch on 8 June 1593 *being in her Majesty's service all throughout the aforesaid time.*'

'I think that covers everything. The Court does, indeed move to Nonesuch on Monday and letters will be brought from Holland to the house of Eleanor Bull, which you can collect and deliver to her Majesty a week tomorrow, on the ninth.'

Cecil returned to his lunch in rare good humour and he was still smiling to himself as he hurried down one of the wide corridors to the room which had been set aside for his use. It was then he was suddenly brought up short, literally, for in front of him stood Thomas Walsingham, a drawn sword in his hand.

Cecil froze. 'Who let you in?'

'Your secretary. Had he not done so, I'd have run him through.'

'You know the penalty for drawing a weapon within the Queen's Court, Thomas.'

'And would pay it, too, along with that for slitting your throat!'

'You overreach yourself,' said Cecil, softly.

Walsingham grasped his arm in a firm grip. 'No, Robert, it is *you* who are the overreacher. Power's gone to your head. I want an explanation.'

'Then let us find somewhere more suitable for discussion

than an open thoroughfare,' and Cecil led the way down the corridor and into a side chamber, Walsingham following behind, reluctantly sheathing his sword.

'You're referring to Marlowe's death, I presume,' continued Cecil, closing the door behind them. 'Have you heard the inquest verdict? If not, I have it here.' He produced the note from Danby. 'You will see that the verdict, with which Sir William Danby agreed, was that the killing was purely in self-defence.'

'You still take me for a fool, don't you? You expect me to believe in this farrago of nonsense over who paid a bill, in the integrity of an inquest held not before the usual Deptford man but the Queen's own personal coroner. Of two men who sit eating their supper, while a third, sitting between them, fights to the death with a dagger and yet they do nothing. It's a tale fit only for children or those born without their wits. You never intended Kit should leave the country alive, did you Robert? This whole farce was designed to lull us all into believing you would let him escape. And all the time you knew, you *knew*, what was going to happen. Please God there'll be a special circle in Hell reserved for people like you.' He warmed to his theme. 'Oh yes, I can see it all now – you intended this from the first, didn't you? That's why he was allowed out on his own bail.

'Oh it was so good of you to arrange that, wasn't it? And get me, the only person he could trust, to persuade him to leave the country! Then you tell me that while waiting to take ship – and common rumour has it in a tavern, though we both know where he was, and the uses to which that house is put, that there is a brawl over who pays the supper bill and Kit, oh so conveniently, dies. And still you expect me to accept it?'

Cecil looked at him steadily. 'Whether you do or not, it would be best you pretend to do so.'

'Do you threaten me? Have a care – I'm no cobbler's playwright son.'

'Suspicion of treason can reach to the highest in the land

and you, like Marlowe, have had strange dealings in the past.'

Walsingham laughed out loud. 'I can scarcely believe my ears. Do you need reminding that it was my uncle who initiated the whole network of spies and agents?'

'No one doubts your late uncle's abilities, but living men change, circumstances alter, men who were once deemed excellent become at best a liability and at worse a positive hazard, which is why we are here now.'

'And you decided Kit was such a one?'

'You know, none better, how careless he had become, what manner of things he said in drink and not only that. When I questioned him upon his arrest, he did not hesitate to tell me that he would name many names of those in high places who had been similarly involved and whom he felt it was in the public interest to reveal; not to mention the light he proposed to shine on one of her Majesty's most esteemed servants, who was once involved in a tawdry and dangerous scandal; a matter which has even been kept from the Queen herself.' He walked over to a table and picked up some papers. 'Since you're here, you might as well cast your eyes over these,' and he handed Walsingham Baines' note and Kyd's confession.

Walsingham read swiftly through both then threw them down. 'They're almost identical – and what tosh! All this stuff about the Bible, and then that not everyone in Judea believed Christ was God's Son. That is, surely, a fact. That such things have also been said by Harriot, Raleigh's man. You can't bind men's thoughts, Robert, or rack their discussions. Was part of your ploy that Kit's fate should act as a warning to Raleigh's circle that they should rein in? To ensure Raleigh never regains his place in the Queen's affection?'

Cecil turned away abruptly and began his habitual pacing. 'There remains one other reason why Marlowe needed to be stopped. His theatrical pieces were highly popular and seen by thousands of people in London alone.'

Walsingham looked at him with incredulity. 'You surely

can't be saying you would have him dead because he wrote *plays*.'

'*Tamburlaine* was well enough.'

'And *The Jew of Malta*? What of that? He's boiled to death in his own cauldron, very salutary.'

'Only after it had been shown that the Christians behaved no better. If any came well out of this tale then, according to Marlowe, it was the Muslims; hardly an edifying moral. He follows this with a piece about a puling, effeminate King and his catamites, and finally gives us a man who challenges God himself.'

'And goes to hell for it. I fear you've lost me, Cecil.'

The fire usually so well banked down in Cecil now set him alight. 'Don't you understand? Most of those who go to the playhouses, Thomas, are ignorant and unlettered. Suddenly, they are exposed to new ideas, ideas of a blasphemous, immoral, even of a treasonable nature, ideas they would never have dreamed of had they not been presented with them in so immediate and vivid a way. What might Marlowe have gone on to write? What would have followed the challenging of God?'

'I take it you are serious,' said Walsingham.

'Most certainly.'

'I can scarcely believe my ears. What will you do then, Robert? Close all playhouses for good? Round up all the playwrights and have them put to death'

'I see no need for such extreme measures, but if I ever thought it necessary, be assured I would do so, if by such means I could ensure the protection and defence of the realm against the Queen's enemies: *all* her enemies, those who corrupt and subvert men's minds as well as those who plot her overthrow.'

Walsingham picked up the papers he had thrown down and put them on the desk in the middle of the room. 'What if I publish what I know abroad?'

'You'll not do that.'

'Why? It might be salutary for it to be known that you authorised this killing.'

'You'll never prove it. And let me spell out for you another reason why you will keep your fancies to yourself. It was, after all, one of your own men who killed Christopher Marlowe. No doubt it is widely thought he is your confidante.'

'He's not and never has been my confidante. Any who know me would also know that he's never had my ear except on the most mundane matters. Certainly he lives on my estate, sees to the collecting of some rents and the signing of leases since he is sharp in such matters, but no more than that.'

'And he has a reputation as a petty cozener.'

'Which has worked to my advantage sometimes, I admit.'

'How perfect a vehicle for you, then, to use to rid yourself of a friend who had become an embarrassment, a friend about to be arraigned for blasphemy and High Treason . . .'

'No one would think . . . no one would suggest . . .'

'Oh, I think they would. Easily. Especially if the word is put about. Come and look out of this window.'

Reluctantly Walsingham joined him as he opened the casement. 'Look up the river, to the cities of London and Westminster, the crowded warrens of the Bankside. Even now rumour is abroad, it stalks the streets and is assisted on its way – Marlowe was killed in drunken brawl, during a quarrel over an unpaid bill, in a fight with a serving man over the favours of some lewd wench, by the hand of God which took him with his mouth full of oaths, even by the Plague . . . oh yes, there will be many good reasons for his death. Shall we add to them that his friend and patron, Thomas Walsingham had had enough and wanted rid of him?'

Walsingham turned away. 'You care for nothing do you, Robert?'

'I care for those within my own family. I care deeply about those who interfere with the smooth running of the state and on them I have no mercy. Consider this also,

225

Thomas, since you purport to be a caring man. What would have been the outcome had Marlowe come to trial? You may mock the evidence of blasphemy and treason, but you must also know that it would have amply sufficed had it been necessary.

'Had the charge been treason it would have ended, almost certainly after torture, with his being dragged to Tyburn on a hurdle and, at the last, the rope, the disemboweller's knife and his entrails burned before his eyes – no swift blow of the axe on Tower Hill for a mere gentleman playwright. Had it been blasphemy, then it would have been a slow death chained to a stake. Instead, he had a clean quick death, once the dagger penetrated the brain. His end was merciful. Be thankful of that.'

Walsingham's energy suddenly drained from him, and he sat down heavily on the desk as Cecil snapped the window shut and said, 'Go back to Scadbury, Thomas. This incident is at an end.' He walked over to the door, obviously signalling that the interview, too, was over. 'I hear you are shortly to marry Sir Ralph Shelton's daughter. A most engaging lady. A lady with a bright and original mind.'

Walsingham looked up in some surprise. 'You know Audrey?'

Cecil smiled a strange smile. 'We have met.' He did not add that he knew the lady intimately.

'We are to wed at the end of the summer,' said Walsingham, dully, following him out of the room.

'Very suitable. Another reason for putting this matter behind you. Go home, Thomas, and breed sons. I wish you happiness in your future life.'

* * * *

Two days later Tom Kyd asked his gaoler if he would bring pen and paper so that he could write to the Keeper, Sir John Puckering. This having been done, he wrote asking first that he be cleared of all charges of atheism. If they thought he belonged to the School of the Night, then surely all they had to do was to ask its members. Then, from the recesses of his mind, he dredged up every single thing he could think of which would blacken Marlowe further, from a joking reference that he was thinking of offering his services to James of Scotland, to another scatter of blasphemies.

He ended 'Of my religion and life I have already given some instance of the late commission and also of my reverence to the state; although perhaps my pains and underserved tortures, if felt by some, would have engendered more impatience, as far less has driven men outside the fold, which it shall never do for me.' He signed it, 'Your Lordship's most humble in all duties, T. Kyd.' The next day he was unchained and moved to a better cell. No one told him that Marlowe was already dead and in his grave.

*   *   *   *

The Rose company was breaking up. Simon had packed his baskets to take to the Lord Chamberlain's Men, and now he, Jenny and Jamie stood with Richard outside the Popes' house ready to say goodbye to him. If they wondered what had made him so withdrawn or why he would not discuss his own future, they said nothing. Probably, thought Richard, they assumed it was because he had been so deeply affected by what had happened.

Hours had been spent discussing the inquest evidence, then Simon had called a halt. 'I think it best, after today, that we never speak of this again. Not to anyone. Unless we wish to find ourselves treading a similar path.'

'Poor brilliant Kit,' said Jamie, 'to challenge everything, even God, and then be brought down in such a way.'

'The Greeks called it nemesis,' commented Simon, soberly, 'which, as you know, walks on the heels of hubris.'

Will Shakespeare was waiting for Richard on the north

side of London Bridge, holding two horses. Before he mounted, Richard looked up, once again, at the heads. Would Kit Marlowe's have been there? Or perhaps it should have been his own, since it was the place for betrayers. Will followed his glance. 'Perhaps it was for the best. We could scarcely have borne to see one of us so horribly and publicly displayed. I'm told he was halfway through a major piece of work at his death. If that is so, then he died as he soared in flight, like a bird on the wing.' He looked long at Richard. 'I do not know what is haunting you, Richard, but whatever it is, I feel as sure as I am of anything, that he was not marked out for long life. If it had not been now, then it would have come soon enough. He had bound himself to the wheel of fate with his own hands.'

They mounted their horses, turning their heads towards Oxford and home.

*   *   *   *

Three weeks later, on a fine summer morning, Ingram Frizer was released from Newgate. He was ushered out by the Keeper, who hoped he had not found his enforced stay too unpleasant. Frizer thanked him and bowed. Two full purses nestled comfortably against him, under his doublet, for he had spent many happy hours playing cards with his gaolers.

Robert Poley, waiting for him outside with a horse, handed him two rolls of parchment. On the first was written the full indictment, the finding of the jury (with a note to the effect that also in his favour was the fact that he had made no attempt to escape) and concluded: 'We, therefore, moved by piety, have pardoned the said Ingram Frizer the breach of our peace . . . for the death of Christopher Marlowe.' It ended 'In Testimony and Witness, the Queen, at Kew, on the 28th day of June 1593' and was signed with the wonderful intricate signature of Elizabeth herself. The second was a grant of land and rents in the gift of the Duchy of Lancaster.

Poley watched him out of sight, then brushed his hands as if at the end of some long labour. It had, indeed, been a tedious business and he was in need of relaxation. Recently, and much more carefully, he had been seeing Mistress Yeomans again. All things considered, he felt he had done well. His view of espionage was entirely justified – that it should be left to the professionals. With the successful conclusion of the Deptford incident, he had ensured that Christopher Marlowe would never be heard of again.

AUTHOR'S NOTE

THE MURDER OF CHRISTOPHER Marlowe has proved one of history's most intriguing thrillers, since the scholar Leslie Hotson discovered, in 1925, the details of the inquest into his death. In the event, the official version raised more questions than answers and this note is for those who, like me, want to know how much truth there is behind a fictional story and, if it deals with real people, what happened to them.

Most of the events leading up to Marlowe's death are as portrayed in this story: the surveillance, the arrest and torture of Thomas Kyd, Marlowe's own arrest and his being released on bail, all culminating in his death in Deptford on 30 May 1593. The evidence given at the inquest is all documented, apart from that of Eleanor Bull which is fictional. In 1986 I had the good fortune to have these events enacted on the stage of the Swan Theatre in Stratford-on-Avon by Royal Shakespeare Company actors. The murder itself proved a point made to me by a forensic pathologist, that the stabbing could not have taken place in the way described at the inquest. Nor was that all; the sight of the actors playing Poley and Skeres sitting stolidly eating their supper, while Frizer, wedged between them, grappled with Marlowe, caused a great deal of hilarity.

The years in which this story takes place, 1590–93, were years of turmoil and disruption; political turmoil as the reign of Elizabeth I drew to its close without her officially naming her successor, and of disruption because the Plague raged more or less continually from 1591 to 1593, an unprecedented length of time.

The People in the Story

Christopher Marlowe was born in Canterbury three months before his rival, William Shakespeare. He went up to Cambridge on a scholarship and, while there, was recruited into Sir Francis Walsingham's secret service by Thomas Walsingham. This is documented.

We know that from when he first came down from university, he was an immensely successful playwright; crowds packed the theatre to see the two parts of *Tamburlaine*. We know he was brilliant, witty, homosexual, that he lived recklessly, drank hard and that when he did he talked too much. He was a member of an esoteric circle founded by Walter Raleigh, known as the School of the Night, which was looked on with deep suspicion by the authorities. Thomas Walsingham, for whom he seems to have felt a true affection, remained his friend and patron until his death. The events leading up to that death are much as described, but we will never really know what happened that

230

Wednesday night in the house of Eleanor Bull on Deptford Strand. I have made what I consider to be an educated guess.

What might Marlowe have known that would make him a danger to the government? The story of Antony Bacon's prosecution for sodomy and other sexual offences is true. While I was researching the life of Daphne du Maurier, I discovered that she had unearthed this fascinating tale when working on her life of the Bacon brothers in France. It was a very real find as there is no trace of the matter in any of the relevant English records, and until she discovered the French documents, no one here, according to Dr A.L. Rowse, knew of their existence. When I noticed that this incident coincided with the time Marlowe was likely to have been at Rheims, I thought it possible he just *might* have known about it.

Robert Cecil remained Acting Secretary (unpaid) to the Privy Council for six years before Elizabeth finally ratified the appointment. He continued to spin his webs of intrigue, using informers, double agents and *agents provocateurs*, as the Gunpowder Plot conspirators were to know to their cost. There is an intriguing sideline on Robert Cecil. Although never known as a womaniser, several sources suggest he had a liaison lasting many years with Audrey Shelton, both before and after she became the wife of Tom Walsingham; and, more fascinating still, that she assisted him in his secret service activities. He was known as a brilliant, but cold and scheming, man.

Robert Poley is now acknowledged to have been a master spy with a string of credits to his name. He did go to prison over an affair with Joan Yeomans (which he picked up again later) and was also arrested and personally questioned by Sir Francis Walsingham once on an unknown matter. The special warrant which was issued to him, dated 9 June 1593, is a curious document as, on the surface, it suggests he was out of the country for a month, yet those who drew it up obviously knew he was present at Marlowe's murder on 30 May. And it stresses that he was on the Queen's secret business throughout the whole period. He continued working for Cecil well into the reign of King James and probably died in his bed. It does seem that there must have been rumours among theatre people about his possible implication in Marlowe's death, or why should Ben Jonson warn people against dining and walking in gardens with him, in his poem 'Inviting a Friend to Supper'? There is no indication as to his personality so I have invented one. He is, after all, a familiar type.

Nicholas Skeres: there are records of payments to him in Sir Francis Walsingham's secret service accounts for the late 1580s and early 1590s, for work undertaken. Then, in March 1595 he was arrested at the house of a Master Williamson, who had testified against Robert Poley. Skeres was imprisoned first in the Counter Prison to wait

further examination, transferred to Newgate, then, finally to Bridewell
– after which he was never seen again! That is all we know.

Ingram Frizer really was arrested for what we would now call a
'scam', in which he palmed off a load of old guns on young Drew
Woodleff in exchange for an I.O.U. for £60. This took place around
the same time as Marlowe's death, but although he was charged with
the offence, there is no record of a subsequent trial or punishment,
which is odd. But then there is much that is odd about Ingram Frizer.
He was given the grants of land and rents from the Duchy of Lancaster
shortly after Marlowe's murder and in 1611 was one of two certified
assessors for Eltham and made an officer of certain charities. Later he
was described as 'one of sixteen good and lawful men of the county',
by several worthies, including the Biship of Rochester, the Vicar of St
Nicholas' church in Deptford (where Marlowe was buried). Again, his
personality is an invention.

Sir Thomas Walsingham married Audrey Shelton some time after
Marlowe's death, was knighted, and became a prominent figure at the
Courts of both Elizabeth and James I, having left the dark world of the
secret service behind him. One can only speculate as to what he knew
of his wife's activities in that field, let alone her possible liaison with
Cecil. He remained a prominent patron of the arts (Audrey took part
in several Ben Jonson masques) and the playwright George Chapman
dedicated his play, *The Conspiracy of Charles, Duke of Biron* to
Walsingham's little son, also called Thomas. Most of his magnificent
house at Scadbury was demolished in 1727 and only parts of it remain.
Somewhere in the grounds, as late as 1937, there was a mysterious and
quite elaborate tomb with no name. Legend has it that Walsingham
had Marlowe's body removed from the grave in St Nicholas'
churchyard and buried in his own grounds. His character is based on
what is known about him.

Richard Baines: scholars differ as to how long he continued as a
government informer. Dr Frederick Boas notes that a Richard Baines
was hanged at Tyburn on 6 December 1594, and that a ballad was
circulated to that effect, called *'The Woefull Lamentation of Richard
Baines'*. It does not seem an unlikely end, knowing his trade. Much of
what he says in this story is recorded.

Eleanor Bull: until Hotson discovered the inquest indictment, it was
accepted that Marlowe was killed in a tavern brawl. Yet, although
records of inn and tavern licences go back hundreds of years, there is
no record of either having been kept by a Mistress Eleanor Bull in
Deptford at the relevant time, and the indictment specifically states
that the death took place in a 'house'. We do not know if she gave
evidence at the inquest. This Eleanor Bull is entirely fictional.

Phillip Henslowe: every single playwright of note wrote at one time or another for this great theatrical entrepreneur. He built the Rose Theatre and ran the Bear Pit. We can gather something of his character from the diary he, most fortunately, kept. This, and his details of plays commissioned and put on, and his inventories of props, costumes, scenery, stage effects, box office receipts and loans to actors, is the single most valuable source of information we have about the Elizabethan theatre. He also carefully noted recipes for medicines, ear drops, etc. When he died in 1616 his papers passed to his son-in-law, Edward Alleyn, who later gave them to Dulwich College. His personality in this book is an amalgam of theatre directors and administrators I have known.

Edward Alleyn: little needs to be said as his life is well documented, including the rivalry with Richard Burbage. His finest roles were Marlowe's great overreachers. After Marlowe's death he gradually withdrew from acting, eventually becoming more of an administrator and director. He remained devoted to his wife Joan, his 'mouse', until her death, after which he married the daughter of John Donne. He founded Dulwich College.

Thomas (Simon) Pope: a leading actor first in Lord Strange's Company, then with the Lord Admiral's Men at the Rose. He left Henslowe in 1593 and became a sharer in the company of Lord Chamberlain's Men (later the Kings Men), run by the Burbages. His name appears on various documents, along with those of Dick Burbage, Hemmings, Condell and Shakespeare, first at the Theatre, then at the Globe. I have taken the liberty of calling him Simon to avoid confusion with the many Thomases in this story – Walsingham, Kyd, Watson and Harriot, to name but four.

Robert Greene was a popular playwright of the late 1580s and early 1590s, also known for his journalistic pamphlets and writings on the world of the low life of London. He really did dress, wear his hair in such a punk style, behave as extravagantly and die in the manner described. He did sell two different theatre companies his script for *Orlando Furioso*, both believing it was exclusive to them.

Emma Ball and Fortunatus: Emma was first mistress to the clown, Tarleton, who provided her with a house. Then she became Greene's mistress. Her brother, Cutting Ball Jack, really was hanged at Tyburn. She spent much time with the players. Her son by Greene, little Fortunatus, died of the Plague in the summer of 1593 and she was not long behind him, succumbing to the same disease later that year.

Thomas Kyd: the true innocent victim, caught up in something he never understood, because a heretical document was found in the

233

workroom he had once shared with Marlowe. He was never charged
with anything and sometime towards the end of 1593 he was released,
crippled in body, his health destroyed and a broken man. His patron,
possibly Lord Strange, repudiated him, the theatres ignored him, even
his family would have nothing to do with him. He died destitute in
August 1594, his mother, Anna, going so far as to renounce the
administration of his 'estate' in the name of her husband. His *Spanish
Tragedy* was the single most popular play of its day. Kyd's character is
based on what is known about him. He is also credited with being the
author of the first Hamlet play (known as the *Ur-Hamlet*). The text
has not survived but we know it was popular long before Shakespeare
wrote his and that it opened with a ghost, dressed in white sheets,
clanking chains and shouting 'Revenge!'.

Other actors: the names of Richard Cowley, or Crawley and Dick
Hoope, appear in Henslowe's diary, but the characters are fictional, as
are those of Will Hunt, Ralph Wilkins, Peter the Bookkeeper and
Jamie, the apprentice. There was no Tudor actor from Cornwall called
Henry Brodribb, but three centuries later a Cornishman of that name
took theatrical London by storm under the stage name Henry Irving.

William Shakespeare remained as resident dramatist with Burbage's
company throughout his professional life and really did rather well.
His plays were *not* written by Christopher Marlowe.